NICOLE A OLIVER

JUSTIFIABLE MAGIC

DEDICATION

This one is for my number one fan, Steph.
Every woman deserves a cheerleader like you
in her corner.
Your support and encouragement along my
writing journey has meant the world to me.
Cheers to many more girls weekends,
charcuterie nights,
and plenty of fresh air among the best of
company.

.

Logan

A layer of ash coats my nose and throat, leaving an acrid trail of oily bitterness behind. I fight to keep my eyes open in spite of the oppressive darkness, but they're as heavy with exhaustion as my body is with pain. Bone deep aches have settled in my body, my joints stiff and sore from the cold dungeon floor.

I wish I could drift away into the blissful numbness of sleep, but every time I close my eyes, I see her face haunting me with its vulnerability. My only comfort is that if he had gotten his filthy hands on her, he would have drained me and killed me. Instead, he's indulging in this slow torture. I've seen him drag other Mages down here, draining them of their power in one quick shot before letting their lifeless bodies fall from his cruel hands with a thud. He's done this in front of me to make his point. He's keeping me alive, tapping into my power and stealing just enough to keep me weak, unable to escape or fight back. I've never been so powerless in my life. Now I understand how Sophia felt when he got that power blocking cuff on her and I'm sorry I left her alone. I thought I was doing it for her own good and look how that turned out. A bitter laugh slips out.

The only thing keeping me going in this hopeless place is the thought of her out there. Vulnerable. If there was any way of doing it in this dark dungeon, I might consider ending myself. That way, he couldn't use me against her. That's all I am. A tool to get to her. I don't even want to think her name, afraid of who might be nearby. Which Mages are on his side or what powers he's currently stolen. I'm supposed to be her protector. Instead I lie here, my body sinking into the cold floor of the dungeon, shrinking further into the shadows every time footsteps sound outside my cell door.

Here, in this prison of darkness, I'm no longer her protector. I'm a liability. A danger. A threat to her safe

Sophia

I blink at myself in the mirror through unseeing eyes, not recognizing the girl reflected back at me. She has dull brown eyes that stare back at me without a spark of life. Her hair trails limp over shoulders that are slumped in defeat.

I've lost so much. I can't even think about Xavier without wanting to double over and lose myself to my grief. It's my fault he's dead. He had his whole life in front of him. He had nothing to do with this magical world and he ended up dead, taking a chunk of my already fractured heart with him.

The thought of my "uncle" has a fiery rage flaring up inside the chill of my numb body. He murdered my best friend, he stole my heart, and he's the reason Garrett is gone, too. The thought of Garrett sparks a new resolve inside me.

I'll never be able to bring Xavier back. I'm not sure how I'm going to rescue Logan yet, but I can do something about Garrett. I have to break him out. I don't know why the council locked him up. I don't know why Mr. Armstrong didn't get him released when he took me yesterday, but none of that matters. I'm responsible for all of this, and I'm going to be the one to fix it. I'm going in and I'm taking Garrett with me, no matter who I have to fight.

With that settled, I yank my hair into an obedient ponytail. I force my exhausted limbs to slide on clothes and head downstairs to face everyone.

I squirm under the sympathetic eyes that zero in on me when I reach the kitchen, itching to avoid the scrutiny. Their concern makes all this real instead of the dream I wish it was. Mom pulls me to her in a tight hug. I let myself fall into her embrace for the merest second before pulling away. I don't have the luxury of comfort. If I let myself feel anything but the anger simmering away, I might lose it. Her face falls when I duck away from the hand that falls to stroke my head.

"Morning." Liz's greeting lacks her usual bright exuberance. Clouds have dimmed her sunshine.

I can't bear to look in her eyes. They're just a reminder of him. Logan. I force myself to think his name, even though it causes the ache in my heart to intensify. A bitter resentment seeps in too. After all, if she hadn't grabbed me from Zeus, maybe Xavier would still be alive. The thought twists my insides with animosity. I know I shouldn't blame her, but I can't help fuming at her interference.

She reaches a hand toward me, but as if she senses the imminent rejection, pulls it back and scoops up a cat instead, staring down at its soft fur.

I scan the familiar room that's usually warm and welcoming. Today it feels empty even as my gaze lands on my mother's strained face. The creases have deepened and dark bruises cast a shadow under her eyes. Mrs. Armstrong's crisply ironed white blouse and the navy dress slacks draping her tall figure contrast with the hollow depths of sorrow lining her face.

"Where's Ivy?" I ask. A flare of panic rises. Have they taken her too? Who would have suspected that I'd be so concerned about the wellbeing of Logan's ex, but she's grown on me just like the rest of this little group.

Liz and her mom exchange a look I can't decipher.

"We're not sure. She left early this morning. Her bag is still here though so maybe she just went to get some exercise or something." The ball of orange fur in her arms rumbles. I don't have the brain capacity right now to sort through her cats. "Dad and Trey left early. They're going to get Garrett out."

Relief floods me, and I finally let my body sink into a dining room chair that creaks at the weight of my limp frame.

A plate slides under my nose and Mom's soothing fingers stroke the top of my head like I'm a little kid in need of comfort. I soak in the feeling. If we get Garrett out, that is one step in the right direction. Then I can focus on Logan and what I'm going to do to track him down and rescue him.

Regret has invaded every crack of my being. I should have told him I loved him sooner. I shouldn't have wasted time being angry at him for our last few days at the cottage. I should have given him everything. My body, mind, and soul. He owns them anyway. Why couldn't I have let loose and showed him what he meant to me? What if I never… No, I can't let myself even think that. It'll destroy me and I can't afford to be immobilized by the pain.

I shove the plate away. The thought of food right now turns my stomach.

"Sophia honey, you should eat something. I know how worried you are, but you need to look after yourself. Your power needs to regenerate after you drained it yesterday." Mrs. Armstrong's voice drops low, but her words still resonate.

I reach deep down past the grief and pain, searching for my magic. A weak spark flickers away, buried away deep, but nothing like the usual current that flows through me. She's right. I need to eat. I need to stay strong.

The toast scrapes my raw throat, turning to dust as I force it down.

After breakfast, I don't know what to do with myself, so I end up prowling around the house like one of Liz's cats. I brushed her off when she tried to talk. I can't sit. I can't read. I can't do anything until Mr. Armstrong and Trey come back with Garrett. At least if he's safe that's one less person's loss off my mind. Then we can focus on Logan. I rub at my aching chest as if I can stimulate the bond back into existence. Zeus must be keeping him in the Nether Realm. I'm making an educated guess that our connection doesn't cross the boundary.

Hope stirs within, sending my heartbeat into overdrive at the sound of the doorbell. A few steps away I slow my pace, trying to exercise a modicum of caution. I know Logan wouldn't approve of me running headlong into the arms of whoever might be waiting on the other side. It's laughable to think of who I used to fear when the doorbell rang. Salespeople, kids selling cookies or chocolate bars. Now it's supernatural bounty hunters and assassins I have to worry about. No big deal.

I peek through the peephole, a relieved breath escaping me at Trey's familiar closely cut black hair and dark eyes. As I swing the door open, my ears prick up at the sound of soft footsteps behind me.

Disappointment grips me when I see Trey is alone. I peer over his shoulder, scanning the area behind him, but there's nobody else there. No Garrett. No Mr. Armstrong either. He must still be back at the compound trying to get Garrett released. Okay, I can live with that.

Trey's hard to read. He's really good at building a wall to protect his thoughts. "What happened? Where's Garrett? How is he?"

"Let me come in and we'll talk. Things are… complicated."

My arms tense up, clasped to my chest in a tight hold, as if I can protect myself from whatever news he's about to drop on me. "I don't like the sound of that, Trey. Talk to me."

He scrubs at the rough stubble that's cropped up on his normally clean-shaven face, slipping past me with his long stride. "C'mon. I'd rather explain this to the three of you at the same time, so I don't have to repeat myself."

Fair point. I follow him into the Armstrong's living room. "Liz." I call out. There's no need to strain my voice when she's got the super sensitive hearing. I haven't gained that particular power yet, but I imagine it could be quite distracting being able to hear the slightest noises all the time. I wonder if she can block that out with a mental shield like the Psychic Mages can.

She walks in from the kitchen at a sedate pace rather than using her speed to zip about, as is her usual method of getting around the house. After yesterday's madness, her powers are probably pretty weak right now.

"Hey, Trey."

"Liz." He bumps his chin up in a quick greeting. His eyes stray over her shoulder. "Where's Ivy?"

"She called to say she was visiting a friend. She'll be back soon."

Liz's words provide a little relief. One less person to worry about for the moment. I was starting to think maybe she had gone off to rescue Logan by herself. She doesn't strike me as the reckless type, but when I think about it, I really don't know her all that well yet.

I squeeze Liz's arm, mouthing thanks at her for passing that on before turning back to Trey.

"Ok, spit it out. What happened and why don't you have Garrett with you? I thought Mr. Armstrong was going to get him released."

Trey sucks in a long breath, eyes tilted up to the ceiling. "There's been a power shakeup at the NAMC. Lawrence Kingston has always opposed the progress your parents have made. He doesn't like Witches, and he thinks Mages are better than mundanes. Losing Ivy's parents was a tremendous blow to the progress that the council has made over the last few decades. We didn't know how bad it was, though. Something happened that's pulled other members over to Kingston's side. Maybe it's fear with all the Mages disappearing. Maybe it's something else. But it's happening."

"What's that got to do with Garrett?" My chest tightens and I take a deep breath to avoid spinning out again at this new piece of bad news.

"They won't release him. Robert tried to use his authority, but Lawrence and his gang put some new rules in place. They're not letting prisoners out until they've gone through a trial. That could take months, and he's pretty sure they'll have a stronger hold on the council and the community in general by then, so it won't go in Garrett's favor." There's sympathy in his dark eyes, but the tightness in my chest turns hot with rage at the injustice of it.

"He didn't do anything. He was helping us. He was fighting for us!" I'm tempted to slam a fist into something out of frustration which is one hundred percent not a normal reaction for me.

"I know, Sophia. I know, but there's nothing I can do either."

The anger settles in, spreading through every limb, and my magic perks up a bit, sparking off my skin at the potent emotions coursing through me. "Well then, I guess I'll have to look after it myself." Resolve forms. First my uncle and now this backward council. They don't get to mess with my friends like that. They already fear my Archimage powers. I guess I'll have to give them a reason for it.

"Whoa, whoa, whoa. Ease up. I can't do anything right now, but when Robert gets home, he said he'll help us form a plan to get Garrett out. Don't do anything hasty and get yourself caught, too. They'd be more than happy to lock you up. Don't give them the chance."

A ball of anger rips through me like a comet across a dark sky, but I need to take a minute to control the emotions and organize my thoughts. He's right. I won't do Logan or Garrett any good if I get myself locked up. I need to take the time to plan this carefully and work with my friends. I drag in a few deep breaths, counting to five with each inhale and exhale to calm the rage and center myself. I focus on the cat in Liz's arms, listening to the rumbling buzz of its purr and studying the individual hairs of its smooth black coat.

"Ok. But we're doing it tomorrow. I'm not leaving it any longer. I won't risk Garrett after all he's done for me. I'm the one who got him into this situation and I'm the one who's going to drag him out no matter what I have to do."

"I'm in." Liz's voice is a little more tentative than usual, as if she's scared I'm going to snap at her.

"Of course I'll help you too. I've already declared my position at the Armstrong's side. No way am I going to back out on you. Besides, I'd kinda like that little sneak to owe me a favor." His dark eyes have a little sparkle in them as he makes light of the serious crap we're in. Probably trying to haul me out of my dark thoughts, and it works, at least for a moment.

A small smile tugs at the corner of my lips as I give Trey a light smack on the arm. "You sound like Log…" The words trail off and a wave of sadness crashes over me, extinguishing that brief spark of humor. My entire body droops, and I let myself fall to the couch.

Liz sinks down next to me. She looks into my numb eyes. I hate that she's feeling unsure around me. She's been warm, welcoming and free with her affection since the day I met her. I don't know how to fix this rift between us. I give her a small nod at the question in her eyes and she flings her arms around me. I sink into her embrace.

"I'm so sorry. This is all my fault." Her shoulders shudder with sobs as she pulls me to her.

She's blaming herself just as much as I've been. I need to let go of my anger at her. Xavier's death wasn't her fault any more than it was mine. She was only trying to save me.

"It's okay. It's not your fault." My hand slides in soothing circles between her shoulder blades until the sobs ease up.

Trey shifts from one foot to the other as we pull apart. He clears his throat, looking from me to Liz as if asking permission to speak. "Um, how about we regroup and make a plan after Robert gets home? In the meantime, we need to rest up and regenerate all that power we used up yesterday."

I nod. As little appetite as I have, I'm going to eat something, anything I can force down up and then try to take a nap, or at least lay down. I'll need everything I've got to get into the compound to rescue Garrett. After that, it'll be Logan's turn. Good luck to anyone, including my mom, who tries to stop me from getting to him.

Logan

Exhaustion weighs my eyelids down, fighting me as I drag them open. Cold stone chills my back and metal shackles prevent me from lifting a hand to swipe at my tired eyes. Torchlight flickers on the walls, giving me glimpses of the grim place. Stone floors, stone walls, and stains I don't want to think about. This is where Zeus takes me when he wants to steal my power and question me. I'm not giving him anything.

I squint around the dimly lit room to find that I'm alone. I scan the room, looking for something, anything to give me an advantage. The barred door is hanging open. He must have abandoned the torture session in a hurry. I struggle against the metal restraints holding me down and swear when they bite deeper into my raw wrists.

The murmur of voices comes from the hall outside the door. I ease up on the pulling to quiet the rattling of the metal chains, straining to hear what's being said.

"Incompetent fool let her off the compound, and she's staying at their house right now."

Is he talking about Sophia? Is she okay? I hope so. A faint glimmer of hope stirs from the shadows trying to drag me under.

Where is his intel coming from, though? I had suspected someone had betrayed us to him, but I have no idea who it could be. Anyone at the NAMC could know she's staying at my parent's house.

"We have her friend. Robert tried to get him released, but we blocked the request."

Friend? Which friend?

"Good. Any chance we can pull him to our side?"

"Nah. He seems loyal. We can't get anything out of him. He's not much use anyway. Just a Witch."

The unknown voice drops the flippant dismissal in a condescending tone. They must be talking about Garrett. I may not have liked the guy at first, but that was mostly because of his over fondness for my girl. Now that I've seen him fight, I know he's not someone to be dismissed that easily. Good luck to them.

"Don't underestimate the Witches. Some of them are just as highly trained as the Mages. Get out of here. Report back tomorrow. I want to know where they are and what's happening at all times."

"Yes, sir." The toady's voice comes back. Some people are so desperate for approval they'll turn themselves inside out to gain the notice of someone more powerful than themselves.

I hate going back into the darkness where I can't see what's coming, but I drop my eyes back closed as he comes back into the room. I focus on the heat from the torch on the wall, urging my magic to uncurl from where it's hiding deep within my core. It flickers to life and hums up to my fingers. A weak buzz that I send to the flames, pulling them toward the soft footsteps approaching me.

I open my eyes as the fireball slams into Sophia's uncle. He swears and the look in his eyes turns malicious as he storms back to the torch on the wall.

I stare him down as he lowers the torch to my torso until searing pain slices through me and the smell of burning skin hits my nostrils.

"Next time you try something like that, I'll use it on your pretty face. My niece won't find you so attractive then will she?"

His words are the last thing I hear as agony turns the edges of my vision red before dragging me back down into a black abyss.

Sophia

Unsurprisingly, I spent the entirety of my "nap" tossing and turning, surrounded by the sharp cedar scent and lingering presence of Logan. Sleeping in Logan's bed should be comforting, but in reality, it's torture knowing he's out there somewhere, cold and alone. None of the parents have even objected to my choice of sleeping arrangements, given he's not here.

On high alert, my ears twitch the second the front door clicks open and I leap up. I take the stairs two at a time, attempting to slide into a skidding halt at the front door and failing miserably. My palms sting as I slam them into the wall to stop myself. The pictures on the wall rattle and one falls to the floor, spewing shards of glass from the broken frame.

I wince. "Sorry." Still getting used to controlling the high-speed stops when my Phys power kicks in. At least that means they're coming back online.

"It's fine, Sophia."

The creases on Mr. Armstrong's face have deepened and his shoulders droop in a way that sends my heart racing.

Liz, Trey and the moms have all popped into the room at his return.

"Any more news?" I almost miss the look of sympathy on his face that tells me it's not going to be good news, but I have to hear it either way.

He sighs, running a hand through his smooth hair in a move that reminds me of Logan so much it causes the permanent ache in my chest to throb with fresh pain. His face remains etched in stone. He's the true master of the poker face.

"I wasn't able to make any progress on getting your friend released. I'm sure Trey filled you in on the details. Garrett's trial is scheduled for February 10th. I'm trying to maintain my position on the council to avoid things devolving any more than they are."

February 10th! That's almost two months away. There's no way I'm leaving Garrett at the mercy of unfriendly Mages for two months. "Well then, we're going in for him. C'mon."

I head for the door, not bothering to check if anyone is following. They said they'd help.

"Wait, Sophia!" Mr. Armstrong grabs my arm in a gentle hold. "You can't go running off without a plan. I thought you were smarter than that. I can't be directly connected with breaking him out, but that doesn't mean I won't help you make a plan."

His words hit me hard and I spin around. He's right. I am smarter than that. Our plan to lure out my uncle might have failed miserably, but we did plan it out. It isn't like me to let my emotions rule my brain. I take a minute to suck in a few deep breaths. "Right. A plan. I'll grab a notebook. Meet you in the kitchen." I zip upstairs and back down with my trusty notebook and a pen. Somehow I manage not to trip over my feet on the stairs or crash into anything on my return trip. I'm leaning over the kitchen table with my palms braced on either side of my notebook as the others settle into their chairs.

"Ok. What's the deal? Layout. Entrances and exits. How are we doing this?" I make eye contact with Trey, Liz and Mr. Armstrong. Mrs. Armstrong and my mom followed us in and are leaning against the counter.

Worry darkens Mom's eyes as she chews on the corner of her lip. "Can't you let Trey handle this? Why do you need to be involved, Sophia?" It's a plea, but I can tell she's resigned to me taking part in the rescue mission.

"I got him into this, Mom. I'm going to get him out, and then we're going to find Logan."

Her brow pinches together, but she nods.

I flip my pink notebook open, my pen flying furiously as Mr. Armstrong talks. "There's a tunnel and hatch that opens outside of the grounds. It's meant for escape and evacuation in the face of an invasion. It's as old as the compound and the only people who know about it are the top members of the council. Unfortunately, this means some of our enemies know about it, but I don't think they'll be expecting a breakout. These Mages don't see the value of Witches other than the services they can pay them for. Their lack of interest in him will hopefully work out in our favor and we'll be able to get you two," he nods to Liz and I "in and out before they suspect anything."

I scribble away in my tidy handwriting. "Okay, so if Liz and I are going to get in and out through this tunnel and across the grounds, we'll need to get away fast, right?"

Mr. Armstrong dips his head in a nod. "Yes, Ivy can handle that, but it won't make sense for you to leave via the tunnel. It'll take too long to get through and chances are very likely that someone will be alerted to your presence. It would be far too easy to trap you down there." His face softens when he turns to his look at his daughter with concern.

"Right, so then the best way out is going to be through the front doors? Then they'll need a distraction. I assume that's where I come in." Trey crosses his arms over his solid chest.

"Exactly. You can go in, provide a distraction, and the two other ladies can get the boy."

"What about locks, cameras, security tech?" I know the Mages are quite fond of mixing magic with tech to provide the maximum number of security layers possible.

"I know someone who can disable the alarms and locks for you, but it will only hold for ten minutes. So you're going to need to get him out quickly. If they catch you in there trying to break him out, they'll have an excuse to hold you, and they will."

That's an extremely tight timeline. "Can we really get to him that quickly? Because we can't use our super speed inside the prison building, right?" A shiver runs up my spine at the memory of the hollow ache of my magic being ripped out of my grasp when they took us into the building. Even in my numb state, it was like my insides were being torn out.

Now that we've decided to make a plan, I want to cover all the bases. I'm not going to do Logan any good if I get locked up.

"You can do it, but you'll have to make it fast. No delays at all. Here's a printout of the layout of the floor. Memorize it." He pulls a piece of paper out of his briefcase and unfolds it. "This is the where the tunnel opens up. You two will have to slip out this door here and follow the hall to the cell blocks." His long slim finger jabs at a marking. "Garrett is being held here in the B wing. Relatively loose security as he's not high risk. He's in cell B12 right here. You may need to incapacitate another guard or two along the way, but I know my Lizzie is quite capable." I hear a gasp from my mother, but Mr. Armstrong beams at his daughter with a pride that I've never seen him show his son. I can't even wrap my head around a family where the ability to knock out a guard in a jail cell is something to be proud of, but it sure will come in handy.

"Ok, so we go in. Get out with Garrett and then we need to get back to the entrance?"

"Yes. Trey will be here, providing a distraction with the guard at the entrance desk. I'll set it up for a time when Felice is watching the desk. You're all going to need to leave together. Ivy can stay with the car, and then we're going to get you somewhere safe."

"Wait, what?" I glanced over at Mom again. She looks stricken. "We have to leave?"

"You can't take her away from me!" Mom cried out. "She's only seventeen."

"I'm almost eighteen, Mom. Only a couple of weeks until my birthday." Not that I'm in any hurry to declare my independence or anything, but I'm not going to let anything stand in my way of rescuing Logan, even my mother. Honestly, it will probably be a lot easier to accomplish if we don't have parents hovering over us.

He braces his hands on the table. "She'll be fine. Would you rather keep her here and closer to danger? They know where she is, and her secret is out. There will be more than one group after her now that they know she's an Archimage." He lifts a stern eyebrow at Mom, trying to stare her down. I have to give her credit. She doesn't so much as flinch under the glare of the badass Mage. "Yes, you won't be able to stay here. For your own safety. We'll get you to a safe house while we deal with this mess within the council. I don't want you anywhere near here. Things are going to get ugly. Throwing an Archimage's powers in the mix could provide the edge someone needs to win this fight and I won't have anyone using you like that." His face is set in hard lines.

"Right. Ok. Where are we going to go?" If I have to leave, at least I'm going to plan for it.

"I have a location, but I'm not going to disclose it until you're on the road. The fewer people that know, the better. You're going to get out of that compound as fast as possible and we'll have a rendezvous point in the woods where you'll switch vehicles and disappear."

That's a lot to take in, but if it means we get Garrett out, it's one hundred percent worth it. "We're doing this tomorrow, right? What time?"

"Yes, I think it's best to get this done as soon as possible. Order is deteriorating fast, and things are unpredictable right now. Janet and I will be here, working away to regain control of the council. Trey has a connection with Felice and she'll be on the afternoon shift, so if you head in at 6pm there will be fewer people on site. Many of the ones that live there will be at dinner. It will be the ideal time. It will also give you plenty of time to recharge the remainder of your powers. You may not be able to use them inside the facility, but you'll need them in the tunnel and once you get out."

I nod and tilt my head at Liz. "I guess we should go over our part of the plan." A tentative smile spreads across her lips, faltering when she sees the hard look in my eyes.

Mom engulfs me in her warm arms and soft floral scent. It's the one place I've always felt safe and now I'm going to be leaving again for who knows how long.

"I love you, Mom." Her strong shoulders shudder under my hands and I bury my face in her neck.

"I love you too, honey. You have no idea how much."

Sophia

The sweet smells of maple syrup, waffles, and strawberries compete for my attention as I walk into the kitchen, but I can't find any joy in them right now. Food is just a means to an end. A necessity to refuel my body and my powers. Mrs. Armstrong and Mom are sharing space in the kitchen. My eyes soften at the sight of Mom with a ruffled red apron tied around her waist. She's always been the best of moms, but not the homemaker in an apron type. Mrs. Armstrong seems like such a fifties housewife type, but I know she's a force to be reckoned with in her own right. Her Psychic powers and position on the council show her strength even without the fighting skills I know she's spent her life honing. Respect to her for being able to be both.

"What can I do to help?" I sling an arm around Mom's waist and snag a bright red strawberry off the cutting board. A combination of sweet and tart flavors explodes in my mouth. Usually strawberries are one of my favorites, but it's not enough to thrill me today.

She clucks her tongue at me. "No snacking." The words are barely out before she sneaks me another berry.

"Morning, Sophia." Mrs. Armstrong turns to me with a smile, but I can see the strain creasing the corners of her eyes. Worry over sending Liz and me going off on our own is taking its toll on her. Not the pain we share over her missing son. "You can start setting things out on the table." She waves a manicured hand at the bowls of fluffy whipped cream, syrup, and is that melted chocolate? Should be tempting, but I can't even seem to get excited about chocolate.

Trey walks in as I'm setting the dishes out. "Morning." I dip my chin in a lazy nod.

"Morning ladies."

"Good morning, Trey. Make yourself useful and set the table, hon." Mrs. Armstrong calls over her back to him as she opens the waffle maker.

Ivy trails in, looking rumpled as if she hardly got any sleep, plopping down at the table.

I give her a curious look. "When did you get in yesterday?"

"Oh, it was pretty late. I had to visit some friends." She slaps a hand over her mouth that stretches in a wide yawn.

"We have a plan to rescue Garrett. I hope you're in," I say to her, not wasting any time to get to the point.

Her back straightens immediately as she perks up, looking at me with excitement shining in her dark chocolate eyes. "Really? What is it?"

"Are you in?" I lift an eyebrow. I'm not giving her the plan until I know she's with us for sure on this.

She jerks back as if my sharp words hit her like a slap and glances at Mrs. Armstrong. "Of course. Of course I want to rescue Garrett, and then Logan. How did that happen? How did we let him get pulled away?" Her eyes darken to almost black, mirroring her pain.

Her words send me off into another spiral. I have no idea how we let it happen. None of this was supposed to happen. Magic wasn't supposed to exist. I wasn't supposed to be this feared and hunted Archimage. Garrett wasn't supposed to get locked up. Logan wasn't supposed to get taken. And Xavier…I force myself to think the words. He was never supposed to die. Not this young. And it all comes back to me. A stream of hot tears rolls down my face before I notice I'm crying.

"Sophia, Sophia. You've got to breathe."

My head whirls as a pair of soft hands lands on my shoulders. The edges of my vision darken. My breathing is coming in quick gasps.

"I'm so sorry."

I'm not sure who the voice belongs to, but it brings me back into my body. I concentrate on taking slow breaths and open my eyes to focus on the room. One thing at a time. The couch. Swirls of a raised darker beige texture pop out on the cream fabric. My mother never would have gotten a couch that color in our house. My brother would have definitely ruined it with his stinky feet. Scott. God, it feels like forever since I saw him. He's supposed to be coming home for the Christmas holidays soon. I wonder how my mother is going to explain our relocation and my lack of presence to him, because I surely won't be around for the holiday. Who knows where I'll be.

My focus and distraction have evened my breathing to a steady rhythm, and I'm surprised to find Ivy's dark brown eyes staring at me with concern. Her small but deadly hands are the ones resting on my shoulders.

I swipe away the tear tracks that have run down my face. "I'm going to go look at some books. I'll be in the library if anyone needs me." I pull away from Ivy's grasp and head for the basement stairs that lead to the Armstrong's training room and office.

"Oh, honey." Mom reaches out for me, but I duck away. I don't know if I can keep it together if she touches me.

"I'm fine. Just need to do some research for tomorrow." There will be enough time to mourn my friend after I've rescued the others. Because I'm not losing anyone else. I can't.

I'm at the basement door before I remember there's a key code and some sort of ward on the door to keep their weapons and secrets safe.

"Uh, Liz." My words are quiet, but I know that her super sensitive ears will pick them up if she's not blocking too hard right now.

As expected, she gallops down the stairs two at a time. She's traveling at a normal human fast pace, letting her magic regenerate. Smart.

"I gotcha, Soph."

Her slender fingers fly over the keypad before she places her palm on the intricate carved pattern of whorls that glows to life, deactivating the ward on the door.

We pass through the training area in silence and she has to repeat the process on the second door into the office. She's still hanging out in the doorway when I reach the heavy wooden bookshelves stretching to the ceiling.

"Want me to help?" Her question comes out with a tremulous quaver. Her usual bravado gone.

"I'm good, thanks." The words come out a little shorter than I intended.

I'm trying not to be angry with her. I know it's not her fault. It's all down to Zeus, and me for putting Xavier in danger in the first place, but I can't help the heat of anger that occasionally rears its ugly head to take over the logical part of my brain. Why did she have to interfere?

The hurt and pain twisting her face guts me, so I try to soften the blow. "I just need to focus, and I don't know if I'll be able to keep it together if anyone gives me another one of those sympathetic looks." My eyes don't quite meet hers as I duck my head away. "I'm going to do some more research. You can come get me for lunch." I have a habit of getting lost in books and forgetting to eat at the best of times. And since the thought of food right now has my stomach flipping in rejection, I know I won't be emerging from here unless someone drags me out.

She pauses for one more moment before backing out. "I'll be right here if you need me. Gotta do some training." I give her a small nod and force a tight smile to my lips.

Now I know she's looking out for me. Logan would probably spend half the day training if he could, but Liz isn't one for a voluntary torture session.

I'm so absorbed in the book I was reading, I startle when the door swings open.

"Sophia dear. I brought you a sandwich."

Mrs. Armstrong settles a piled high plate on the desk in front of me. The lines on her face are deeper than before and worry creases her brow.

My manners kick in. "Thank you."

"Is there anything in particular that you're searching for? Maybe I can help you find the right book."

I appreciate the offer, but I'm not sure what I'm looking for. A spell? A death curse? I don't know. I mostly retreated into the books to settle my brain, but there's got to be something in here that can help find Logan, or put my uncle out of commission.

I heave out a long sigh. "I'm not even sure. There's got to be something, though. I've got a question for you? Why do you have all these books with spells and what not if the Mages don't even use them?"

A small smile turns up the corners of her lips and she looks a little out of place in her fitted black skirt

when she perches herself on the edge of the massive desk.

"It's true we tend to rely more on our innate magic and physical training than on exterior spells. There are some Mages who focus on the spells and objects of power that are usually the domain of Witches. I guess we've just gotten to a point where we rely on them for those types of things. Despite what it might seem like now, relations between Witches and Mages are the best they've ever been. And with that trust and reliance on each other, we've gotten soft in those external areas."

I guess it makes sense. "Then that means it's extra shortsighted of the anti-Witch component to persecute them."

She nods. "Exactly. I don't understand what Lawrence and the others are thinking. It makes no sense."

It doesn't make sense, but then many people do things that don't make sense in the pursuit of power. Persecuting another group to gain the upper hand is only one of the myriad awful things people do. I guess Mages are no different from mundanes in this respect.

"Well, I'd definitely like to study spells and things more…" I trail off, but the implication is there. One day. When I can live my life without checking over my shoulder for fear of someone I love getting snatched away. If that's even an option anymore.

Sophia

The weird vibe in the house all day drove me down to the training room. Guilt tugs my shoulders down like a weighted vest. I should spend some of my limited time with my mother, but the tears threatening to brim over whenever I look at her are freaking me out. I also can't afford to be in a distracted mindset when we leave on our rescue mission this evening.

The tingle of my magic has gone from the sparse and erratic sparks of a couple of days ago to a powerful buzz ripping through my veins. The raw energy surging through me is overwhelming. I'm having difficulty resisting the urge to let some out in order to gain relief, but I have to remember to save it for the potential battle ahead. Potential, yeah right. Judging from all our previous adventures, there's no way we're getting through this one without some sort of epic magical battle.

The satisfying thunk of my fist hitting the punching bag and the jarring pain in my knuckles helps, but the sad lack of movement to the bag is a little disappointing. I toy with the current in my veins. Maybe just a bit of magic?

"Not your best idea."

Trey's velvet voice booms out behind me, startling me enough to jump. I lose the thread of magic I was weaving into it and the punch goes wild, my fist sliding off the smooth edge of the bag.

I spin around with a sheepish smile at him. I should have known someone would end up down here with me. Someone in this house is always down here training. His company is not unwelcome. Out of everyone in the house, he's the one least likely to give me sympathetic looks or tearful glances. They mean well, but their sympathy threatens to send me off the ledge I've been balancing on since I watched Logan get dragged away.

"Want to do some sparring?" he asks.

"Yeah, sure."

He saunters over to the black mat in the center of the room and beckons me over with a curl of his fingers and I find drawn to his invitation.

His usual black cargo pants have been replaced by loose black track pants and a white sleeveless top that shows off the curves of muscle etched across his shoulders and down his arms. I'm used to him in both guises, but relaxed Trey at a training session has a way of loosening the tight hold I have on my feelings. I often find myself sharing more information with him than I intend. He's quietly dangerous in more ways than one.

"We're not going to go too hard. We need to conserve our physical energy just as much as our magic." The disapproving look that he's wearing tells me he could feel my magic building and knew I was about to waste some.

I settle into the starting stance that's becoming familiar to me, but his raised eyebrow and tilted chin have me shuffling my feet a little wider. We've trained together enough now that it's easy for me to read his silent commands and requests.

"Start with some blocks," he says before throwing a right jab at me.

My arm comes up automatically, but I'm not fast enough and he gets in over my guard.

"Come on, Sophia. If you end up facing off with anyone tonight, they're not going to go easy on you. Focus. Anticipate. Watch for my tells. Slight shifts of weight. Small eye movements."

I blink a few times and take a breath, sending the air deep into my diaphragm before releasing it and zeroing in on Trey. I see it this time. The slight shift of his right foot indicates he's about to throw a punch with his left. I'm ready this time and block him.

"Nice. See, it's all about the focus."

Everything in the room fades away except for his solid presence in front of me, the gentle thuds of flesh connecting with flesh and our quick breaths.

He drags me off the floor to do some stretches after I collapse in a sweaty heap. That definitely helped work off my excess energy. My skin is still a little itchy and tight, eager to let off some of the magic, but I'm a little more relaxed within my skin.

My neck cracks as I roll it to the back and side, loosening up the tension that's been sitting there for days, maybe months now. Ever since everything changed. A lot has changed for Trey too.

"How are you doing with all this, Trey?" I narrow my eyes as if I can laser past that calm façade to figure out what's going on in that stoic head of his.

"I'm getting through. Keeping you safe and getting Logan back are my priorities now."

"Yes, but I mean, with Ivy back, and your job is kind of up in the air now." He always seemed to me as if his identity was his job, but having trained with him, I know there's more to him than being a soldier.

"It's great having Ivy back. Weird, but good. She's..." he reaches for the sky in a long stretch. "...different, but still the same. I don't know how to describe it."

My head bobs in a small nod. I never knew Ivy before, so I don't really know, but from what I've seen, she's strong and self-sufficient and a total badass. Someone who I can totally see in my new friend group even if it is a little weird given her past relationship with Logan.

"But how are you handling the job thing? Like have you officially defected from the MED now? How does that work?" I don't want to poke at a sensitive subject for him, but it seemed like that was his life, and I wish he wasn't in this position.

"Only temporarily. We're going to have to regain control of the council eventually. I know Robert and Janet are working on it, but who knows what hold Lawrence has over these people or what he's told them to sway them over to his side. We have to get Garrett and Logan back first and then figure out how to fix what's broken with the council. I wouldn't want to be working for them now anyway. They're on the wrong side of the law. I'd probably be in charge of hunting you down rather than protecting you, and that's just unacceptable."

It's hard to smile, given my current state of worry, but I do my best to project a little warmth into the curve of my lips. It's good to have someone like him on the squad. My high school friends seem like a lifetime away now, though I know Charlotte would be there for me in a flash if she could. She has her own brand of witchy powers after all.

"Thanks."

His eyes light up with warmth and he pulls me in for an unexpected hug, giving me a face full of sweaty tee. "Gross, you're all sweaty."

He barks out a laugh before releasing me. "Right back atcha."

True, I should probably grab a shower before we head out. The thought of our plans for the evening cranks my anxiety dial back up to an eleven and all the tension settles into its new home in my shoulders. There are so many things that could go wrong on our mission. We're breaking into a secure magic facility guarded by both magic and technology. My mind skips around all the ways this could end in disaster.

Sophia

The scenery sweeps by in a blur of changing colors and dark silhouettes during the drive that brings us closer and closer to danger. As we're pulling over to the side of the road, the sun is slipping away for the day, settling a blanket of shadows over the forest. The hovering branches sway in the breeze that tugs at them. Not creepy at all.

I never used to be afraid of creatures lurking in the night. Not even when I was a kid. The world was logic and science and there was no possibility of ghosts, or demons or monsters of the non-human kind. Now, well, now I've met some of those creatures, and I don't even know what else could be lying out there waiting to get me, or more important, my friends.

Trey twists around in his seat to look at Liz and I. "You two got this? You need to get through the tunnel and wait until six to go in. Watches synced."

"We got this. Stop fussing." Liz rolls her eyes as she swings her legs out of the car. I have no idea how she can be so chill about the whole thing, but that seems to be her way. Not me. I'm a tangled mess of jangling nerves and racing heart.

"We'll be fine." The reassuring words are meant for Trey, but maybe they'll work on me as well. I really hope this doesn't all fall apart in another disastrous mess.

I lean in to give Trey and Ivy awkward hugs around the back of the car seats. It's nothing the tears and embrace my mom pulled me into before we left. It was like she was trying to prevent me from leaving. I'm a little surprised she's even letting me go. Not that it would stop me if she tried to forbid it. Maybe that's what it is. She knows she couldn't stop me if she tried and she'd rather not alienate me or have me sneaking off and disappearing into the darkness. Kinda like I did when I coerced Garrett into helping me find Logan and Ivy. I really owe him after all he's done for me. We're going to get him out.

Adrenaline junkie that she is, Liz is bouncing from one foot to the other with a gleam of excitement shining out of her eyes. This sort of thing will help take her mind off of Logan until we can get him too.

I try to keep up as she winds her way through the forest like some nocturnal creature finding a path where there is none. I, on the other hand, trip over multiple tree branches and get smacked in the face by a couple of others like a baby deer that hasn't learned how to use her feet yet. Scratch that. Newborn fawns are probably way more graceful than me.

After about an eternity of uncomfortable darkness and a couple of sore toes, we reach a small clearing. It's gotta be the right place. Something feels a little off. Like it doesn't quite belong in nature.

"We're here." I wince at her voice breaking through the gentle rustling of creatures and plant life. Those sounds belong in a forest like this. Our voices not so much.

I squint at our surroundings in the dim light of the setting sun gleaming through the branches until I spot a large rock to our right.

"That's it."

Dry leaves crunch under our hands, giving off a dusty fall smell as we clear the layer of dirt and dead foliage covering the entrance.

Our efforts reveal a round utility hole that would fit in fine on a city street but looks weird out here in the middle of nowhere. The only safeguard is a large metal padlock that we have the key to.

I run my hands over the cold, ridged metal. "Are we sure there's no magic warding this?" The Mages are anything but sloppy. It doesn't feel like they'd leave anything to chance or half assed. They use a combination of magic and technology to protect their most valuable secrets. I can't feel a buzz of energy, but it's not like I'm that in touch with my magic side yet.

"Nope." She pops the p on the word. "Like my dad said, it would be easier for a Mage or Witch to find the entrance if it was magically warded. Here it just seems like a mundane infrastructure thing."

"Okay." I pull the key out from under my shirt and hold my breath while the key slides in and turns with a click, releasing the latch.

No alarms go off, so I let the air flow out of my lungs and Liz helps me pull open the heavy door. It groans with a creak of disuse that echoes through the forest, but other than the rustling from the trees as a bird takes off, we seem to be safe.

Liz plunges down into the darkness without hesitating, and I follow along with a little more caution.

I grab the sides of the hole and lower myself into the unknown until my legs dangle. I tried taking gymnastics for a year when I was a kid. Turned out dangling from bars was not my thing so my mom let me give it up and went back to my at home science experiments.

"Just let go." Liz's voice pulls me back, giving me the confidence to follow through.

The ground rushes up and a sharp pain buckles my knees when I hit the soft dirt floor.

I have to blink a few times until my eyes adjust to the dim light emanating from the caged lights high on the wall lining the path. At least there's some light down here. A creepy tunnel with horror movie lights is better than one that's completely dark, I guess.

Liz's soft hand closes over mine and she pulls me along behind her. "Come on. We can't waste any time."

Right. We have a job to do. Rescue Garrett and get the heck out of here.

"We'll be fine."

Liz is trying to reassure me. "I hope so," I reply.

"What?" She turns around with a curious look.

"I hope we'll be fine."

I bump into her when she stops in her tracks. "Did you hear me?"

"What do you mean? Of course I did."

"I didn't say that out loud."

"Oh." I glance down at our joined hands. Are they providing a connection, giving me a path into her thoughts?

"Are your Psyche powers emerging?" The light above her flickers with a buzz casting an eerie glow over her curious face.

That's a scary thought. All the other magic has been wild. Wild but cool. The thought of hearing anyone else's thoughts or being able to control them sends a small shudder down my spine. That's an uncomfortable amount of insight into someone else's head.

"Maybe? Not that I can even think about that right now. What a nightmare."

"I think it would be cool. Not as cool as my awesome Phys magic, but still could be pretty useful."

"Or horrifying. I can't imagine hearing all the things people think about me all day long." Bad enough when they say them out loud.

"True. Ah well. You've learned some blocking techniques to avoid Psych Mages getting into your head, right? You can use them to block out the noise as well. My mom can definitely help you with that."

The thought of working with Mrs. Armstrong is comforting. She's becoming like a second mom to me. The edges of my mind darken at the realization that I don't really know when we're going to see her again.

Our silence amplifies the pounding of my heart as we traverse the rest of the twisting tunnel. The damp, earthy stench of the ground is getting to me, and the concrete walls feel like they're closing in the deeper we get.

"There it is."

I follow Liz's finger, pointing to a metal ladder that scales the wall at the abrupt end to the pathway. I guess this is a one-way tunnel. Seems safe. Yeah right. Gotta be against some fire code. I flip my wrist up to check the time on the watch Mr. Armstrong gave me for this adventure. We're stuck here waiting for another twelve minutes.

I hop up and down, rubbing my arms to stave off the cold that's seeping into my bones.

"So, we're gonna head up the ladder and open the hatch at thirty seconds after six, then head right down the hall. Garrett is being held in cell 509 on the third level up, so we need to hit the stairwell at the end of the hall." I recite the plan out loud, more to reassure myself than for Liz. I know she's got this. She might be impulsive sometimes, but she knows when to stick to the plan.

"Sounds right. We got this, Sophia. We went over the plan like five bazillion times already."

I know she's right, but I can't stop my mind from jumping to all the scenarios where everything goes wrong. They don't get the alarms shut off, or they come back online too soon. They have moved Garrett. We encounter too many guards to handle on our own. Liz is a total badass, but I've barely begun training. Pure luck or wild magic are the only things that have gotten me out of the situations we've encountered recently.

"I promise it's going to be fine. We're going to get Garrett out and then we're going for my brother. I won't accept anything else." There's steel in my friend's usually flippant tone and her face has hardened into a determined mask. Good, we're on the same page here. Failure is not an option.

"Me either." I give her a fist bump and check my watch for the millionth time. "It's time."

I clamber up the rusty ladder after her and we count down the seconds.

Logan

The world fades in and out in a blur of pain and darkness. Zeus has left me alone for the a day…or three. I have no idea how much time is passing. Meals and water are delivered sporadically. I'm sure it's on purpose so I have no way of tracking time.

Boots slapping on pavement with a harsh ring in the hallway slow down as they get closer to my cell, and I'm not sure if it's food or more torture, but I drag myself up the cement wall behind me into an exhausted sitting position. It doesn't matter how shitty I feel right now I have zero desire for Zeus to catch me lying on the floor.

I hear the chirp of the alarm on the door being disabled before it's jerked open.

"Boy, how are you doing down here?" There's an evil smirk on the chiseled face that doesn't match the dapper suit and slicked back hair of the older man.

I don't bother answering him. He isn't worth my time.

He strides over and jerks on the chains attached to my handcuffs. "I was talking to you."

I grunt in reply before keeling over as agony shoots up my tender ribs from his sharp kick.

"Well you're coming with me now and you'll speak to me whether you like it or not."

"Never." I don't even recognize the rusted metal creak of my voice. He must have left me down here longer than I thought if I've completely lost my voice.

"It's not really up to you."

I find myself dragged to my feet by the chains he unlocked from the thick metal ring that juts out from the floor.

I do my best to stay on my feet despite stumbling a few times at his rapid pace. Between the battered body and the cuffed hands my usual balance is thrown and I hate it. I hate being weak. I've spent my whole life trying to prove my strength and my worth and now here I am useless.

After an endless number of turns and identical hallways we end up in a room I've never been in before. Tiny needles pierce my eyeballs at the bright light in the room. Every where I've been down here so far has been dimly lit. I'm not sure what I was expecting in the Nether Realm, but this wasn't it. Unless he's taken me out of there and moved me somewhere else. I wasn't exactly conscious for the journey here.

Wariness overcomes the slight relief that I'm not in the room he usually takes me to for a little light torture. A bitter snort escapes.

"Something funny? Well don't worry. We'll fix that soon enough."

I have no idea what he has in mind here but it's definitely not going to be sunshine and sandy beaches.

I struggle against him as he shoves me toward the metal chair that looks like it belongs in the office of a sadistic dentist. I never liked the dentist.

I manage to get my balance enough to kick him hard in the kneecap. It crumbles under him and I try to push past him to the door but he jerks on my chains with a sharp tug that sends me sprawling before rising to his feet brushing himself off and kicking me in the face. My cheek bursts into flame but I don't let out the scream that's begging to escape. My magic is raging inside me in a tumultuous thunderstorm.

Two more beefy guys join us in the room. My shoulders scream as they're wrenched up by the bouncer types. They unceremoniously drop me in the chair and lock my chain into another floor ring. This guy is into some serious kink clearly.

They also snap some more cuffs around my ankles to really lock me in place. Like I had any hope of escaping before. Glad to see I've made an impression though. Sophia's evil uncle is scared enough of me to lock me down tight.

He reaches out to clutch my chin tilting my head up so I have to meet his gaze. I hate looking at her eyes staring at me out of that cold, cruel face. The ache in my chest where I can't feel her again roars to life in an inferno.

"You ready to talk?"

"Sure, how's the non magic life treating you? Must suck being powerless, huh?" I know I'm going to pay for that comment, but I don't care.

"I have more power than you can possibly fathom. And soon to have more when I get ahold of that girlfriend of yours."

"You'll never get her."

"That's what you think. I'm this close." He holds a finger and thumb up an inch apart. "And you're going to be the one that helps me."

I snort even as cold fingers of dread clutch at the back of my neck. "As if."

"Oh, just you wait and see. I've got a treat for you." He strides over to the door. "Watts!" he calls out, sticking his head through the door to summon someone.

A man with thin wire glasses and pasty skin appears a moment later. He's carrying a black leather briefcase that has me wondering if he really is a sadistic dentist.

I bare my teeth at the man as he gets close and his shirt sleeve rides up to reveal a tattooed symbol of an eye set dead center in the middle of a swirling cloud of lines. Looks witch like.

He proceeds to open his suitcase. It's lined in black velvet (very dramatic) and has several small glass vials set into the material that lines it. Does not bode well. I doubt he'd poison me. If he wanted to kill me that would have been easy enough to do. No need to break out the fancy stuff.

I cringe at the appearance of a needle in his gloved hand.

"Now Watts is a bit of a potions master, but one of his specialties is a truth serum."

"No." I try to twist away and my locked up limbs refuse to take me where I want to go.

My heart had given up fighting, but this, this causes it to race into overtime. My skin's going cold and clammy and there is absolutely nothing I can do about it. He's going to question me, and I'm going to be forced to spill my secrets. Whatever he wants to know. Sophia could be hiding out in the cottage. I'll compromise my family's safe space. I will myself to pass out or anything. Anything that will get me out of here.

A silver flash glints off the needle he pulls out of his case. The needle holds no fear for me, it's the viscous red liquid he's drawing out of the bottle that's making my skin crawl.

A vice of a hand locks around my wrist straightening my arm out. If I ever get out of this place, each and every one of these guys is done.

That's the last coherent thought I have before a sharp prick pierces my arm, and a scalding heat spreads through my veins. My thoughts start to dull around the edges progressing to to cloudy haze as if I'm in a dream.

"There. I'm so glad I found Watts. I didn't even have to threaten any of his family to get him here. He seemed almost excited. Now, Logan. We'll start out simple. Make sure you're fully under the sway. The effects don't last long, and the serum takes a very long time to brew, but this will be worth it."

"Are you dating my niece?"

The cloudy haze over my brain makes it feel like I'm in a dream. None of this is real. This man's face is a blur in front of my eyes.

"Well?"

The shouting voice in the back of my brain is telling me to fight this. Fight this until the very end.

"She's not your niece." Is what I manage to grind out in a weak gasp. It's the truth to me. He's no blood of hers. To be family, you have to be there for each other.

"Ah. Trying to get around it I see. You're stronger than I thought. Are you dating Sophia?"

I try to fight it. I try to resist with everything in me but the word still comes out short and succinct. "Yes."

"There we are. And where is she right now?"

That ones easier. The despair even comes through in my words. "I don't know." Because I genuinely don't. I don't know how long I've been down here or where she is.

"Of course. Where was she staying when you last saw her?"

A picture of the cottage floats into my head. Her standing out in the snow, flakes falling to kiss her rosy cheeks. As hard as I grind my teeth the words come out. "The cottage."

"The cottage. Excellent and where is this cottage?"

He jots down the address as I mumble the address, defeated.

"Tell me about her powers."

It all comes spilling out. The things we've been working on. Her training and abilities that have shown in the various magic classifications. I can't stop the flow of words once they've started, and he soaks up every word.

He asks me a few more questions about my family and the council before the haze starts to lift and I clam up, fighting every word a little hard.

"The effects seem to be wearing off now, sir." The tinny voice of the weaselly man is tentative as if he doesn't want to anger Zeus.

"That's fine. I got everything I needed. Get him back to his cell."

The big guys drag me off the table and back to my new home. I don't even fight it this time and a raging headache is pounding my temples by the time they've slammed the door shut on me.

My knees give out on me and I crumble to the floor in heap of guilt and despair. The cold floor sends shivers through my body, and I let the darkness pull me under.

Sophia

I hold my breath as I slide the reluctant key into yet another padlock.

"It doesn't want to…"

"Come on. Hurry." As if I need the added pressure of Liz's urging.

A metallic clang echoes around me and I glance around as if anyone is around to hear it.

"Crap. The key broke." My heart races at double time.

"What?" She hisses at me. "Use your strength."

"Won't that send out the alert that we're here?" I really don't want to give them a heads up that we're here with my super special Archimage signature that I've been told my magic gives off.

"Right. Shove over. Let me up there."

I dubiously eye the narrow old ladder I'm perched precariously on. Does she actually think she's going to fit on here with me? I guess we'll find out. She does a one armed pull up and turns to me with a smile.

The ladder groans when she places a foot on the rung beside mine, but it holds.

It's hard to believe her tiny hands are capable of wrenching the heavy lock open, but it's not the first time I've witnessed her superhuman strength. I've barely touched the surface of the things I've seen her do. Makes me wonder what I'll be capable of when I fully come into my magic.

Her head swivels around, and I give one last glance at my watch, giving her a nod.

"It's go time. Brace yourself."

Bright light streams in through the hole in a piercing stream as she pushes the door open nice and easy.

I peek up to scan the area. Looks clear, so I climb up the last few rungs to push through. My feet slip out from under me and I drop with a squeal, scrabbling for a handhold before I go plummeting back into the abyss.

The offending padlock that tripped me up tumbles to the ground with a clang that's gotta be reverberating through the entire building. It wouldn't surprise me if Garrett could hear it from his cell.

"Sorry. Probably shouldn't have left that there," Liz says as she hauls on my arms to drag me up after leaping up with her usual feline grace.

Passing through the ward is like a punch to the gut that sends all the air shooting out of my body. I rub my chest at the uncomfortable but now familiar feeling of emptiness that accompanies the disconnection from my powers. After having those infernal cuffs on you'd think I'd be used to it, but no, seems like getting a major portion of your being ripped away never gets easier.

"You think?" I eye the room we've ended up in. It's a large space full of metal shelving overflowing with cardboard banker's boxes. Good to know the map is accurate. We're right where we're supposed to be in the back of the records room.

The lit up emergency exit sign leads us toward the way out. The timer counting down in my head urges me to pick up the pace. I'm calculating whether we can make it to Garrett before anyone catches on to our presence in here.

A sigh of relief escapes after we pass the booth at the front, but my heart doesn't stop pounding against the wall of my chest. Even though Mr. Armstrong said no one would be watching the desk at this time of night, you never know if some workaholic is going to be staying after hours.

Footsteps alert us we've got company as we make it through the door and into the long white hallway. The stairwell that leads to Garrett's floor is tantalizingly close.

I glance around at the rooms surrounding us. This entire floor is supposed to be storage, so that door two up on our right should be the maintenance room if the map in my head is accurate.

I give a tug on Liz's arm and tip my chin at the door I think we should go through. She nods back and we duck in. Shelves of toilet paper, paper towels and cleaning chemicals prove my calculations are correct.

We press ourselves flat against the wall on either side of the door, giving a surreptitious peek through the window until the man passes by without a glance. After too much time, we slip back out through the day and run to the stairwell.

The stairs disappear beneath my feet in rapid succession as we fly up them to the floor Garrett is being held on. This is going to be the tricky part. There are likely to be guards here, and we need to avoid notice for as long as we possibly can.

Liz seems to be so nonchalant right now, as if breaking into a secure facility is an everyday occurrence for her. Not me. I'm afraid my stomach is going to leap right out of my mouth at any second. That would be a great way to go down. How'd you get caught? Oh, you know, vomited all over the floor before we even got to Garrett's cell. I swallow hard and check my watch. Five agonizing minutes have passed. Every second that passes brings us closer to a horde of guards descending on us when their system comes back online.

Our luck holds as we emerge from the stairwell. No guards yet.

Luck is a fickle thing though, and a moment later it vanishes in a poof as if we displeased the genie watching out for us.

A hint of red flashes from the chest of the otherwise stark black uniforms of not one, not two, but four guards. Two at each end of the hallway. The light glints off the metallic B12 on the door, taunting us with Garrett's freedom. If we can just get around, under, or through those guards without bringing the force of the entire building down on us we can get to him.

I yank Liz back into the stairwell before they catch sight of us, painfully aware of our time running out. Once they get the cameras and alarms back up, they'll be on us. She's dancing on her feet with her eagerness to take action.

"We have to go. I can take them. There's only four," she pulls at the arm I've restrained her with.

Even without her magic active, I believe her. Liz can kick ass even without her powers, but it's not the smart decision.

"No, we wait. They'll pass by and we'll have our chance. I'm not willing to risk Garrett's freedom out of impatience."

"Fine." A hint of disappointment creeps into her tone as she sighs and peeks longingly through the window in the door. "They're stopping for a chat."

I didn't think it was possible for my heart to race harder, but it picks up another couple of impossible notches.

The rapid tapping of feet racing up the stairs fills the area. Resignation sets in, replacing the anxiety that's been keeping me on high alert since we got here. We're trapped. Looks like we'll be using a combination of Liz's stellar fighting skills and my dubious ones sooner than I'd hoped. Hopefully, her skills and the element of surprise will tip the balance in our favor.

A gleam hits her storm-tossed eyes and I give her a nod. It's time.

I yank one of my knives out of the calf sheath and take a deep inhale. One advantage of coming in through the back entrance is the stockpile of weaponry we brought with us. Not that I'm really into the idea of actually using any of them on another human, or Mage, whatever.

Liz's petite frame bursts out the door and she bolts for the guards that are farthest away, leaving me with the man and woman closest to us. They've turned to chase after Liz without noticing me, so I've got the advantage of surprise. Thank Curie, I need all the advantages I can get against these trained warriors.

I use both hands to grip the hilt of my blade and slam the butt into the back of the male guard's head, wincing at the crack as it bashes his skull. He stumbles for a moment before his knees give out, sending him to the floor. I'm so surprised at my success that I pause for too long to watch him go down and the female guard gets the jump on me.

I've got no defense against the arm she slides around my neck in a chokehold. A shot of pain shoots through my foot, followed by a metallic clang as the knife slips from my sweaty palm. My hands scrabble at her hold, but she tightens her grip, cutting off my breath. I swing a leg back and attempt to kick her or step on her feet. Anything to get her to release the breath stealing hold. All the defensive training I've been doing has been to avoid getting stuck in a situation like this. I can't believe I let her get her hands on me so easily.

My body is limp and my vision is fuzzy and black at the edges when the arm around my neck releases. I gasp in a breath that's like knives sheering down my windpipe, reaching out to grab something to keep from toppling over. I felt the warmth of another body as my hands connected and then a familiar arm embraced me.

"C'mon. We haven't got much time. None of them sounded the alarm. Idiots. But the system is going to come back online soon and then we'll have a bit more of a challenge."

Right, four guards and a near strangulation wasn't much of a challenge for my friend. The screaming pain in my throat finds this laughable. I shake off the unsteadiness, remembering why we're here and pull away from Liz, making it the ten feet to Garrett's cell in record time. Well, record time for me anyway.

I'm praying to any dead scientist that's listening that they didn't deactivate Trey's keycard yet as I slide it out of my back pocket. Relief makes me almost woozy again when the light flashes green and the door opens with a satisfying snick.

Garrett's mouth flies open when he catches sight of me. The anger that was simmering behind his eyes flashes to shock, and he half rises to his feet from the small metal bed.

"Sophia." His eyes dart behind me. "Liz. What are you doing here?"

"Really? For an intelligent person, that was not the smartest of questions. We're here to rescue you, obvi."

A small laugh escapes him in spite of the dire circumstances he's in. I run my hands over the coarse fabric of the ugly outfit they put him and he seems no more damaged than he was when we got here.

"Hurry up, nimwit. We don't have all day."

"Of course." He rushes toward us. "You shouldn't be here. It's too dangerous for you, Soph."

"Maybe so, but there was no way I was leaving you here to fester at the hands of hostile Mages. You should know better than that. That's not what friends do."

I slide my hand into his, and yank at him to hurry.

"Welp. Here we go. Prepare for anything." Liz calls the words out over her shoulder as we head back to the stairwell we came from.

Three floors and a few hallways to get out the front, I remind myself, counting the steps as each one brings us closer to our escape from this place.

The door between floors swings open. Liz grabs hold of the railing, swinging up and sending the guard who dared to walk through the door flying backward. I didn't even have a chance to consider our options. That's one more out of the equation.

We continue taking the stairs two at a time, but the sharp sound of an alarm pierces straight into my soul. The slightly nicer carpeted hallway we skid into indicates we've made it to the admin/exit level. So close.

My breath comes in rapid pants and my vision has narrowed to the door at the end of the hall where our freedom lies. Get through there, meet up with Trey, and make it out the front door before they can lock it down. I push my legs faster than they've ever gone, trying to keep up with Liz. Garrett's holding back, keeping pace with me.

Guards spill from the doors behind us, and we almost make it to the last one between us and Trey, who is supposed to be waiting at the check-in desk out front.

I spin around when a rough arm catches mine. I slam the palm of my hand into the soft spot at the crease of his elbow and he releases me. I don't bask in triumph this time, pushing through the door after Liz.

The woman at the front desk is slumped over onto her arms. If I didn't know better, I'd think she was sleeping on the job, but I know it must have been Trey's doing. She's the first one I spot, but then my gaze falls to the crumpled heap of Trey's body on the floor. What happened? I glance back at the woman and my stomach exits my throat when I spot a lying on the counter inches from her hand. She shot him?

The guards burst through behind us as I push open the front door. Darkness spills through, reminding me of the time. It's so lit up in here with fluorescents it feels like daytime.

A glint of something catches my eye, drawing it to the deadly looking gun pointed at me. Aren't they all deadly looking? I didn't think they carried those around here, but I guess with the lack of magic inside the building, they've learned to rely on other sources of defense.

I duck down and a small pop sounds as something flies over my head.

I grab Trey's arm and try to drag him along with me, but without my extra strength, there's no way I can manage the densely muscled weight of his body.

Liz and Garrett each join in, grabbing a limb and we tug him along after us, making it to the main entrance without getting swarmed by the guards.

Liz leaps out the front door first, giving one last heave and throwing Trey's prone body over her shoulder. Now that she has her magic back, she makes it look effortless. All we have now is the brief distance between the door and the car where Ivy is waiting, hopefully with the engine running.

The path is clear, but fresh snow is falling, leaving a slippery dusting that's trying to steal my feet out from under me as I push myself to the limit. The rush of magic back through my body is a little distracting and Liz has blurred out in front of me to get herself and Trey into the car as fast as she can. I don't want to boot up my super speed, because there's no way I'm abandoning Garrett after all that.

When I glance over my shoulder and spot a couple of guards with their guns out, a fiery anger courses through me. It swells my powers until an electrical buzz is shooting down my arm, begging for release. I let the energy flow out the palm of my hand in a flash of flames so powerful it almost knocks me off my feet. It definitely knocks a couple of guards off of theirs. Oops. I hope they're ok. I didn't intend for it to be that huge, but the pent up magic compounded by the fear and anger inside was too strong for me to temper.

Another rush of guards spills out after us. Looks like the whole compound knows we're here now. Here I thought the hard part would be getting out of the building. We still need to make it through the front gates with the entire Magical Enforcement Division coming after us. At least the ones that are loyal to Zeus and Lawrence.

One problem at a time. Gotta make it to the car first.

"Go, Sophia." Garrett is running hard and still trying to get me to leave him behind. As if I would after going to all of that trouble.

I ignore his plea and throw a hand out to my left, trying to focus my mind to send a surge of wind at our pursuers to the left. It escapes my control again with another surge that rips a sapling out of its roots before sending the handful of guys sprawling.

I turn to the other contingent on our right and they've stopped in their tracks, eying me with a level of fear I never expected to inspire in anyone. I shove the sick feeling down and keep running. I have to make a sudden stop to avoid the car that screeches onto the grass in front of us, spinning out to the side as the door is flung open. The move wouldn't look out of place in a blockbuster action flick.

Garrett drags me to my feet and shoves me in to the back seat before leaping in the front. The car shoots off before I've quite slammed the door shut.

My chest aches from sucking all the cold air into my lungs in huge gulps and my throat is burning from the chokehold, but I shove down all that pain and turn to Trey.

I run my hands over his body as the car barrels toward the gate, tossing us around. I'm expecting a pool of blood to be spreading under his body, but there's nothing. Liz flips her hand open to reveal a red feathered dart. I almost cry in relief that Trey didn't get shot for me. I can't lose another friend. X's face swirls behind my eyelids and a fresh wave of pain claws at me.

"Tranq darts. They don't carry real guns. Haven't stooped to that yet. Although, after today… they might rethink their stance."

"Right." I don't know that much about this sort of thing. Not exactly a major component of my pre-magic life. "How long will the effects last?"

"Shouldn't be longer than an hour, two tops," Ivy's voice is way cooler than mine would be if I was trying to keep a racing vehicle from skidding off the road.

Other cars are keeping pace with us now, but we had a head start, so no one is catching up. I'm sure Ivy's foot is touching the floorboard as we follow a steady path between the trees lining the driveway. It's way too long and curving for my comfort.

Pain blossoms in my shoulder to join the rest of the aches when I'm thrown into the window as Ivy swerves, barely scraping past a tree trunk. I turn around to see a row of spikes poking up through the formerly empty road. Smart defense. I'd be impressed by it if we weren't the ones trying to escape. Just as I'm hoping there aren't more where that came from, she makes another sharp turn that sends me on top of Trey. Liz is now buried beneath the both of us, but she shoves him off as I right myself again and the massive black exit gates loom into view.

Show time. I don't even try to hold back this time as I shove both arms out the window and gather as much magic as I can. It's swirling around inside, eager to be let loose and unleash havoc. I'm not afraid of it this time. I'm not going to hurt anyone, so I can put as much power behind this as I want. The freedom is amazing. I focus on the snow, and the cold air biting at my cheeks, pulling moisture from the air and sending it to the gate. I imagine the droplets freezing in a cold snap that would rival the energy needed for cryogenics.

Energy rushes through my body in a constant stream, but I have no idea if this is going to work. I continue to send the magic into the gate as it rushes at us faster and faster.

I squeeze my eyes shut tight as we slam into the gate with a force that hurls our bodies out of the seats. This had better work. It does. The frozen gate shatters, sending a rain of icy particles clattering all over the vehicle. We make it past the gate before a loud pop sounds sending the back of the car swaying. It slows as Ivy tries to get it back under control, but other vehicles are in a race to catch up.

Three dark SUVs come careening through the gaping hole that used to be a gate, but we keep going. I'm sure they're going to catch us after all that, but then a creaking sound echoes through the woods beside us. A massive tree topples to the ground barely a foot from the back of our car, effectively protecting us from our pursuers. I send up a thank you to Mr. Armstrong. I knew he was watching out for us, but I didn't know he had this planned out.

The car sputters along despite the one deflated tire as we turn into the woods to our rendezvous point. There should be another vehicle for us to swap to containing our prepacked bags and zero trace of a connection to the Armstrongs.

We get everyone out and transferred to the new vehicle and hit the logging back road that will take us out of reach of the hostile council and their army.

Sophia

My terror finally eases after twenty minutes on the road with no one in pursuit. A shiver that turns into full body quaking accompanies the relief as the rush of adrenaline makes its rapid departure. A deep cold seeps through my skin and muscles settling right into my bones.

Liz pulls one of the neatly folded blankets off the floor of the new car and wraps it around my shoulders. Ah, now they make sense. My brain is analyzing the inputs and has figured out the reason for the shivers. I must be going into shock, but the knowledge does nothing to help me deal with it.

"Here." Garrett leans into the back between the two seats and tries to hand me a silver thermos.

My shaky hands can't quite close around it, so Liz grabs it, unscrewing the top and holding the rim to my mouth. I take a long pull and am pleasantly surprised when the rich chocolate floods my tongue. I inhale the sweet smell, pulling the fleecy blanket tighter around my shoulders to further ease the shudders. I guess caffeine probably wouldn't be the best option to bring me down from this. The hot chocolate is much appreciated. I take another sip, not even caring about the scalding it's giving my ravaged throat.

When I start to warm up, the shivering eases up and I curl into Liz's side. She somehow scrambled out from under the dead weight that is Trey to snuggle up next to me.

I toss my blanket around her shoulders so we can share each other's warmth. Something about the danger, adrenaline, and goal we shared to break out Garrett washed away the anger and blame that had been souring our friendship since Xavier's death. I know deep in my gut that I would have done the same thing for her. I would have saved her regardless of the consequences, and she had no reason to suspect Zeus would go that far. All this talk of disappearing Mages and people turning up dead never really hit home until we actually experienced my uncle's cruelty. I can't wrap my head around anyone trying to kill another human being, even after seeing it with my own eyes. A deep shame and disgust has set in, knowing that I share blood with that monster,

"I'm sorry." My whisper brushes a lock of multicolored hair off the delicate shell of her ear, revealing some black cat studs in her ears. Of course.

"For what, babe?" She looks genuinely confused.

"I haven't exactly been nice to you the last couple of days. I know it wasn't your fault. I think I was just blaming you to avoid pointing the finger at myself."

Her icy fingers close on my cheeks, turning my face toward her. "You have nothing to feel guilty about. None of this is on you. And you've been through some serious trauma. Of course I don't blame you for your feelings."

I relax against her. I haven't even known Liz that long, but she's already one of my closest friends. I feel like I'm living a world away from all my high school friends, except maybe

Charlotte. With her witchy powers, I know she'll be able to stay a part of my new world, but she's still stuck at home finishing up high school at the moment. But I wonder if I've lost the rest of my mundane friends forever.

A moan breaks me out of my reverie, and I lean toward another member of my new squad. Trey's dark eyelashes flutter a couple of times before he reaches his hand up with an obvious effort to rub his head at the temples.

"Hey there, Trey. How you doing?"

"Wha…what happened?" He gets the words out with some difficulty.

"You got shot with a tranq. Taken down like a rabid lion."

"Ugggghhh. Well, that explains it."

My hands are still freezing cold, so I place one on his forehead, hoping to ease a little of his pain. He jumps a bit at first, before letting out an appreciative moan.

He takes a look around after dragging his eyelids all the way open. "Did everyone at least make it out?"

"Yup. All here, safe and accounted for. A bit battered and bruised, but I think maybe you got the worst of it." My hand instinctively goes up to rub at the Logan sized hole in my chest where the bond usually warms me. All safe except one. He's next I vow to myself. It might be an impossible task to get down to the Nether Realm to find and rescue him, but I'm doing it with or without help. It's still comforting to know that everyone in this car will be there for me.

I try to push Trey back down when he tries to rise to a sitting position.

"Let me up, Sophia. I've suffered worse. Just a bit of a headache." I've never been hit with a tranq dart, but I seriously doubt his claim. Not that I'll ever get him to admit it.

I reluctantly pull away, and he slides into a sitting position. Trey extends a hand up front to give Garrett a slap on the back. "Good to see you made it out, man. I would have hated for all that effort to be for nothing."

"Gee thanks, dude," Garrett replies. "Glad you care."

A snort escapes Trey. "C'mon, I didn't mean it like that. I'm glad you're safe."

Garrett turns around with a glare in our direction. "I can't believe you all risked Sophia for me. I'm not worth that."

My heart aches for him. I know he's still got a lot of survivor's guilt about his own family. What I'm feeling about Xavier's fresh loss is nothing compared to what he's been living with for years, but I think he's well and truly proven himself lately. He is the good person he kept hidden for all those years. He's been there for us multiple times, risking his own life and freedom.

"Don't talk like that. You're totally worth it, and do you really think any of these jokers could have stopped me from getting you out? I would have gone in alone if I had to."

"So true," Liz says. "She was ready to go in powers blazing, literally, the next day. We had to pull her back from the fire and convince her to make a plan. And since you know she's the queen of not jumping in to things without a plan of action, you know she was determined."

"Still." Bitterness twists his features.

"Garrett, recently you've become one of my closest friends. I have no idea how it happened, but here we are. I'd do the same for any of you weirdos."

A brief flash of protest comes over his face before it turns into resignation. "Same for you." He turns back to the road. "Where are we headed?"

"Back to the cottage," Ivy says. She's been super focused on the road, so hasn't joined in the chatter much since we peeled out of the compound and transferred vehicles. "We're actually not too far now. I've been keeping an eye on the rearview mirror and that, combined with all the back roads on this route, seems promising. Doesn't look like anyone followed us."

"That's good," my words come out in between a yawn.

"Yeah, this day has been exhausting. Even for me. I can't imagine how the rest of you mere mortals are holding up." I'm glad to hear Liz's usual sass come back in her playful jab at us.

The car easing through the front gates of the cottage wakes me up from the brief nap that pulled me under, and I blink to clear away the fog. It's comforting to be back here. Feels safe, where no one can find us.

Sophia

A hint of moonlight peeking through the window is the only illumination to light up my repetitive path through the dark house. Somehow, despite our exhausting day, I find myself up and pacing in the middle of the night. The conversation at dinner was sparse. I think we were all drained after existing on adrenaline to get us through the heist. I tried to sleep, but Logan's big bed feels so empty without him, and my mind wouldn't stop racing. I wonder where he is, and if he's ok. What kind of question is that? Of course he's not ok, that's why I can't sleep.

I'm so intent on my endless loop I don't notice that I've got company until I bump into a hard body coming through the arch that leads into the kitchen.

Red lines of exhaustion trace out from Garrett's multi hued irises and purplish bruises have settled below them. He looks about the same as I feel. As if I just spent the evening breaking into a secure facility to rescue a prisoner. I can't even process that this is what my life has become.

"What are you doing up? You should be getting some rest." There's a hint of scolding to my tone, as if I'm not also in desperate need of some sleep.

"I've been locked up in a tiny room. I've had more than enough time to rest over the past couple of days. And you're one to talk." He reaches a hand out as if to brush my cheek, pulling it back before he makes contact.

I'm not surprised he called me out on my hypocrisy. "Yeah, but you look…"

A pale eyebrow arches up. "Like shit?"

A snort escapes through the fog. "Not what I was going with."

"Ah, but you were thinking it." There's the tiniest hint of mirth lightening his expression for a moment.

"I'm just worried about you. We just got you back. Can't be losing you all over again."

"Plus, you're going to need my tracking skills to get your guy back." I don't like the shadow behind his eyes that hints at bitterness.

"That's not why I rescued you, Garrett. You're my friend now, and I don't leave my friends behind." The words ring a little untrue even to my own ears as I think of my high school friends and the life I left behind. But that's for their own good. At least, I thought it was until Xavier… I can't even think the words without a wave of nausea slamming into me.

"Sure." The single word is weighed down with doubt, and I'm not sure how to convince him how much he means to me. If the big rescue didn't do it, I don't know what will. Talk about a grand gesture. I've never broken into a prison before and hopefully never have to again.

"Seriously, I mean it." I reach out to place a hand on his arm, flicking my eyes up to meet his so he can hopefully see the truth in there.

He shakes my hand off. "Either way, I'll help you find him. You're important to me, and he's important to you. He's kinda grown on me, anyway. Like Rhizopus on a slice of old bread."

And with that comment the angsty look is gone replace by careless teasing. My snort turns into a full-fledged laugh at his nerd joke. Sometimes I forget that the smart guy I first met in debate wasn't a lie. He may have been pretending to be someone else, but deep down, we share that nerdy core.

"Wanna join me for a midnight snack?" He nods, but as I'm reaching for the cupboard, a piercing alarm rings out through the house. My heart is pumping out of control for the second time today, if it even is still today.

Garrett's arm swings out as if to hold me back from whatever danger is approaching. The guys in my life seem to have this habit. Protect Sophia. It's getting a little tired. I know I started out helpless to defend myself, but I'm starting to get a grasp on my powers. And this has gotta be a fancy smoke detector or something, right?

As I'm sliding out from behind his protective blockade, a breeze rushes past my face, sending my hair whirling. Liz materializes in front of me, eyes wide with panic. She pulls me away from Garrett with a grip that makes me wince and threatens to disconnect my arm from its socket.

"We've got to go, now!"

"What's going on? Is there a fire?" I swivel my neck, searching for smoke or heat or any sign of fire. "Carbon monoxide?"

"No, intruders. Someone's here. They've breached the first set of wards."

What? This place is supposed to be safe. No one is supposed to know about it. My mind jumps from Trey to Ivy to Garrett with suspicion. Did someone give us away? No. I shake my head as Liz drags me along behind her. They wouldn't do that. I can worry about the how later. We need to get out of here.

"What about Trey? Ivy? We need to get them." I pull away from Liz using a normal human effort before remembering my power. I grasp at the tendrils buzzing around at a frenetic pace. The shock of the alarm sent my magic into high alert and it's itching to come out to play. I shove some force into my struggle and pull away from my friend with ease.

She spins around. "Good job, but there's no time for that. Ivy and Trey are coming. Don't worry."

"I'm not leaving until they're here with us." I cross my arms over my chest.

Her exasperated sigh does nothing to move me. "They're heading out front to protect our backs. We're going to head out the back through the woods. There's a back-up car on the other side of the property. They'll meet up with us."

That's not right. I can't leave them behind after all we've been through. "Nope. Unacceptable." I shake my head at her. "We leave together or we fight together."

"Sophia. We're no good to Logan if we get captured or killed."

Her plea tugs at my emotions, and I rub at the empty place where we're usually connected by the protection bond as I falter. No, it's not right. I pivot and head for the front door to collect my friends.

"Do something?" Liz hisses behind my back.

I can almost picture Garrett's flop of sandy hair falling into his eyes as he shrugs. "I can't stop her. Plus, I kind of agree with her. After all, they helped get me out. I wouldn't feel right abandoning them, either." A grim smile lifts my lips at his words, and I grab his hand in solidarity when he joins me.

"Fine. You guys. Going to get us all killed with your heroics." Liz's words are a jumble as she transitions to her super speed and darts ahead of us, bursting out the front door with a crash. I admire her dedication, not even bothering to use the handle.

I guess I could have done that. Maybe not in quite so dramatic a fashion, but it's not automatic yet for me to use my Phys powers. I don't even remember I have them ninety percent of the time. Not like for Liz. She's always had her powers. It's natural and easy for her. I hope one day to get there, but I'm going to have to stay alive long enough for that to happen, and honestly, at this point, that forecast is looking pretty dismal.

Logan

There's not a single part of me that isn't aching when I blink awake in the stark stone room that has become the beginning and end of my reality. Nightmares twisted my dreams last night that I couldn't drag myself out of. Maybe the potion messed with my head, or maybe it was the guilt that's settled deep into my bones. My stomach lurches at the memory of what I told him. Of my betrayal of her secrets. Forced or not, those words came out of my mouth. I should have protected her with my life, my mind, everything, but I didn't.

Now I'm lying here useless. Worse than useless. I'm the one who is going to get her captured.

The dark thoughts threaten to pull me under again, but I'm afraid if I let myself go there, I'll never get back to myself. As much as I deserve that, it's not what she'd want. She'd expect me to keep fighting like she has through this entire ordeal. Since her life was set ablaze, and she got tossed into the fiery and dangerous world of magic. The thought of her face, her bravery, sets a spark off deep down. It burns through me, lighting up the darkness and setting my soul back on fire.

I need to get out of here. I need to get to her. I've got to think this through. Use the logic and planning Sophia is so fond of. Use every bit of training and discipline my father instilled in me. If there's one thing he taught me, it's that no situation is ever inescapable. There's always an exit, an out, a plan. I just have to figure out what mine is.

Sophia

The figures of Ivy and Trey are like a matched set of statues standing guard over the cottage. They're planted at opposite ends of the front porch in the same ready-for-battle pose. Hands loose at their sides, feet planted shoulder width apart and alert gazes sweeping the front lawn.

The driveway is excessively long, but I can pick up the rumble of engines and the faint glow of headlights in the distance, disturbing the peace of the night. They seem out of place out here. This place of solitude and nature.

"C'mon. You're coming with us."

Trey's gaze lands on me as my words snap him out of his focused wait. "Sophia. What are you still doing here? You should be on your way out."

I wince at the echo of his booted foot on the wooden porch as he advances on me, but I hold my ground. "Nope. I'm not going unless you guys are with me. Everyone or no one."

"We'll catch up with you. I promise. We'll just hold them off for a bit and then we can rendezvous later." He turns back around as the cars rumble closer. "I promise."

"Those are some pretty lies, but there's no way you can promise me that."

Ivy's hickory eyes land on me. "Please, we've got this."

"No. Liz couldn't stop me and neither can you guys. We didn't come all this way to lose more people. If you want me out of here, you're coming too."

Liz pipes in. "Trust me, I tried to drag her out, but she's stronger than she looks. Now get your butts back in here and we'll all head out the back way together. The longer we argue, the closer they get."

My hands latch on to Trey's elbow and I don't let go until he follows me back inside, struggling to shake off my grip. Liz gives me a nod, doing the same to Ivy.

Tension in the air is thick as we head back through the busted open front door. We find Garrett swaying back and forth from one foot to the other as if he's still not sure of his welcome. All of us coming to rescue him wasn't enough to convince him of his place in our little fam.

"Hurry up then. All present and accounted for. Let's get the frick out of here." Liz heads for the back door, dragging Ivy behind her.

We all spring into action. I push off my heels and jog out the back door. The cold steals my breath and burns my lungs, but I push through and pick up the pace. The faster we run, the warmer we'll get.

"Follow me." We all obey and trail after the teal ends of her hair bouncing on her shoulders as she runs ahead toward the massive forested area behind the cottage.

The property is so huge I barely even touched on exploring the grounds during our last stay here. If you didn't know the place well, it would be easy to get lost in these woods and become a missing hiker statistic. Luckily, we have Liz.

I have no idea how we're going to evade capture at this point. The crunching snow underfoot gives us away with the trail of footprints we're leaving behind. I whip around at the crashes and shouts that announce our pursuers. My head grows light at the sight of way too many men and women bursting out the back right before we make it into the cover of the trees.

Once we make it in a few feet, I skid to a stop and spin around. "Guys, stop."

Surprisingly, everyone listens to me. Not sure I'd do the same if the tables were turned, but I'm grateful. "We need to create some obstacles. Slow them down. I can slick up the path, turn it to ice. Trey, can you knock some of those trees down without taking any of us with them?" I could probably accomplish the feat, but my precision and control are not great yet. I'd probably end up taking out one…or all of us.

"Got it." He glances over at Liz and she gives a nod to his unspoken question.

With no further questions, blue electricity crackles down his arms a moment later. He directs a tremendous blast at one of the larger trees near the entrance to the trail. The wood creaks and the tree sways for a moment, but Liz darts forward as it starts its descent. She puts her strength into directing its fall and, after an agonizing moment, it falls in a neat line to block the path.

It's not enough to stop them, but it gives me a moment to pull the moisture from the air. I picture a slick ice rink and channel my energy into freezing the snow covered lawn that a couple dozen people are racing across at the moment.

They've started shooting fireballs and bolts at us. I duck as one of the trees shivers above me, dropping a large bough in the spot I was just standing in.

I duck behind the tree and redirect my energy to the snow. It's working. I can see the snow start to slick up with a top layer of smooth ice. The legs of the guy leading the charge spin out under him as he hits my icy patch. The sight of it revs up my magic, and I gather a wave of energy to coat the entire area. A white hot burst of agony rips down my arm as a fireball makes contact and I lose focus. The magic spills out in an erratic wave and all the snow melts into a foot deep flood of water.

Not quite the effect I was looking for, but it slows them down.

I back up and Trey fells another tree, Liz stacking it neatly beside the first one. I think I can handle some branches, so I send some small bolts up into the canopy above. Branches rain down and Trey pauses for a moment so Liz and I can speed over and stack them up.

Some dormant bushes and saplings shoot up around the fallen trees and pile of branches we've started building. I glance over at Ivy to see her whispering to the plant life, encouraging it to grow at a rapid pace.

"Time to go," Garrett says when our wall has grown to a solid height. We've blocked off a good several feet around the entrance to the forest and the surrounding trees are densely packed. It's not going to stop their pursuit, but it sure will slow them down.

I ignore the searing heat in my arm threatening to pull me under and head off at a run with my friends.

Liz grabs my hand as she darts off the path, veering into the tangle of trees. "Follow me. That'll hold them off for a bit, but we want to be well into this forest once they break through."

I glance over my shoulder and do a quick head count to make sure everyone is with us as she pulls me deeper into the dark canopy of trees. They crowd around us, branches and roots tearing at my skin and trying to knock me off my feet. I recite the words on repeat to keep myself going, in spite of the fiery burn radiating down my arm.

The shouts and bangs behind us are too loud. Run faster, push harder, don't fall. My inherent lack of balance was never a problem in my old life. But there was much less running for my life back BTM (before the magic.)

We all stop in our tracks and spin around when a massive crash rings in our ears. The sky behind us is lit up with a flickering orange and red glow as flames lick at the forest.

"Keep going." We all heed Liz's words and start back into action, following on her heels once more as she takes us on a twisting path through the tightly packed trees. "Faster."

Her small body is almost vibrating ahead of me with the urge to take off at a superhuman pace. Since I'm the only one that would have any chance of keeping up with her, I give her arm a squeeze to remind her to remain steady.

My breath is coming in painful gasps and a vicious stitch is ripping up my side when she finally slows down. I drop my hands to my knees, bent over, trying to catch my breath after we come to a full stop.

Our pursuers may have broken through our wall, but we left the sounds of them feels like several hundred turns ago. Thank goodness Liz knows where we're going. If it was up to me and my sense of direction, we'd be living in these woods for the rest of our lives. Wandering aimlessly among the identical trunks.

I pull myself back upright and glance around the small clearing we're in. A sliver of moonlight speckles the ground around us as it fights to clear the branches and boughs of the evergreen trees. The woodsy smell of green growth and cedar trunks hits me in the chest with a reminder of Logan. I make a futile effort to rub the ache away.

"Where do we go from here?" Now that I've caught my breath, I spin around to check out our surroundings. Trees, trees, and more trees, as expected. There's a wide gap in the forest to my left. That must be our path out. I nod toward it. "That way?"

"You got it, and I'm not sure of the where, but I've definitely got the how covered."

"Planning on enlightening the rest of us? I don't see any giant eagles handy to catch a ride on." The exhaustion must be getting to Garrett. He's using the tone he usually reserves for trading barbs with Logan. He's usually nicer to Liz.

"Better than eagles. Well, maybe not, but unfortunately I haven't befriended any of those. C'mon."

We're all following behind her and I have to blink to double check I didn't miss something when she vanishes from my sight.

Sophia

"Liz!" I call out. Panic has me pushing my aching feet into a jog. The buzz of magic in the air should have been a warning, but I'm too upset to stop. I slam into a wall of magic with a wince, knocking my bruised body to the ground in a painful heap.

Liz's disembodied head pops out above me. "Sorry about that. You're going to need to back up. Get over to the side. All of you."

She waves us over to the right of what I realize now is the mouth of a cave. The moss crawling up the sides has it blending into the woods like a Bob Ross painting. Makes me think of days spent watching episodes with Dad.

I back away, right into a warm body. Strong arms circle my torso, steadying me on my feet. For an infinitesimal fraction of a second, my eyes flutter shut with happiness when I think it's Logan keeping me safe and steady. But it hits me like a bucket of ice when I realize that can't be true. I twist around to see the specks of gold dotting the browns and greens of Garrett's eyes looking down on me. There's a shadow behind them, deeper than the usual darkness that lurks there.

He releases me. "You ok?" He clears his throat to get rid of the gravel in his tone.

"Yeah," I say. It shouldn't be awkward, but it is. He's a friend helping another friend, but I know about his feelings now, and it makes things a little weird between us.

His tongue darts out across his bottom lip and his mouth falls open. The rumble of a car engine breaking the silence of the forest chases away whatever words were about to escape, and his arms tighten around me in a protective hold.

We take a step back in unison as a nondescript, dark gray car materializes through whatever magical barrier is protecting the cave mouth. It's a strange sight here and the trees seem to loom in a little closer in protest of the unnatural machine threatening their peace.

Once the car emerges, Liz's head pokes out the driver's side. "Get your butts in here."

I end up stuffed in between the boys in the back seat in the scramble to obey her and get the heck away from this place that used to be a safe space.

"Exactly how many cars does your family have stashed away in random places?" I ask Liz.

"Oh, I dunno. I'm sure I don't even know about half of them." Liz's reply is so nonchalant, as if this is a completely normal thing, but I guess in her family, it is. It's weird though. Things seemed to be pretty stable in the magical community until I came on the scene. There must have been trouble brewing before then if they've got all these precautions in place. Makes me feel the tiniest bit better that it's not all about me.

"So, any clue where we're going?" I need to know there's some kind of plan in place. "Has your family got some other safe house somewhere we can hide out in?"

"Nope. Anyone got any ideas? Ivy? Boys?" she asks.

My heartbeat spikes thrumming in my chest faster than it was when we were racing through the forest.

There are some murmurs from the guys, but no helpful suggestions.

"We can't go to any of our family's places. Way too easy to track. You got any secret hidey holes, Garrett?" Trey's contribution to the discussion is no help.

When I look, Garrett's eyes are closed and he's dropped his head against the back of the seat.

Suspicion rides me. "Garrett, I thought you were all in. Are you hiding something from us still?"

He's so close to me his deep sigh sends tangled strands of my hair fluttering around my cheeks. "I might have a place where we can regroup. We can't stay long, though. I'll give you instructions once we hit something resembling an actual road."

I'm mildly annoyed he was thinking about holding out on us, but at least there's something of a plan in place now.

As I settle back in my seat, my heartbeat returns to its normal rate and the ache in my arm glares back into an inferno. It's like now that the immediate peril has turned into a slightly more distant peril, my brain is allowing my pain receptors to kick back into high gear.

I glance from side to side before rolling up the sleeve of the baggy sweatshirt I'd thrown on for my nighttime wanderings. A large hole with blackened edges mars the arm of Logan's sweatshirt and I wince as the fabric sticks to the burn. Eyes fly open on either side of me at my pained cry.

A large angry red patch covers my forearm, and it feels like it's still on fire.

Garrett's horrified expression does not help at all. "What the hell! Sophia, that looks terrible."

I'm rocked into him as the car swerves when Liz whips around to see what's going on.

"Liz, should you even be driving?" I ask her.

She waves off my concern. "It's fine. We can swap once we get out of the woods. I have my learners." Of course. Add an illegal driver with dubious skills to our list of potential problems.

"I don't suppose you have any of that witchy healing salve hidden away anywhere?" I eye the red plaid pajama pants Garrett was wearing when we made our unplanned departure.

My attempt at humor clearly fell a little flat, given his pained expression. "I wish. I don't know any healing spells either. I'm sorry. I've always been a little more focused on stealth and combat. My dad…" His words trail off. I catch a hint of his anguish before he shuts it down with a blank expression.

I'm thrown forward as the car jolts to a halt and Trey's arm swings out to stop me from ending up halfway in the front seat.

"What the hell, Liz!" Trey says. "You're definitely losing your driving privileges as soon as we hit the road."

She's out of the car, slamming the trunk and stuffing a white metal box through the back window before anyone else has time to protest her reckless driving.

"First aid kit. There's also a survival backpack back there, some cash, and spare clothes. You're welcome."

She's back in the driver's seat, drumming her fingers on the wheel as Trey snaps the box open.

"What you need is some cold, running water, but since we don't exactly have access to that right now, I can put some of this on."

He rips open a pack of some burn treatment and I tense up when he lays the cool gauze on the seared skin of my arm. I relax as the liquid soaked gauze hits my skin, dulling the pain. His fingers deftly pull out a bandage roll and he wraps it around my forearm with the ease of someone who has some practice with this sort of thing.

As if he feels like he needs to contribute, Garrett roots through the box until he emerges with a tiny bottle of painkillers. "This should help."

There's no water to be found, so I reluctantly swallow the chalky pills dry, my face twisting in disgust at the bitter taste lingering on my tongue.

"All good?" The words are barely out of her mouth before Liz is peeling off again, branches scraping the side of the poor car and thumping the underside.

"We'll survive," Trey replies. Famous last words. At this rate, I can only hope they're accurate.

Sophia

Thankfully, Trey swapped places with Liz and took the wheel as soon as we hit the road with Garrett, directing him to our unknown destination.

I've lost track of time, but pale lilac and cotton candy pink streaks are marking the sky when he tells Trey that we're here and to make a right turn. I do a double take at the hand painted sign out front that declares we've reached Cedar Creek Cabins. A snow covered tennis court sits neglected for the winter to our right with a children's playground on the left. Tall evergreen trees line the driveway of the small resort.

I lift a questioning brow at Garrett. So many questions.

"I know the owner." Is his only response.

There's a cheery hand-painted sign that says 'Reception' in forest green letters hanging over the door of the large wooden building Trey pulls up to. Garrett shoots out of the car before it even comes to a proper stop.

"Be right back."

He darts out and up the driveway.

"Anyone got any thoughts on this one?" asks Ivy. She's been strangely quiet for much of our journey. Not that she's usually that exuberant or anything, but more quiet than usual. I don't know if Logan's loss or something else that has her down, but she's a little off.

The door opens again, letting in a fresh rush of extra crisp winter air along with the sharp scent of evergreen trees. Garrett slides back in next to me, not bothering with his seatbelt.

"Head straight, then turn right at the fork. We've got Cabin 14. There's a spot to park right in front of it."

I tap his shoulder. "What is this place?"

"We can only stay a couple of days. It's slow here in the winter, but they have some guests coming on the weekend, so we've gotta be out. That should give us some time to regroup and make a plan." I notice how he ducked around my question again, but I don't push him.

"Thanks." I tell him. I truly appreciate that he's let us into his world. I know how hard it's been for him to trust anyone since he lost his family. He clearly has some kind of connection to this place.

A comfortable, musty smell weaves itself around me as we walk through the creaky pine door. The place is bigger than I expected, with a rustic sitting area with a dark green couch and assorted chairs, but a noticeable lack of a TV. This place is definitely perfect for an escape from regular life. Or in our case, to hide out from the rest of the world while we figure out what our next step is.

He waves at the two closed doors at the far end of the space. "There are two bedrooms and a pullout couch if you girls don't all want to share one room."

"I'll take the couch." Ivy is quick to jump in, so Liz and I head to door number two, while the guys veer to the left.

The twin beds with matching friendly red and white checked comforters are nowhere near as swanky as the Armstrong's "cottage" but my exhausted body isn't complaining.

The guys brought our limited baggage inside, so I don't feel bad about giving in to the call of the bed. Every joint and muscle groans in relief as I collapse on the surprisingly soft mattress.

"Just a small nap." The squishy pillow muffles my words, and even the rising sun is no deterrent to my eyes sliding shut. I don't think I've gotten more than a few hours' sleep in the last few days.

I blink blearily awake. Liz is nowhere to be seen, but Ivy is perched on her neatly made bed. If the sun is bright and hanging low in the sky is any indication, it looks like I've slept away most of the day. That thought yanks me upright. There's no time to waste. We need to figure out how we're going to get to Logan like yesterday. My mind snaps from dazed and half awake to alert and panicky in a rush that has my head spinning.

"We shouldn't still be here. We should go after Logan." The words mirror my thoughts.

"What was that?" I ask.

Her head jerks up from its spot resting on her hands and her narrowed eyes are wary. "I didn't say anything."

My forehead scrunches as I scan. Was I dreaming? No. Definitely not. "Yeah, you said we shouldn't still be here."

Her eyes widen bigger than a deer facing down a semi. "What? You must have been dreaming." She pushes her slight frame off the bed. "I'm going to go for a walk. Check this place out."

I mean, I could have been dreaming… No, I heard her; I swear. But why would she be lying to me? It doesn't make sense, but then nothing does anymore, so who am I to judge? Was it my psychic powers kicking in again? Is she scared of me?

I shove the hair out of my eyes, wrinkling my nose at the greasy strands, and sit up. My body is basically a mass of sore muscles, and my burned arm is still aching with an intensity I'm shocked I could sleep through, but no major damage. I don't think I've ever needed a shower more. Personal hygiene has unsurprisingly hit an all-time low on my to do list of late, apparently. The rest of the world can wait five to ten minutes while I remedy that situation.

Liz and Garrett are engaged in a fierce card game that involves a lot of yelling when I emerge fresh and clean from the shower. I'm choosing to ignore the wet hair, leaving a damp patch down the back of my only shirt.

"What's up?"

"Shhh, I'm about to take him down." Liz slaps a card down on the table and Garrett throws his hands up in defeat.

"Ok, then. What's the food situation like?" I eye the small kitchen area off to our right, hoping the food elves have dropped off some groceries and left us a fully stocked fridge.

"Nothing yet. Trey went to the closest store to grab some supplies. He should be back any minute now."

"Should he have gone by himself?" Tendrils of fear curl around my heart thinking of my friends off by themselves.

Her shoulders rise in a quick shrug. "He's a big, strong boy. He can look after himself. Garrett was still passed out when he left, and Ivy was off somewhere. I couldn't leave you all asleep and vulnerable for anyone to attack, now could I?"

She has a point. After what happened at our last "safe place" I don't feel safe anywhere. I'm actually kind of surprised I managed to sleep that long. Now that I'm awake, I can't seem to settle down. I'm weaving a restless path around the small space. From the coffee table, to the kitchen and back on a loop.

"Sit down. You're making me dizzy." Liz pats the spot next to me on the couch. "You can help me gloat to Garrett that I'm the queen of cards, and he's the loser."

Garrett takes her teasing with a good-natured eye roll, settling back into the comfy cushions with folded arms.

I take a seat, but my fingers immediately find their way to my mouth. I'm going to nibble them down to the quicks if I keep it up, but I can't seem to stop myself.

"I wish I had my notebook."

"You'd take your notebook all the way into the deepest, darkest pits of the Nether Realm if you could, wouldn't you?" Liz must immediately spot the shadows that have darkened my face at the mention of that place. "I'm sorry. We'll get him back. That's a promise."

"Oh, I know." There's no other option. "But you're not wrong. I would take my notebook with me if I could."

"Wait a sec." Garrett launches himself off the couch and starts ripping open random drawers around the place. He disappears into the guy's bedroom, only to return triumphantly a moment later, brandishing a notepad in one hand and a pen in the other. "Will these help?" His dimple pops out for the first time since we rescued him, and I return the smile.

"Thanks." I grab his treasure and hug it to my chest for a moment. "Ok. When is this going down and how are we doing it?" This isn't a question of if. We're going to face whatever is out to get us down there and we're going to get Logan back. He's rescued me enough times. It's about time I returned the favor.

"We obviously need to use the spell we found before to open a portal to the Nether Realm. Garrett and I have that covered." I jot that down as my first note in my tidy handwriting.

"You made us practice it about a gazillion times before our last attempt, so I think we've got that covered." Garrett pokes at me.

"Maybe so, but I'm pretty happy I did that. Now we have at least one task we don't have to worry about accomplishing." I tap the Cedar Creek pen on the pad in a rhythmic beat. "I know we were hoping to find some way to direct the portal. You know, so we end up close to wherever Zeus is keeping Logan, but that's not happening now that we're stuck here with zero resources. Are you going to be able to track him from down there?"

The sun glints off the smooth green surface of his tracking crystal when he pulls it up from where it lies beneath his shirt. I knew I didn't have to worry about that. He never takes it off. "As long as the Nether Realm doesn't mess with its magic, we're good."

"I don't want to be a downer, but what if the atmosphere down there does mess with it? What are we going to do then?" Liz asks.

"We'll deal with that if it comes to it." I never thought those words would pass my lips, but we can't wait. We have no idea what Zeus is doing to Logan down there. The ache in my arm is a mosquito bite compared to what he could be enduring right now while we're up here wasting time.

"I'm shocked to hear you say that, but I'm in. I love a challenge. Plus, my brother will owe me for like I dunno…eternity if I'm the one to rescue him."

Of course she's all in. I once saw her take down two giant men with an excited glint setting her sea-blue eyes dancing. "Big surprise."

"If it comes to that, we'll reassess the plan and figure out our next step from there."

"What are we likely to face down there?" That's the bigger concern for me. It could be inhabited by mutated zombie bears, for all we know. The literature on the Nether Realm is slim at best.

"Well, definitely shades. We have some experience with them. Other than that, there's obviously Zeus and his minions. Who knows what other kinds of unholy creatures could be lying in wait for us." Garrett is gnawing on his lower lip in a show of nervousness I haven't seen since I first met him. When I thought he was an entirely different person. I've always thought that he showed parts of his true self back then. When he was pretending to be an ordinary human.

"Fine. We've all got varied skills in physical combat. Hopefully, our magic won't be offline or wonky when we get down there. When are we going to go?"

Trey walks in at that moment, powerful arms curved around a ridiculous number of paper grocery bags. Looks like he carried it all in one trip. Silly boys. We could have helped him bring them in if he'd taken the time to ask.

"Are you making plans without me?"

"Dude, chill out. We were just talking about the logistics of getting into the Nether Realm and what we're going to be looking at once we get there." Garrett smirks at his impatience.

The careless toss of the groceries onto the small kitchen floor itches at my brain, begging me to organize them, but I ignore the compulsion. Not the most important thing to worry about right now.

He sinks into a low chair across from us, dropping his elbows onto the denim-clad legs sprawled in front of him. Where did he get jeans?

"What's the scoop?"

"Nothing new. Garrett and I have the portal covered. Only problem being that we can't target our entry spot, so we might have a bit of a journey when we get down there."

Trey shakes his head. "Wish I could help with that, but I don't even know how you two pulled that off the last time. Once we get there, though, I'm all yours." He curls his arm in a flex before flipping his wrist and unfurling his fingers to reveal flames dancing over his palm.

"We get it. You have super cool elemental skills. Put that away," Liz scolds him.

"When are we leaving? And where's Ivy?" He scans the small space as if he might find her tucked away in a corner.

I shrug. "She went for a walk. I think I heard her thoughts and freaked her out. I didn't mean to. I was half asleep." Should I have shared that? I don't want them all scared of me.

I change the subject to avoid the scrutiny of Liz's curious gaze. "I think we should leave tomorrow." The less time Logan has to spend down there, the better.

"Are you sure it's not too soon? Should we be doing more research? Seeing if we can find any more info on what might be down there or whether we can narrow down our landing spot better? That was, after all, our initial plan." Garrett is the one to voice the words that I would normally be thinking. I'm usually the one who thinks things through and makes a very detailed plan, but my heart protests every delay.

"It might be nice, but I don't know how we're going to do that. I mean, it's probably safer down there for us. Up here we've got Zeus after us, Lawrence and the council. Too many variables."

Liz snorts. "You think we'll be safer in the Nether Realm? What have our lives come to? I'm game though. Trey? Garrett?" She tosses a sharp chin at each of them.

Trey's long fingers are rubbing his temples, but the look of resignation in his eyes says we've won this battle. "I don't suppose you'll listen to me if I advise caution and a little more planning. For the record, I'm going to let you know I do have concerns about rushing into it like this. That said, I'm there for you. Whatever you need."

The grim look in Garrett's eyes tells me he agrees with Trey, but he gives a quick nod to let us know he's in. I've always had a few close friends, but these people. They're family. The kind that sticks with you through life, death, and everything in between.

Trey's passes his hand over his stomach with a groan as he stands up. "Ok, now that's settled, I'm going to make us some food. I'm starving."

His words kick off a sharp pang inside as I realize how hungry I am, too.

Everyone chips in, pulling food out of the paper bags and assembling dinner. There's lots of dry food and snacks we can hopefully bring with us to the Nether Realm. I have no clue what the eating situation will be like down there.

Garrett has just thrown a bag of spaghetti noodles into the bubbling pot of water when the door creaks open. My nerves are in a constant state of high alert by this point. The knife I was chopping carrots with clatters to the counter as I whip around with the rest of the crew at the sound. The tightness in my shoulders only eases up when I spot Ivy walking in the door, cheeks flushed red from the cold, her hair messy from the wind.

"Ivy! Where have you been?" Trey asks.

She glances down through her lashes and back up again. "Needed a walk. I guess I kinda got lost out there." Her voice is quiet.

"I see how it is," Liz says. "You waited until we had dinner almost ready before you came in. Skip out on the work. Scammer."

Ivy halts in her walk across the room. "I…I didn't…"

Liz bounces over to her, pulling her into a big hug. "I'm just teasing. Man, you're freezing. Come on and warm up in the kitchen." She drags her over to the rest of us.

We dump all the food family style on the table to dig in. For a little while, it feels like we're somewhere safe as our conversation veers to lighter subjects. It's punctuated by the sounds of chewing and forks clanging off plates as we gobble down the delicious meal of spaghetti, garlic bread and salad. It's like we came up with an unspoken rule to enjoy this one meal before heading off on our dangerous adventure.

Liz is the last one to declare defeat, leaning back in her chair with a sigh.

"Ivy, we were talking while you were out, and we decided we're going to open up the portal tomorrow. Commence the rescue mission." Second one in a week. No big whoop, right? Breaking into a secure magic facility was hard enough. Now we've got to head into what is basically the magic equivalent of hell, so that should be fun.

"That's fine. Whatever you guys decided is fine with me."

I don't know what's going on with her. She seems so subdued, but she's going to need to be all in if we're going to make this happen. "You know you're part of the team? We were talking while you were out, but I want your input. If you have any concerns or suggestions, let us know." The timeline isn't going to change, but I'll still listen to her opinion. Like everyone else, she gets a voice.

"Thanks. I'm sorry. I'm just worried. About Logan, my family. I'm not myself right now. I'm sorry."

"You don't need to apologize. We're all anxious, and stressed, and quite frankly I'm terrified right now. What if we can't save Logan? What if I lose someone else? I know where you're at, and I get it. But we've got each other, and that's what matters. I don't know what I'd do without you." Pretty sure I'd be falling to pieces right now, but together we're all stronger.

The pained look doesn't ease up on her beautiful face, but a tight smile tugs at the corners of her lips. "Thanks. You're right. We can do this together."

Logan

I've been keeping track of the food and water deliveries. At first they seemed random to throw me off, not let me plan or figure out any sort of routine, but I've realized they're on a two-day cycle. The constant dim lighting and irregular routine did what it was supposed to at first, but now that I've gotten past the disorientation, I've figured it out.

The best time to make my attempt is during the third meal of the second day of the cycle. I've gauged that it's somewhere between 2 and 3 in the morning. One guard delivers the meal, usually with a yawn.

I've been wearing a groove in the cement all day, waiting for my chance. My feet are sore and exhausted, but I can't stop. Because that's it. I'll only get one chance. I don't even think he'll bother to keep me alive if I'm caught. He got the information about Sophia out of me. I don't even know why I'm still alive at this point. I assume he still thinks he can use me as some sort of bargaining chip.

As the time creeps nearer, I have to force myself to settle down on the floor. I tuck my hands under my body, pressing my palms into the unforgiving stone floor.

Each heartbeat marks another moment closer. I strain my ears, listening to the dark silence until I hear it. Faint footsteps outside of the thick door followed by a pause and a flashlight beam scanning the room as someone peers through the window to make sure I'm down. I've been shouted at to get to the floor, so I know they always do a check before opening the door.

A few more agonizing heartbeats pass as the beam disappears and a key scrapes into the lock. The stone surroundings amplify any sounds in the place. I use my hands to shove up from the floor, springing to my feet and reaching the door in a single bound. I press myself against the wall right beside the door before it swings open wide enough to slide a tray through.

I let my leg fly into the face of the unsuspecting guard. It connects with a satisfying crack to his nose. He scrabbles to swing the door shut, but I grab his hands that are still holding the tray of food and yank with every last reserve of strength.

His face collides with the floor and I drag him in a foot, but he's he continues to struggle, scrambling to gain his feet some purchase on the slippery stone.

My energy is dangerously low, my entire body aching, and my feet are on fire. Forward progress seems almost impossible under these circumstances. If I can just knock him out. It will still be tough to move his heavy body, but at least he won't be fighting every inch of the way.

I don't have much to work with. I'm barefoot and exhausted. The only way I'm going to do this is with some leverage. I swing a leg over his back, taking advantage of gravity to land in the center of his twisting back. I throw my weight down with a thud, pinning him down as I grab his head. The crack of his head hitting concrete twists my stomach, but I swallow the feeling down and jump up to drag him the rest of the way inside.

He doesn't stir, and I hesitate a moment before sinking my first two digits into the soft spot under his chin. A sigh of relief escapes when the faint thrum of his pulse beats against my fingertips. I'll do whatever it takes to survive and get back to Sophia, but I don't relish the thought of killing someone. Particularly someone like this. Human, maybe Witch. Likely coerced or threatened into working down her for Zeus. Nobody would choose to live down here.

With a last glance at the hellish hole I've been living in, I peer through the door. Silence and darkness greet me from the long, dark hallway. I'm nowhere near out of danger, but it looks like there are no immediate threats.

This place is a maze. Could be underground, could be multiple stories up. With no windows, there's no way to tell where I am or how to get out, so I take my chances, heading toward the faint flicker of a torch that's visible in the distance.

Sophia

I've been ready to go since dawn. The anticipation of our journey was enough to keep me up. Add that to the fact that I slept most of the day away yesterday and my eyes didn't stay closed for more than two minutes at a time last night. But I know how badly everyone needs their sleep, so I let them rest.

A yawn stretches Garrett's mouth as he appears from the room he shared with Trey. He scrubs his palms over his face as he walks over to me. His hand falls on my shoulder, stilling my restless pacing for a moment.

"Hey. How long have you been awake?" he asks.

I shrug. Not wanting to admit I'm operating on minimal sleep. I don't want anyone's concern for me delaying our mission.

His nod letting me know he's onto me, but makes the wise choice of refraining from commenting. "Have you at least eaten anything?"

My lack of reply is enough for him. "Let's make a decent breakfast for everyone. We've got some supplies to bring with us, but who knows how long we'll be there or if there will be any demon squirrels to hunt down."

My mouth falls open. "Demon squirrels?"

His mouth pulls up in a smirk that makes his dimple pop.

"Right. You're messing with me." I give him a shove.

"Hey, made you smile."

He's right. The crease between my eyes and permanent frown disappeared for that one instant.

"What do you think demon squirrels would look like?" I ask him as we work together in harmony, pulling items from the fridge and cupboards while we prep breakfast.

"Red eyes, definite must," he says.

"Obviously. And fangs? Sharp ones."

"Yeah. Big. Like Golden Retriever big."

"But hairless." I shudder. "Because hairless things are creepy."

Trey trails in giving with a weird look as he catches the tail end of our conversation.

"Maybe no fur, but scales. Definitely scales."

"May we never meet a demon squirrel in real life."

Trey slips in beside me with a longing look at the coffeepot. The life giving brown liquid is taking its sweet time to drip out. "What are you two on about?"

"A little wild speculation about what we're going to find in the Nether Realm," I say.

"I can tell you one hundred percent there is no such thing as demon squirrels." His long arm reaches above me, pulling open the cupboard to grab five assorted mugs.

Everyone is rushing around grabbing last minute items as I wait by the door, tapping my foot impatiently. Garrett talked to the owner. She's letting us leave the car here. We don't have too many other possessions after our forced departure from the cottage. The supplies from the trunk and the things Trey picked up yesterday are all waiting in a pitifully small pile by the front door.

I stroke one of the knives resting in my calf sheaths. One thing I've learned lately is you should never be caught unaware without a weapon. Even if it's nighttime or you think you're safe. At least if you're me. After the second surprise attack by the Ferrebat, I've kept my knives on my person or as near as humanly possible at all times. I'm pretty sure the rest of the crew already knew that rule, because they all have some weaponry with them. Ivy's been known to walk around the house with her sword strapped to her back.

"Where are we doing this?" My ponytail whips up off my back as Liz skids to a halt beside me.

My hand flies up to my heart. "Liz. Don't do that. You're going to give me a heart attack."

"Logan always says I'll put him in an early grave, but if his constitution isn't strong enough to handle a little jump scare from his sweet little sister, then that sounds like a him problem. Survival of the fittest, you know?" Her words may be careless, but I catch the smile on her face falter at the mention of her brother's name.

"There's a small beach on the other side of that boathouse." Garrett gestures to the wooden structure by the water. The fading blue paint puts an image in my head of years of guests enjoying this place on long, hot summer days. "Should be private enough. It's not crowded here, but there are a couple of cottages rented out to mundanes. Not sure how Gilda would explain away a portal opening up on the tennis court."

"It would probably damage the tennis court too," I say.

He gives me a weird look. "Right."

Yeah, maybe property damage is kinda the least important of our concerns right now, but she was nice enough to let us stay. I'd hate to destroy her business on the way out.

"Let's get on with it." Trey claps his hands, slinging the largest backpack over his shoulder. It's the survival kit that came with the car.

The sun is high in the sky, light glinting off the fresh snow we're crunching through.

The closer we get to the boathouse, the louder my heartbeat sounds in my ear until it's a deafening roar threatening to take my breath away.

Even draped in a heavy blanket of snow, the beach is pretty with the sun sparkling off the frozen lake. Garrett and I went over the spell a few dozen more times before bed last night to make sure we don't mess it up. That could be bad. Really bad. But we've done it before, so I know we can do it again.

The weight of all their expectations presses on my chest, leaving me short of breath. Like I'm not putting enough pressure on myself. "Can you all maybe?" I wave my hand at them. "Not stare."

"Sorry," Ivy says, spinning around, followed by everyone else.

Garrett's hand reaches out to clasp mine even as he swivels away.

Staring at the stark whiteness surrounding us helps me clear my mind. It's like a real-life version of the white room I go to when I need to clear my mind. I focus on the magic rather than the words. I know them off by heart, so I can let them flow from my lips as I concentrate on the awakening thrum of my powers unfurling from my core. The familiar buzz spreads from my shoulders to the tips of my fingers and I draw it into the spell.

Tendrils of gold and pink wrap around the words I'm reciting on repeat.

I send the power away from myself and my friends until the magic streams from my fingers, melting the snow under our feet. I keep feeding more power and intention into the words until a thunderous crack shakes the ground under our feet. A dark void looms in front of us. Flames licking at the edges of the circle are the only light coming from the thing. That's not terrifying at all.

A high-pitched squeal accompanies Liz's clapping and I glance over to catch her leaning forward on her front foot, ready to launch herself forward.

"You did it." Ivy sounds a little too incredulous given this isn't the first time I've done this, but since I'm kinda surprised myself, I guess I can't blame her.

"Yeah, I did. Shall we…go?" I know we have to, but a pit of dread is lurching in my stomach now that we're actually facing the reality of leaping into the unknown.

"Uh yeah. That's why we're here. You didn't just rip open a giant black hole between the realms for funsies."

"Thanks for the info, Liz." I don't think I could roll my eyes harder if I tried. She does have a way of lightening my grim thoughts.

She shifts her weight back and forth with a bounce. "I'll go first."

Trey takes a long stride toward the gaping hole. "No, I should do it." Ah yes, Manly man being all noble and manly.

I steel myself. It's gotta be me. This is my rescue mission, after all. That is a portal of my creation. What if I did it wrong? I suck an icy breath deep into my chest and take off before anyone can beat me to it. I know the portal will only last for five to ten minutes.

"Sophia!"

Garrett's voice follows me to the edge where I pause for a whisper of a moment, close my eyes and leap.

My skin crackles with power as I pass through the tear. Flames lick at me as if they're trying to grab hold of my body. My legs bicycle, searching for solid ground to land on, as I sail through the air. I bet they regret it when the hard ground finally catches up with my fall and shattering pain shoots up my shins when they make contact with a painful thud. I tumble to the ground in a heap of tangled limbs and wince as the heat flares up in my injured arm when it slams into the hard-packed dirt.

I roll out of the way as Liz comes flying at me in the dim light. She lands in a neat crouch like one of her cats, rushing over to me.

"Are you okay?" she runs her hands over my skin searching for injuries.

"I'm fine." I shake out my arms and ignore the hand she's holding out for me as I push myself to my feet.

Our other friends land next to us one by one. All of them land on their feet despite a little stumble from Garrett. Of course I'm the only one who crashed to the ground like a newborn foal still trying to work out how to use its legs. Here I am summoning all my bravery and trying to lead the way.

The world around us is dim and barren. We're standing on hard packed dirt and there are no buildings nearby. There are skeletal trees lurching out of the ground at odd angles. There's no snow down here, but the trees are bare of any life. No leaves, or buds or anything, just black bark and cracked limbs.

At least there's no sign of other people around. Shades, demons, whatever awfulness lives down here are absent for the moment.

Garrett draws the crystal hanging around his neck out from under his shirt. "Have you got something of Logan's I can use to track him?

"Sophia?" Garrett's voice breaks into my thoughts.

"Right, yes." The smooth hilt of his knife somehow warms my palm. The one piece of him I've been carrying with me.

He tugs at it when I pass it over, but I'm reluctant to release my only token of Logan. Garrett's warm hand closes over mine and he leans in.

His words are a whisper of warmth in my ear. "I got this. I'll give it right back."

The assurance loosens my fingers, and he pulls the dagger away. My now empty hand flies up to my chest, rubbing at that spot near my heart where the bond lies.

The crystal dangles from Garrett's fingers with a mesmerizing sway. Time to find out where we're heading.

Logan

Heavy wooden doors break up the monotony of the rough stone walls. I try not to think of who might be behind them as I follow the path to the wide arch at its end. Torches flicker high on the walls down this next hallway. An unbroken stretch of stone faces me. No doors, no crevices, no hallways branch off from here. The lack of escape routes sets every instinct on edge, but I don't have too many choices. Need to get through here as quick as possible and then I can see where we're at.

I give a last scan to make sure no one is coming before sprinting. The ground slopes slightly upward. I hope that's a good sign. That maybe this hallway will take me somewhere closer to an exit. Closer to Sophia. Closer to home. My next step is still a mystery, but any action is better than none at this point.

My lungs are burning, and I still can't see the end of this stretch. I ignore the ache in my thighs pushing forward. By the time I reach the end of the long stretch, my breath is coming fast and my heart is racing. My endurance has already taken a solid hit during my time in this place.

As I pause to catch my breath, my luck runs out. The footsteps ringing out down this new hall have me searching for an escape route. I could fight, but if I tip them off too soon, I'll bring the whole building down on me.

I can duck behind the pillar dividing the two corridors or I can roll the dice and choose one of the two paths. Either could lead me straight into another guard or five.

Playing it safe is for suckers, so I choose the latter option. I edge around the pillar and use the shadows between the lit torches to conceal my presence. The heavy thumps of booted feet are getting louder, but I still can't spot a body to match them. That's good. If I can't see them, they probably can't see me either.

I've plastered myself so tight to the wall that the rough surface snags at my clothes and scrapes at any exposed skin. I continue to inch along even after the shadowy figure finally shows up under the flicker of a torch. Looks and sounds like only one guard. That's good. I can definitely take a single guard if push comes to shove, but that's not my first choice. I'd like to keep my escape quiet as long as I can. I don't imagine it will be too long before someone's going to notice the missing guard I locked in my cell or he'll come to and call for reinforcements. I kicked his radio out of the cell, but I didn't have time to hide it.

I'm so focused on watching the guard's steady approach, I'm caught by surprise when the wall gives out behind me and I stumble into nothingness. The footsteps quicken at the scraping sound that rings out through the space. Rookie mistake. Stay aware of your surroundings. I know that. Adrenaline is coursing through my body, but my mind is still a little sluggish from lack of sleep. And yeah, the torture.

I guess that made my decision for me. I give a quick glance down the hallway I've stumbled into before moving back into a jog. Looks clear and the brightening light at the end of this way gives me some hope that I'm getting somewhere. Somewhere probably has more people, but also hopefully an exit. I'm nearing the light when the guard catches up, turning down my hallway.

There's an actual door with a window ahead. His shout rings out, pushing me on through the door. I explode out of it into a room with a handful of unfortunately occupied chairs. The heads all swivel toward me and a cry rings out.

So much for getting out of here quietly.

Sophia

I'm prepared this time for the blinding flash of light that emanates from Garrett's tracking crystal once the spell kicks in. It was startling the first time he did it in his car, but here in this shadowy place full of potential enemies, it sets every nerve in my body on edge. It's like a beacon in this dark place. Like sending out an SOS on a deserted island. Only instead of getting help, we're attracting nothing but trouble. Like some kind of monster beacon. But I guess that's kind of what I do all the time now with my Archimage powers. Come and get me. Fantastic.

I avert my eyes to avoid burned retinas and get my first thorough look at the landscape surrounding us. Skeletal trees, check. Dirt ground, check. I got a taste of that on my landing. The first sign of life or something like it is off in the distance. Looks like a cluster of small buildings. Probably houses. Not interested in finding out who lives there. A handful of larger ones surround it. Maybe the most surprising part is the moon hanging low in the sky. There's a sallow greenish yellow tinge to it. I don't know if I'm more surprised to see a moon in the sky at all or at its strange coloring. I guess it tracks that this place would share some similarities with our reality. This place is basically a parallel universe.

A shiver runs up my arm when a small hand closes over mine. "Liz, your hand is freezing!"

"Don't let go."

"I won't." I tell her.

"What?" Liz's head tilts, a curious gleam lighting her eyes.

"I won't let go. Don't worry." In spite of the cold, I have zero intention of letting go. The comfort of being connected to another person is reassuring.

"But I…" My friend is not one to stumble over her words, but she does this time as she glances at our interconnected fingers. Her voice drops to a whisper. "I didn't say that out loud."

A shiver of a different kind pops goosebumps up on my arms. Great. The thing I've been fearing. Psychic powers. I don't know what scares me the most about this aspect of my powers. Mrs. Armstrong is a Pyschic Mage, and she seems remarkably well adjusted. Intruding on the private thoughts and feelings of others seems so horribly intrusive though. I know there are ways to block them so you're not inundated by a constant stream of stray thoughts, but I only have minimal training in this so far.

Liz is bouncing on her heels. "What color am I thinking of?"

Yellow invades my brain. An image of Liz swathed head to toe in yellow, hurling a yellow ball at me. "Um yellow. Could you maybe not shout it at me? I think a little subtlety would be fine."

She bounces up and down, clapping her hands. As soon as the skin-on-skin contact is gone, the image fades. It's still there, but just a muted idea of the color yellow in my brain. If I wasn't concentrating, it might drift away on the wind. I need to see if that's the key, so I grab her hand, and the image sharpens along with a billion other thoughts buzzing through her busy brain now. She's excited about this recent development. I drop her hand again to cut the too intense connection.

"Why are you so happy about this?" I hiss at her. Not quite ready for the rest of the group to hear about this. Although given their proximity, I'm sure they're all aware. I'd like to at least try to maintain some illusion of privacy.

"It's cool and could come in very useful. We don't have a Psych in our group."

"Right. But aren't you worried I'll like read your thoughts or something? Dig around in your brain?"

"I've got nothing to hide." She drops her voice. "Try it on someone else."

I don't know if I could shake my head harder if I tried. "No! That would be a massive invasion of someone's private thoughts. I wouldn't do that." If it happens by accident, there's not much I can do about it yet, but I wouldn't purposely dig into the minds of my friends. That wouldn't be right.

She actually looks disappointed at my show of moral fortitude. I love Liz but man, I'm glad she's not a Psych.

"But I want to know what Trey's thinking. Is he still digging on Ivy? I need to know. I'm missing all my reality tv right now. I need some drama in my life." Yeah, because the constant threat of attack lurking around every corner lately isn't enough drama.

I reach out for her hand, but think better of it and grab her elbow instead. Probably best to avoid bare skin contact as much as possible for the time being.

"What are you ladies doing back there? We really should get going. Garrett has a lock on him." The chime of Ivy's voice rings out as she glances back at us. As the pools of her deep brown eyes meet mine, a thought intrudes. That moment. When I thought I heard her say something. Was that in her mind? Maybe that hazy state between sleep and full consciousness left my mind in a more open state that let me hear her thoughts? No wonder she looked so alarmed and ran off after that. She wasn't lying. She never said those words out loud.

Garrett and Trey are pointing to the left. It's in the direction of an area that looks uninhabited. I don't know if it's better or worse to be surrounded by life. I don't imagine too many people or creatures down here are of the friendly sort.

Garrett slips over, sliding the comforting weight of Logan's knife into my hand. I squeeze it tight, relishing the pain as the cool metal ridges of the hilt dig into my palm.

He hesitates a moment before sliding his arm over my shoulders in a quick side hug. "Shall we?" A wave of sadness washes over me as he pulls me in close, fading when he lets go. His pain piles on top of my own, and I realize the other complication that could come with Psyche powers.

I swallow hard and nod, leading the way with him. Liz darts ahead, blurring out for a moment before she slows down to rejoin the group.

"Was that a good idea?" I ask her, glancing around.

"Thought I should make sure my powers were working right. So far, so good. Not to mention, Garrett already lit up the whole place with his spell. If anyone was nearby, they'd already be on us."

She has a point. But I'm not risking breaking out my powers until I absolutely have to. First, I want to save all my energy for when we get to Logan. And second, that whole unique Archimage signature thing might be a problem. Not the best idea to leave a trail of Archimagey essence across the entire Nether Realm. I'd be like the pied piper of nefarious creatures. I shudder at the thought of the demon rats we thought were so funny in the bright light of our world. Not so much down here.

I'm yanking at the sweatshirt that's hanging off me as we near the buildings. It's cold down here, but there's oddly no snow. Just a weird greenish mist clinging to the forlorn branches of the trees we've been traveling through. We're going to have to leave what little protection the barren branches offer soon to cross over a large open space that will leave us visible and vulnerable.

"We should stop for a quick snack before we head out there." No surprise that Trey is the one looking out for our well being. I know I'd keep going until I collapsed on my feet, but that would clearly not be one of my better life decisions.

He drops the heavy pack he's been carrying and we all settle down onto our packs or the random tree stumps or fallen branches.

Ivy opens the pack she was carrying and produces a stash of protein bars. I grab a mint chocolate one, taking a few dusty sips of my water. I've been drinking it conservatively. The noxious smell of rotten eggs has been lingering in my nose since we got down here, so I don't imagine I'd want to drink any sort of liquid we might happen across.

I'm ready to jump up the moment I finish my bar. The longer we stay in this place, the more the sensation of watching eyes on my back intensifies. When I scan the area, I don't see anything other than the eerie green mist drifting lower.

Ivy's face is drooping with exhaustion, and I can see the strain on Garrett's face from maintaining the tracking spell. I resort to drumming a rhythmic beat on my knees instead of dragging everyone up like I want to.

I'm surprised to see Liz's mouth stretch in a wide yawn. She's usually the one with the perpetual battery running. Except, of course, before eleven in the morning.

It causes a chain reaction, and we all join her with sympathetic yawns. My eyelids get heavier even as my brain screams at me that something isn't right. The last thing I see before the world grows dark is the greenish mist twining around my friends as they succumb to sleep, one at a time.

Logan

I'm surrounded immediately. The worst part is that this room has windows showing me a taunting view of the outside world. I'm so close. I do a scan of the semicircle of men I have to get through to get out of here.

Six men, a couple of whom are already wielding magic of some sort. One has lightning sparking off his palms, and one cracks his knuckles before speeding over with his arm drawn back. I leap off to the side, narrowly avoiding his fist as it crashes through the stone wall behind the spot where my head used to be.

I boost myself up and swing over the back of the ugly leather couch, ducking behind it for cover as the Elemental shoots some warm up bolts my way. I peek around the side to pinpoint my targets. The current of my powers is rushing in a euphoric race through my veins. Being reunited with my powers after I escaped the cell renewed my flagging energy and gave me a fresh rush of adrenaline. I can take them down. Each and every one. The thought brings a grim smile to my face. I'm sure I look this side of psychotic right now.

The idea of using fire or electricity in this small space wouldn't be my first choice, but the room is too dry to pull any water to make ice. And it's certainly not stopping the rest of these jokers.

I pull on the threads of my power, weaving it into an electrical current. My first shot flies wild as a red and orange ball of heat comes hurtling at my face. I duck back just in time to miss it and catch one man coming at me from the side. Big mistake. Brave idiot that he is, I don't sense any magic in him, but the huge sword in his hands is calling to me. I send a strong current of wind at him that has him stumbling. His grip on the sword doesn't loosen until I twirl it into a whirlwind that lifts him off his feet for a moment. The blade falls with a satisfying clatter, and I dart out to snatch it up, releasing him from the mini tornado until he crashes to the ground. There's a sweet satisfaction in slamming the hilt of his own steel into his head, taking him out of the equation. One down, five to go.

The sharp crack of an elbow in my back steals my breath before I can turn around, but I'm not one to lose hold of my blade, so I'm spinning back to take on my next foe. He backs away, drawing his own blade when he notices the one his companion was so kind as to give me. I step into him, forcing him back while still keeping an eye on the others.

He takes advantage of my momentary disadvantage when I duck down to avoid a fireball spinning at my head. The Mages are keeping back, letting the mundanes wear me down with a physical fight. Smart strategy, but they haven't fought me before. They got comfortable thinking they could take me with a six on one situation. They were wrong.

I take out the one in front of me and the one creeping up behind with a sword hilt to the gut, followed by a spin and back kick. My fury and desperation have risen to an urgent pitch. I don't even have time to enjoy the moment with three men lying crumpled around me before a volley of lightning and fire shoots over the back of the couch.

Enough of this. I grab the back of the couch and swing myself back over, avoiding all but one bolt of lightning. A quiet gasp is the only sign of the fiery pain in my thigh from the hit.

My leg threatens to buckle on the landing, but I will it to hold. If these guys want to play with fire, I'm all in. This whole place can burn for all I care. As long as it takes Sophia's uncle down with it. He's probably not even here right now. He's probably off, using my information to capture her. The dark thought tries to drag me under, but I don't have time for that.

"Yes." The triumphant yell escapes as I take down the one who must have gotten me with the bolt. The blue current dancing down his arms sparks out as he falls. I'm so focused on him I don't notice the insidious vines that were creeping closer until they twine around my ankles trying to trip me up.

Not today. I take turns slashing the vines with my captured sword and ducking the streams of fire trying to roast me where I stand. I've practiced with Ivy enough times to know how to handle a few vines.

Sweat stings my eyes at the intense heat from the flames, but I'm an Elemental. I can handle a little heat.

I kick the broken vines off my feet and make a run at the Bio Mage that sent them for me. He doesn't look ready for a direct attack. I guess coercing people into working for you might not get you the best of the best.

He glances at me with a nervous look before turning and fleeing. Coward. While I'd like to chase him before he sounds an alarm, I don't have time to do it.

This last one might prove to be a bit of a challenge. His well-muscled arms give me the impression he might not be a stranger to a physical fight. However, he has been burning off his powers at a tremendous rate. He can't have that much juice left.

I zigzag toward him, encouraging him to waste his power. That'll give me the advantage I need. He takes the bait, but his fireballs are getting smaller.

I send out another gust of wind powerful enough to knock chairs over and it snuffs his faltering flames right before it hits him. I've always wanted to send a cow flying like you always see in tornado movies, but I wouldn't hurt a poor, defenseless bovine. This guy. I'm happy to experiment on.

I build up an even stronger whirlwind, noting the fear on his face with satisfaction. The wind sweeps him a few feet in the air. I let him spin for a few moments longer than necessary. The pounding of footsteps in the hallway is the wakeup I need. Everyone here is down. I need to get out of this place before they catch up.

The guy moans as I send him to the floor with more force than necessary. He doesn't stir when I nudge him with my bare toe. I spin in a circle to assess the rest of them. One of them's gotta be awake enough to give me some information. The coward who ran would have been my best bet, but the mundanes will probably break easy.

I spy my target as I walk back around the couch. The former owner of the sword I'm now holding has come to and is edging back toward the door. I slam a foot into his gut. It loses some of the usual impact with my foot bare of anything but filth and scratches, but it gets my point across. His eyes widen at my mouth, bared in what is likely an unhinged grin.

I lean in close, placing his own steel at his neck. "Tell me how to get out of this hellhole."

Terror fights with indecision in his eyes, so I lean in just a little closer to get my point across. "Keep in mind that I'll make sure to you suffer before I kill you if you even think about lying to me."

"Uh, that way." He cracks like an egg tapped on a glass bowl, waving his hand in a vague gesture to the left.

"Be more specific and fast." A drop of blood beads at his throat at the extra pressure I apply to the blade before easing it up just a little to let him speak.

"Straight through that door. Take a right at the first branch and you'll be at the main entrance. There's guards there though. Don't kill me, please. I have a family."

"You should have thought about them before you started working for such an asshole."

I almost feel sorry for the man, but he probably should have made better life choices that didn't get him stuck down here working for a psycho.

I start to rise before realizing I should grab his boots. The sounds in the hall are getting louder as I fumble with the laces on his boots. I mutter a curse until they finally give way. No time to put them on. I tie them together with a quick knot and sling them over my shoulder, taking off at a run in the direction the mundane pointed to.

I direct one last blast of wind at the couch until it slides in front of the door, blocking the way. I imagine there's more ahead, but if I can stall the ones behind me, it'll help.

The lack of guards along the path has me glancing over my shoulder with paranoia. I need a plan before bursting through to the main entrance. When I spot my turn off, I slow down, taking a moment to catch my breath. I channel every lesson I ever had from my father, every training session with Houston. Every fight I've ever been in and draw on my powers. I let them build and build. They're more than happy to respond, having been cooped up for too long. The very blood in my veins is tingling as I let every ounce of rage, fear, and terror loose. Maybe my father was wrong all along. Maybe letting my emotions cross over into a fight might help me out this time.

When my powers are swelling in a rising tide of the perfect storm, I push through the door. Man, sometimes I hate it when I'm right. Dozens of Mages, Witches, and mundanes circle the room. The shadowy figures of shades hovering above me swoop down as one unit. But before their icy darkness can engulf me, I let the power loose like never before. Even when I was a child, everything was controlled, measured, guided. For the first time in my life, I just let it go and it's a powerful thing. It's like the magic has it's own mind. It flows through me in a flash fire of heat and energy. The magic travels from deep in my core out through my fingertips in a blast of flames that has me stumbling back.

Flames stream out like massive wings to either side of me, rising from the cold stone floor all the way to the high ceiling. The shades pull back from the flames disappearing through the thick walls. Everyone else clears out of the path or gets thrown back from the blast. Smoke and chaotic screams fill the air.

The blast ripped the massive wood doors off their hinges, so I make a run for the path I've cleared. A couple brave souls rush in to stand their ground in front of the gaping wound that was once a door. One of them shoots a couple of laughably small fireballs at me while another sends out a pitiful stream of water that evaporates as it hits the heat of my wall of fire.

They make the smart choice to run, and I don't even give them a second glance as I burst out the front doors into the unknown that lies past it. Don't know where it'll take me, but I'm going.

The flames are licking away at the entrance but they're mine, so they pull back to allow me to pass before resuming their blockade of the entrance.

I run without a backward glance. Out into the darkness, my uncaring feet pounding on dirt, rocks, tree branches until.

I run and run until I can't push myself any further. My heart is pounding so hard I'm afraid it's going to quit and my entire body is quaking, but I think I'm far enough away. I need to find somewhere to take cover.

I've made it to a strange forested area. It doesn't provide much cover though, as the dark branches twisting from the trunks are bare of any leaves. There's got to be somewhere. I push myself forward, knowing that someone is likely following me and if Zeus is anywhere nearby, he'll be after me. He won't let this slide and with my powers drained, I'm not going to be fighting back.

I finally find an area filled densely with the strange trees. There's some sort of life here. Odd purple flowers dot the surface of a copse of bushes. Sharp almost metallic thorns claw through my tattered clothes, scraping my already raw skin. I ignore the pain to keep tearing through them until I'm in the center of the patch concealed by the bushes.

The shreds of my clothing that are left get soaked through, but my body is so exhausted and numb I barely feel it. Sleep is pulling at my conciousness trying to drag me under when it hits me like a bullet train. The bond snaps back with a rush. Sophia. She's down here. In the Nether. Was all this for nothing? Did he get her? That's the last thought I have before tumbling into a deep sleep.

Sophia

Terror grips me as my feet pound the dirt.

The sting of a thousand tiny needles pokes my feet, my legs, my arms. What am I running from? People, flames. Something is on fire. I'm running from the wall of heat behind me. Flames licking at my heels. Never ceasing. Almost catching up.

The world looks wrong. Blurred, out of focus. Where am I?

Pain stabs me in the temples when I shoot up with a start. Not me. It's not me. It's not my pain. It's Logan. I can feel him. His fear, his heartbeat galloping in a race that drags mine along with it. My hand flies down to the sheath where his dagger has been resting next to my skin in a strange version of a comfort toy.

My panic rises when my fingers meet the smooth leather of the sheath devoid of its usual smooth metal occupant.

"Logan!" I cry out. I can feel him, but he is still too distant to hear me.

He's not here, but the rest of the gang is. They're all splayed out on the damp ground. Liz, Garrett, Trey, Ivy. They're all here, but something's wrong. Why are they sleeping? Why was I sleeping? I reach over to shake Liz, who is lying closest to me.

She's already stirring and blinking her eyes blearily when I my hand falls to her arm.

"Liz! Wake up."

Her usually neat black bob tangles her around her face in a wild birds nest and her eyes have a dull look to them as if the sea that fills them is polluted.

I hear a yawn and a groan from one of the others. "Why does it feel like someone took a pickaxe to my skull?" Trey asks squeezing his forehead.

"We've been asleep. Something happened." I search my mind, trying to remember what we were doing when we fell asleep. Endless walking and then taking a break in the woods. "The green mist!"

"Whaaaa cha talking about?" A huge yawn interrupts Liz's statement.

All grogginess has cleared from my mind already, so I don't have time for them to catch up.

"The green mist. We were sitting. That weird green fog descended on us and we all got sleepy. It must have been magical. The question is why?"

I reach back for the knife again and am once again reminded that it's gone, so I pat my waist, looking for my own set. Nothing.

"Wait. Where's my crystal?" A mask of horror twists his face as he tears at his shirt and starts scrabbling in the dirt. "It's missing. Where is it?"

I reach for my neck and realize my necklace is missing too.

"Our packs are gone." Ivy sounds almost resigned. "We've got nothing."

"So someone or something knocked us out and stole all our shit. Fantastic," Liz says. "I guess we'll have to hurry this mission and get the heck out of here."

It hits me with a rush and my hand flies up to my chest. To the warmth there that's been missing since he was taken. It's there. I can feel him. I think the bond must have snapped back into place. I can't believe I was so distracted by the frightening dream and our stolen stuff that I didn't realize it. I should have recognized it immediately. The knowledge itches away at my brain. That means. Maybe that wasn't a dream. Maybe Logan really did escape, and I was seeing things through his eyes. He was running, terrified.

I reach out, testing the bond, but pull back at the emotions coursing through it. It's faint, but there. Pain, fear. He's scared, and the only time I've felt Logan scared before was when he was worried about me. My heart aches for him. Some teleportation skills would be helpful right about now. I need to get to him.

"How are we going to do that, Liz?" Ivy asks. "Garrett's tracking crystal is gone. How are we going to Logan now?" Her hand is running through her hair as if she's stuck in a loop.

Right. They don't know the bond is back in place. I tap away at my chest. "It's fine. He must have escaped or something. I had a dream while we were sleeping. Only I don't think it was a dream. He was running. There were flames behind him." The confusion twisting all of their faces lets me know they're not following the inner dialogue that accompanies my wild rambling. "The bond. It's back. I can track him through that."

There it is. The realization dawns on them. Except Garrett. I realize he hasn't joined the rest of us. He's sitting on the ground with his head in his hands.

"Garrett?" He doesn't respond to his name, so I kneel beside him and pull his hands away from his face. Looking into his eyes is like staring into a dark abyss. They're empty of all life.

I cup his face between his palms and try to avoid getting sucked into their void. "Garrett, what's wrong?"

He shakes his head. "It's gone. It's all I had left, and it's gone. I've got nothing."

Before my mouth can form another question, it hits me. His tracking crystal. The thing that gives him his main Witchy power is gone. "Your crystal. I'm so sorry. I'm so, so sorry."

He yanks out of my grip. "What are you sorry for? Did you take it?" His words slap me like a lash striking my cheek, but I don't pull away.

"Of course not, but it's because of me you're down here, so I'm sorry for that."

"Everything is not all about you, Sophia. Get over yourself."

"Dude!" Trey calls out, but I shake my head at him.

Garrett's words hurt, but I get it. That was the last thing he had that tied him to his family, and every time he looked at it or touched, he still felt the fragile connection to them. I've been a little lost, a little adrift, a little further away from my dad since Mom and I had to leave our house, but I've still got her. I've still got my brother as far away as is right now. Thankfully. He's safer away at school. But Garrett lost his house, his family, all the things that provided that connection and then he ran from all his former friends. That was it. It's not about the power. It's about that last thread of his family ties being snatched away. I know it's not about me, but I can't help the guilt that swells up every time one of my friends or family members gets hurt merely by being in my presence or helping me out.

I know words won't change anything, but I need him to know that I'm here for him, no matter what. "I understand, Garrett, and I'm here for you. No matter what."

He unfolds himself from the ground without another word or glance in my direction before walking off. Everything about him screams don't talk to me. His stare off blankly into the distance and his arms are crossed tightly across his chest as if he can somehow hold himself together, but at least he's up.

"Let's go." His husky voice is like sandpaper shredding my heart. I hope we don't lose him to this. I hope we can get him back, but Logan is still out there, and he needs us.

Logan

The landscape down here is a never-ending expanse of despair. Exhausting expanses of rocky terrain are occasionally broken up by lifeless trees. The colors are all off too. My feet fall on dirt that's got a grayish tinge to it and the sky looks like it's on fire all the time. Lightning bolts zigzag across the sky with a startling regularity, but they aren't accompanied by thunder or rain. Nothing seems quite right.

I've been keeping my distance from any villages or buildings that dot this rural hellscape. I can't risk running into anyone or anything down here. I got a couple hours of restless sleep last night, but I blew out my powers escaping that place. The only sign of my magic is an occasional faint hum that fades to nothing after a moment. I've got zero energy, one sword, and maybe one small burst of power to defend myself at the moment. I could probably scrape off a win against one opponent, but my odds would sink astronomically if I happened across multiple attackers.

Maybe I'm being optimistic even thinking I could take on a single foe right now. The only thing that's keeping me on my feet, pushing forward one at a time, is Sophia at the other end of the bond. It's pulling me in her direction at a steady pace I might not be able to maintain if I didn't know she was out there.

The lack of fear or distress is another positive. We're still too far away for too much to come through, but I'd know it if she were suffering from any intense feelings of terror or pain. Those should be strong enough to travel the distance. She must be relatively unharmed. Whatever that looks like.

My toe catches on a rock, sending me to my knees as the luminescent yellow moon sinks lower in the sky. The pinkish lines streaking across the lightening sky remind me of Sophia's magic. When we're connected, I can see her magic swirling around in that exact shade. The reminder gives me the strength to push myself to my feet.

Emotions that aren't my own are intensifying. She's tired too, but determined, focused, a little sad. Nothing that makes me think she's in imminent danger.

Each step has been bringing me closer and closer to what looks like a small village. I've avoided all signs of life so far, but the bond is trying to lead me straight through this area of full of small buildings.

I could try to go around it, but the extra time it would take has me hesitating. I barely know how I'm still standing. I don't think I can afford any delay. Maybe I can blend in? I'm sure I look wrecked with my torn clothes hanging off me and several days' worth of stubble. I suck in a deep breath and press on.

A loud bark has me almost jumping out of my skin, but it's just a couple of stray dogs. At least that's what I think until one of them swings it's head around to reveal blood-red eyes and saliva dripping off razor sharp death. The thing looks terrifying, but doesn't seem to have a problem with me. One of the other dogs distracts it with a nip and it spins around to chase it away with a playful bound. I guess even demon dogs like to play.

I edge through the village. There's no sign of people, although a few shades swoop around the corner in a shadowy chase.

I'm halfway to the safety of the barren land beyond and each step has the bond pulsing stronger in my chest. Sophia's so close, I swivel my head around in search of her golden head. My tired steps quicken into a slow jog. I'm never going to make it to a full run, but I can feel her. Tantalizingly close.

I should know better than to loosen up my guard. If there's anything my father taught me, it's to remain constantly vigilant. Blame it on the exhaustion, but I never see it coming. The sharp pain is my only warning before I tumble into darkness.

Sophia

We made a solid trek through one small village, but our luck can't hold out for a second. Logan is on the move. The bond that ties us together is pulling at me with every step.

When we reach the edge of the village, we creep in. There's a few too many of us to hide, but hopefully the old safety in numbers theory will hold up. He's ok. Exhausted, sure. In pain, some. Hungry, definitely, but nothing life threatening.

My heart is thrumming like a hummingbird until I'm almost light headed and then pain. My hand flies to the back of my head as if it's my own, but it's not. Pain and then nothing. He's gone.

"Nooooo!" I shout, breaking into a run. Where is he? I look around frantically.

"What's the matter?" Liz grabs my arm.

Her voice pulls me back, and I realize he's not dead. The bond is still there. He must have lost consciousness. I follow the thread of the bond that was there before. "Logan, something's wrong."

I've barely gotten the words out when she blurs out. If I had time, I'd smack myself. Super speed, right. I blur out after her. My teeth rattle at the force of slamming into her back when she comes to an abrupt halt. Graceful as always. Maybe one day I'll get the hang of all this.

"What the heck?" I peer over her shoulder and spot him. He's there.. Lying in the dirt in the middle of the dirt road in between ramshackle houses.

Her arm swings out to restrain me when I try to run past. "Wait. It's probably a trap."

"I don't care." I smack at her am.

"Stop it. You won't do anyone any good if you go rushing in and get yourself captured."

She's not wrong. Always weird when Liz is the voice of reason rather than rushing in with magic blazing.

"Fine. What's the plan then? He's right there." It's like someone slipped a dagger past my guard and slid it right through my heart. The pain is so bad it's like a physical injury being so close and not being able to get to him. Not to mention the phantom throbbing at the back of my head.

"Wait for the others to catch up. If we're going in, at least we want the numbers."

Right. We can use any advantage we can get since we have no idea what we're going to be up against.

My foot taps at the ground as I peer over her shoulder at Logan's still figure. I really don't like seeing him like this. If it weren't for our connection letting me know he's still alive and breathing, I wouldn't be waiting.

All three of them are breathing hard when they catch up, so I bite back the completely unfair response of 'took you long enough' that wants to sneak out.

"What…?" Ivy catches sight of Logan. "No!"

"He's ok. I can feel it, but we thought we should wait until you guys caught up so we have our best defense."

"And by we, don't you mean me?" Liz pokes me.

"Helpful." I turn to Trey. "How do you think we should approach this?" I know they're all trained to fight, but Trey is the one with actual experience leading a team. Don't say I don't know when to defer to someone else with more knowledge.

He scans the area. "Don't see anything, so if someone is waiting here for us, they're well hidden. We'll approach with caution. Surround Logan to protect him. Everyone face out and keep an eye open in all directions. Ground, sky. Who knows what could be out here?"

I nod and meet everyone's eyes to make sure we're all together. My heart sinks when Garrett averts his gaze at my attempt.

"Ok, go."

We all sprint off, stopping in an outward facing circle. I'm dying to turn around, touch him. Make sure he's really there and this isn't some messed up illusion.

The air around is silent in a way that has my skin prickling with discomfort. Something's here. Watching us. Biding its time.

A howl rends the quiet as soon as I bend down to shake Logan out of his unconscious state. Rays of sunlight glint off the black coats of a pack of black dogs that are rushing at us. Red eyes flash at me as one of them leaps at me, baring a set of decidedly unearthly teeth at me. Maybe not so much of a dog.

My magic comes to life with a jolt, happy to respond to my call for lightning. I wince as the dog thing falls back with a whimper before going limp. My powers were so anxious at the chance to get out, I might have let a little too much seep into that one.

I try to ease up on my next blast. The creatures are falling around us on all sides when another creature swoops in toward

Logan's prone form. It raises it's furry little triangular face to look at me as it descends.

"Oh, no you don't." At least I know what this one is. A handful of Ferrebats have joined the party. Sharp talons poised to rip at our flesh.

I tamp down on the magic, afraid I'm going to hit one of my friends instead of the creature. I'm getting the hang of switching between the various branches of my power. I let a rush of Phys strength flow into my arm, slamming it into the Ferrebat.

It falls to the ground, and I go tumbling after having not been prepared for the strength of my swing.

I land across Logan's chest with a thud, happy to see his ocean eyes blink open at me.

"Sophia?" he groans.

"Yes, I'm here." The world around me vanishes as I fling my arms around him.

Until a booted foot thuds into my thigh and everything comes rushing back. The growls of angry beasts, slams of flesh on flesh and the shadowed form of a bunch of shades who have come to join the party.

It seems like any time we've encountered shades, they've been under the control of my uncle. I find my eyes darting around expecting to see him lurking around somewhere waiting for his minions to wear us out.

There's no time for relief, but there is a bit of comfort to be had when the warmth of Logan's body surrounds me from behind. He can't be that hurt if he's up already.

Liz is whipping around in a blur, knocking shades out of the sky, and Garrett and Ivy are flat out taking the dogs down with swift kicks. I build up a strong wind to help Trey whip the shades out of the way, but there's nowhere to send them since we're already down here in the Nether. They keep coming in an overwhelming rush. Some of them only have enough strength to whip around our heads, causing everything from minor distraction to temporary blindness. There's a handful that are corporeal enough to be firing elemental magic at us. You never know which ones are which until you're ducking a lightning bolt.

Fire worked on them, though, as I recall from the last time we faced them. I let the magic build to a high level of intensity. Burning through me until I have to release it and then I let it fly at a cluster of shades. The flames disperse them immediately, but I have to duck to avoid another streak of lightning aimed at my head. Heat sears the top of my skull as I narrowly avoid losing the top of my head.

Warmth flows into me as a solid hand lands on the back of my neck and thoughts that aren't my own intrude. *Useless. Drained. I can't even protect her.*

I'm so mad that Zeus has put Logan in this position. I focus on the thread that ties us together, sending a golden glow of warmth through it while I continue to roast the shades.

I can feel Logan's internal struggle as he tries to build his own depleted magic. *It's ok. We're good.* The words flow from my mind to his with an ease I've never felt before when we've been connected and the warm flows along with them, taking my magic along on the current.

It's like it stokes the fire of his magic and suddenly his powers sputter to life with a jolt that has his hand falling from my neck. As soon as he drops the skin-on-skin contact, the flow stops like a tap shut off. I slide to the right to avoid a fireball and then grab his hand. Once we've reconnected, the magic flows again. His magic curls around mine and it's like our powers are feeding off of each other, roaring to a blaze. Our dual focus allows us to send off a blast even more powerful than the one one I let loose that leveled the abandoned store we battled at.

Shades evaporate around us as the force throws the whole group back. Ferrebats rain down and pitiful yips follow the remaining demon dogs as their paws stir up a cloud of dust around us. They're fleeing around the blackened crater we left in the middle of the road in droves.

We have to send a final, smaller stream of flames at the remaining shades.

Ivy, Liz, Trey, and Garrett all have some pretty wild eyes and gaping mouths when we spin around.

"That was interesting," Ivy says.

"Um, yeah, what just happened? There was like a cloud of magic surrounding us. I've never felt anything like it," Trey says, rubbing at his head with a worried crease folding his brow.

Garrett's fingers are dancing curiously in the swirl of magic that's surrounding us. His fingers close over as if it's a ball of hard packed snow he can scoop up to hurl at an enemy.

"How about we get the hell out of here and figure out the logistics later? I, for one, will be happy to never return to this hole." I lean into the arm Logan slides around my shoulders.

The prickle of magic is still dancing in the air around us when a slow clap echoes through the seemingly deserted town. I don't even need to turn around to know who it is.

"Zeus."

Sophia

My stomach churns at the sight of my "uncle" casually leaning on a run-down shack with boarded-up windows. He couldn't look more out of place if he tried. His crisp blue suit is spotless, in sharp contrast to the rest of us. After the chaos of the fight and the explosion of our creation, there's dirt coating the dirt on my ripped clothing.

"Impressive. This is a new development I was not anticipating."

Logan squeezes me in tighter into his side as Zeus takes a step forward. I did not get her back to lose her again. If he thinks he can take us now, I guess he's in for a surprise.

"Come on. Let's get out of here," Ivy urges.

I pull out of Logan's arms to move a little closer. I know he's itching to pull me back, but he hesitates, thinking of how annoyed I'll be if he does that, so he settles for hovering behind me like a warm shadow. He's close enough to yank me back and away, given the slightest provocation.

"Wait. I have some questions." I want to get out of here, and I want Logan away from him, but I need to know. Why is he doing this? Why the constant pursuit?

"Right. We didn't get a chance for too much conversation the last time we met."

"Maybe because you were in the process of murdering my friend and kidnapping my…Logan last time we met." My throat catches on the words and a surge of pain washes over me, threatening to knock me off my feet.

"That mundane?" he waves a dismissive hand. "I did warn you."

A broken laugh escapes my lips. "He was one of my best friends." The image of him falling to the ground flashes in front of my eyes. That picture has been branded on my brain. I'll never be free of it.

"You don't need that kind of influence in your life. You're better than that now." Wow. This guy has zero value for his life. My soft pink magic is deepening to crimson with my rage. The hairs on my arms are lifting at the energy swirling through me. In spite of the massive amount of power I just expended, I feel like I could do it all over again.

Logan's words whisper across my ear on a shiver of heat as he leans in close. "Come on. We don't need to do this. Let's just get out of here."

"He's probably right. You should go. I'll be seeing you soon enough." He heard Logan? I wonder what Phys he stole that power from.

"The next time you see me, I'll be the one taking your life." Logan's husky threat has deepened his voice a couple of decibels. He's lost his mind if he thinks I'd let him be the one to kill Zeus. It makes me even angrier that he has me considering murder. Something I've never thought of before in my life. But then, no one has ever taken this much away from me.

"You're just letting us go?" *Something's wrong. He wouldn't just give us up after all that.*

Maybe so, but we're taking him up on his offer. Let's get out of here before he changes his mind. Logan's thoughts are as clear as my own in my mind.

"Of course. You're free to go, but I'm going to extend this offer once. Come and work with me. Together, this world can be ours."

"I would never work with you. Not in a million years."

"That's what you say now, but you'll be coming to me. And I was planning on letting you keep your…Logan. He was, after all, quite helpful. But that's only on the table if you come willingly. Although having seen what the two of you are capable of together. That's interesting. It changes things."

That's it. I've had enough of the nonsense spewing from his mouth. As if I would ever work with him or trust him. It makes me uneasy that he witnessed whatever just happened with Logan's and my powers working together. I don't even understand what happened. I definitely don't like the idea of him having any extra knowledge of us.

"You don't know anything about me if you think I'm just going to cave."

"I might not know as much as I like about you, but I think you're going to find that the world you left behind is not quite the same as the one you're going back to. Let me know when you need my help to navigate it."

I'm so over it. My magic has been begging for a release anyway, so I let it build until sparks dancing off my palms before releasing a volley of lightning at my uncle.

The electricity leaves a frustrating series of burn marks in the patch of dirt he just vacated, and I back away.

"That is one weird dude," says Liz.

"Weird is maybe not the word I'd go for. I'm thinking more along the lines of psychotic or criminally insane myself."

"Yeah, you're probably right. Now, can we get out of here? I'm starving, and I miss my cats."

Love Liz, but I think she needs to work on her priorities. She is right. We need to get out of here.

Logan

The giant gaping void in front of us is evidence of how good Sophia has gotten at the spell to open up portals between our realm and the Nether. She didn't seem to have any trouble reversing the spell to get us home with a little help from Garrett. She must have practiced with him before they came here. Only a dull edge of jealousy creeps around the edges of my brain at the thought of them working together. I know I can trust her, and he hasn't let us down so far.

"Ok, here goes nothing." She squeezes my hand. "Come on."

We step forward together, and the uncomfortable feeling of losing track of my senses only lasts a moment before we step out onto a sidewalk.

The squeal of a car's tires is the first thing that lets me know we're back in the world of the living. The murmur of voices is next, followed by cries of surprise that ring out just as Trey appears out of the portal and joins me at my side.

I blink away the bright light that's sending a pulse of pain through my eyeballs that have gotten used to the dim lighting of the Nether Realm.

"What?" Sophia's chocolate eyes are wide with horror and I follow her gaze to the group of people ogling us with their cell phones out.

Liz hops out. "What's going on?"

"Um. They're filming us. That can't be good, right?" Bit of an understatement from Sophia. This is catastrophic. We just walked out of a giant portal in the middle of a street full of mundanes.

Liz steps forward, flashing a huge smile. "Not the time for showboating, little sis."

"Hey, if you got it, flaunt it."

"We need to get out of here now. Then we can find a phone to call Robert to get this mess sorted out."

"Before we go anywhere. Anyone happen to know where we are?" I didn't even notice Ivy popping out of the portal until she speaks.

My scan of our surroundings looking for any familiar signs or locations is a failure. I don't have a clue where we are. I brush a loose tendril of gold behind Sophia's ear. "Any clue where you've brought us?"

Judging by the way her mouth pulls down, that's a no. "Uh no, sorry. We planned to do some research to figure out a way to pinpoint a precise location with our portal. Unfortunately, we ran out of time, so I'm as clueless as you."

The surrounding crowd is getting a little rowdy. It seems thicker and people are jostling each other to get a better look at us even as the portal behind us shrinks. This is ten shades of shitty.

"I think we really need to get out of here, like now. We can regroup and figure out our next step once we get away from all these eyes." I'll be the one to state the obvious. "Come on."

I hustle everyone into a quick march, unfortunately some of our oglers are trailing after us. We need to lose them, and fast. I spot a tall building with a sign that indicates it's a multi-level shopping mall. Perfect place to get lost in a crowd. Lots of small shops and corners to disappear into.

"Hey, guys. Lets head for there. We can lose all the gawkers in there and call our parents." I nod at Liz.

"I vote you to make that call," says my ever helpful little sister.

"Of course you do."

Our ragtag group is hustling around the corner to the entrance when something catches my eye. A dark paneled van swings into a parking spot near our portal and out spills a team from the Magical Enforcement Division. Their distinctive black uniforms with the red crest give them away.

"Guys, there's a MED team over there. They must be here for a cleanup. We can grab them to use a phone or get them to call Dad," I call down the street waving an arm.

Ivy grabs my arm. "That might not be the best idea. Trey basically defected. We broke Garrett out of the prison at HQ. And last we checked, the council had booted your parents and Lawrence had taken over."

"What? What the hell did I miss when I was down there?"

"You don't even want to know, big brother." Liz rolls her eyes at me. "But good job. You've now alerted them to our presence. So yippee for that."

I can't even wrap my head around the things they're telling me. No time for that, anyway. The MED team has broken into a run, and they do not look friendly. Shit.

"Ok, go!"

We scramble through the revolving door that's moving entirely too slowly and spill out into the main lobby of the mall.

This was a good choice. The ceilings tower up three stories and there are lots of stores to hide out in. We're getting some pretty odd looks, so I glance down to see what's wrong. Right. I look like I just escaped from prison. I'm filthy and draped in tattered clothes. The rest of them don't look quite as bad, but everyone's got some bruises or cuts, and not too clean clothes.

This place is pretty good strategically. There's got to be multiple exits. If we're going to find an alternate exit to get out of there and lose ourselves in the city, we should probably do it fast. I imagine if they're really here to get us, they'll call in reinforcements to surround the building.

It's a strange feeling getting pursued by the MED. I've always considered them to be the good guys. I've spent my life in and out of our local headquarters. My family has been on the council for generations. I can't even fathom what's gone down to bring this abrupt change about, but I imagine it has something to do with Zeus. There has been unrest and division between the leaders, but Lawrence would never have the power to bring this about.

Tension surrounds us like a weighted blank pressing down. The sound of my stolen boots squeaking on the shiny floor is like a drill stabbing into my eardrums as I weave around the endless crowd of shoppers. Forest green garland, and giant gaudy ornaments deck the windows and railings throughout the place. That explains why it's so busy. It's almost Christmas. I lost track of the date around Halloween. Life has basically been a whirlwind of fighting and running for our lives since then. It's not going to be the kind of holiday I'm used to spending with my family, but I'll at least have Sophia, my sister, and the rest of these weirdoes around. If we can get out of our current situation.

The smells of greasy fast food and burned coffee overwhelm my senses before we even reach the food court at the center of the mall. Plastic tables ringed by all the food options. The scent of fried foods and grilling meat punches my empty stomach.

A large sign points out where all the hallways branch off. There's a nondescript gray door at the end with a parking sign above it. That might be a good place to make our escape. I nod my head at the door. We've reached a master level of silent communication.

"That's a good plan," Trey says. "Maybe we should send someone over to the customer service booth to see if we can figure out where we are and maybe use a phone to reach your parents."

My eyes bounce around each of my friends. We can't let someone go off alone. I shake my head. "No. Too dangerous to get separated."

Ivy's wide eyes look unperturbed as she blinks at me. "I can do it."

"No, Ivy. I'm not going to let you go off alone." What if I lost her for real this time? I haven't really had time to appreciate her being back since we've been jumping from one fire to the next. But I know for sure that the thought of losing her for good sends a shiver of fear through me.

"Hear me out. I'm the least recognizable and most presentable of the group of us." She slips her torn jacket off to reveal a clean black sweater. "You're disgusting." She wrinkles her nose at me, then turns, pointing to Liz's hair. "Liz's hair is too recognizable after they aimed those cell phones at us, and Trey is way too intimidating. I'll slip over there and then meet you in the garage. Trust me, no one will notice me all by myself.

They won't be looking for us alone. They're looking for the group."

"I really don't like…"

"It's not up to you, Logan. I can make my own decisions." Sophia's mouth pulls back in a small smirk. These women are trying to kill me. So much for thinking they care.

"I'll go with her." Garrett jumps in. "I'll hang back and keep an eye out, so at least she's not alone." He still might not be my favorite, but he moves up a tiny notch in my books with his offer.

Sophia elbows me and gives me a dark look when my mouth falls open to make another protest. "Fine. Meet you in there. We'll try to find somewhere to take cover where we can monitor the door. Be fast. I suspect we need to get out of this place as soon as possible so we don't end up trapped." The thought of being confined again sends me right back to that cold, dark place in hell.

With one more scan of the area, we part ways with our group, pushing through the heavy fire door into a landing. The stale scent of sweat and urine matches the graffiti stained walls. The landing branches off with a set of black metal stairs heading up, one going down with a green painted door straight ahead with a P1 stenciled on the door. While I'd rather go up or down to put as much distance as possible between us and the MED team, we need to take the straight path so Ivy and Garrett know where to find us.

There's not too many cars moving about the packed parking lot. Looks like all the spots are already full on this level. There's got to be somewhere in here we can duck away to avoid notice.

"Over there." Sophia tugs on my arm, pointing at the green ticket machine tucked into an alcove across from us. We can probably make that work.

We cross the lot and duck into the shadowed corner behind the bank of machines. I tug Sophia back into my side, needing her as close as possible.

"What did I miss while I was down there?" I hiss under my breath. I don't want to draw too much attention to us as people move about the lot.

Her nose wrinkles in thought and her eyes dart back and forth. I can almost see her brain racing. "Ummm. A lot? So I pretty much leveled that building after my uncle dragged you off."

"It was totally epic!" my sister chimes in at a volume ten levels too loud.

"Awesome. Maybe a little louder? Don't think the people on the next level up caught that."

"Right. Sorry. My senses are all buzzing after that escape. I think my hearing is out of whack and throwing me off."

Makes sense. Her enhanced hearing must sometimes make it hard to judge her volume. Although I would think she'd be talking quieter rather than louder, but that's hardly Liz's way.

Sophia ignores the interruption to continue her story. "Then, we got picked up by a MED team."

Liz is bouncing on her toes while Sophia talks in her even tone. "But there's crazy madness going down with the council and they wouldn't release Sophia or Garrett!"

"What?!!!" A crimson haze blurs my vision as I look around for someone I can punish for containing my girl, and after she just watched one of her best friends die. My hands curl into fists so tight my nails dig into my palms, and I struggle to keep my emotions in check as I imagine the horror she was going through.

Her hand falls on my arm and she sends a wave of calm through the bond. "But I'm fine. Obviously. Your dad got me out, but he couldn't get them to release Garrett."

My gaze flicks back to the door we came through once again. "But he got him out, eventually?"

"Yeah, no. We had to look after that ourselves." A small smirk pulls up the corners of her lips.

I level Trey with a look. "And you couldn't do anything about it?" He's pretty high up in the MED ranks for being so young.

He's trying to be nonchalant and brush it off with a shrug, but I've known the guy since we were kids. The pulse in his clenched jaw and the thin creases of stress between his eyes give him away. I shouldn't be badgering him, but he makes an excellent target to aim my frustration at.

"I tried, but the council is not the same one you remember. Lawrence has taken over and installed his own people. Your parents are hanging in by a thread. They basically told me to leave it alone or I'd be fired. So here I am."

My eyes widen as shock and guilt ripple through me. Trey's job is everything to him. I might have used this fact to poke fun at him, but honestly, I respect him for his dedication. Things must really be bad if he ended up quitting. I've never spent too much time worrying about my self sufficient parents, but it sounds like they're in a dangerous situation.

"I'm sorry, man." My hand connects with his back in an awkward pat.

"It's fine. We just need to figure out what's going on and put a stop to it. Restore things to their previous balance." His face hardens with determination. He's right. We've gotta to fix this, if for no other reason than to protect Sophia. I glance over at her to see a small smile turning up the corners of her face. There's still a constant shadow of grief marring her beautiful features. I'd do anything to wipe away that pain, but it's not the sort of thing you can just erase with a kiss.

Sophia

My fingers curl into the coarse fabric of Logan's shirt. I can't stop my eyes from darting from Logan back to the door in an endless loop of checking that he's still here and ok, and watching for our friends to reappear. His strong hand rubs in soothing circles every time the creak of the heavy metal door causes the muscles in my back to tense.

I'm not the only one who tenses when I spot a pair of legs clad in black cargo pants entering the garage. He's not in the full uniform of a MED agent, but the distinctive red crest embroidered into the black Henley on his chest gives him away. We sink further into the shadows, Logan pulling me behind him in that protective stance he falls into no matter how many times I prove to him I can handle myself. Sort of. Most of the time.

The soldier's eyes scan the garage in a thorough sweep before he turns around to speak to someone behind him. Here's hoping there aren't too many others with him. We can quietly take down a few, but any more than that and we might end up bringing the whole unit down on us.

I can't tear my gaze away from the door even after the sound of it slamming shut echoes through the garage after a second man joins him. We can do this. I'm about to rush forward when Logan's hand closes on mine, pulling me back into him.

Let Liz get in behind them.

The thought comes through our bond as clear as if it came from my own mind. It still amazes me every time we're able to share our thoughts like that. As she darts past me in a blur, her speed lifts my hair, sending it across my face in a move that causes a tingle in my forehead. I hold my breath, trying to stop the sneeze that threatens to erupt.

Sounds about right. After all we've been through, I'm going to give away our location with an inconveniently timed sneeze. I screw my eyes up tight until I'm jerked into action.

As we take off to meet the MED partners head on, I lose it. The sound shatters the silence and rocks my body, alerting them to our presence.

I don't think when I see the first agent reach for his radio. I dart ahead of the others, putting power into my moves. My hand goes numb and I pull back with a yelp when I attempt a brilliant martial arts style chop to his resist. On the plus side, my overexuberant attack apparently has some unexpected power to it as well. A loud crack accompanies the clatter of his radio hitting the floor and he cradles his right arm to his chest. Did I break it? Oops. I almost apologize before remembering that he's here to catch me and my friends. That eases up on the sympathetic thoughts.

The other guy is sprawled on the floor in a Liz induced heap next to us. Her sneak attack was quick and efficient. The poor guy was probably down before he could even reach for his magic.

Logan looks way too satisfied, sending the guy whose arm I may have broken to the ground in a chokehold. The guy probably further injuring his arm by flailing it about as he tries to catch his breath. It's not pretty, but it works. The satisfied rage Logan is inadvertently sending my way doesn't seem to abate, though. I tug on his arm to bring him back to me. I don't think I could send any calm vibes at him, given the current speed of my heartbeat.

His arms close around me in a quick hug.

Trey's head gives a jerk back to our hiding spot, but I glance down at the men sprawled around our feet. Maybe not the best idea to leave a couple of unconscious men in the middle of the parking garage. Don't want to raise the alarm too soon.

"I got this." Liz jerks the first guy up and over her shoulder, then darts off to stash him…somewhere. She's only just got the second one settled when the door bursts open again.

I let out one relieved breath at the sight of Ivy and Garrett intact, but tense up again at the wild look in their eyes. Garrett's legs are swallowing the concrete with his huge strides as he tears past us.

"I'll grab us a ride! Keep them busy." He yells the words at us as he whips by.

A handful of dark clad agents are right on Ivy's heels as she approaches. My jaw drops as her back leg flies out in a spin, kicking the most eager one in the face before he catches up to her. I doubt I'll ever be that quick thinking in a fight. He stumbles, recovering quickly with a lightning bolt shot she ducks easily. The current that misses her slams into a car that was parked quietly minding its own business setting it's alarm wailing with a screech that sets my teeth on edge.

Logan advances, a little more cautious with the magic. His face is set in concentration as he analyzes all his options in the situation. I can logically analyze any scientific situation, but I recognize and admire his ability to use it in a battle type situation.

The other guys seem to have realized their team members' error in sending off that bolt, so they've resorted to yanking out all manner of weapons. Thankfully, there are no guns to be seen, just a range of swords and daggers. Our group is woefully outmatched in that department, given the loss of all our stuff in the Nether, but that doesn't prevent a determined advance on our part.

There are eight of them to our five. Not terrible odds given the mad skills I've seen my friends use on more than one occasion. They've got a couple of Phys Mages on their team though to match Liz and I. She's clocked a beefy guy with silvering hair at his temples and is matching him in a whirlwind of punches and kicks that are invisible in their speed. It's the flashes of silver glinting in the dim lighting of the garage that worry me. They're probably equally matched on a speed and strength level, but he's got a wicked looking piece of steel that he's wielding at the same frantic pace.

Logan who's engaged in a fight with not one but two guys. A small yellow current flashes in the middle of the scuffle and I really hope he's the one using the lightning.

I don't even have time to assess if he's ok when a tall woman zips in behind him. I use my extra speed to dart over, grabbing the woman's hair before she can slam him into the kidney. Not the most elegant solution, but her deadly punch goes wild, and she turns her attention to me, looking pissed. I've still got her long, dark ponytail wrapped around my fist. She uses this to her advantage, sending a punch into my torso that sends me hurtling into the hard cement, stealing my breath.

I gasp for air that I can't quite reach, but roll away before her booted foot makes contact with my face. That would have cracked my mandible if it had made contact.

I'm struggling like a fish that's been tossed on the shore when she comes at me again, returning the favor with a yank on my hair that drags me to my feet.

"I'm not one to stab someone when they're down, but now that I have you on your feet…" A malicious smile spreads her lips as she spins a dagger in her hand. Not good. Not good at all.

I force a stream of fire out of my palm. Using my magic is not the best idea, but it might be my only option at the moment. She's able to use her speed to avoid the flames, but it's enough to give me some much needed space.

A vehicle hurtles towards us all at a speed that sends us scattering. The squeal of the tires competes with the car alarm that's still echoing through the area as it swings around to a stop.

"GET IN!" Garrett shouts through the window.

I don't think twice before I grasp the cool metal of the door handle, yanking it open, and tumbling into a gasping heap in the back.

Ivy and Liz leap in after me, and I scramble up to make sure Logan doesn't get left behind.

"Go, go!!!" His deep voice reassures me as his hand grabs the roof to swing himself in as Garrett eases onto the gas, pulling away from our pursuers.

A volley of fireballs follows him, a couple rocking the van on its wheels. One slips through the door before Logan can slam it shut.

"What the???" Ivy calls out.

I yank at my sweater in an unsuccessful effort to get it off so I can beat the fire out with it. Before I can get to it, Logan just pulls water from a couple of sippy cups sitting in the cup holders, sending it in a stream to cool down the flaming carpet. One day

I'll reach for my magic first instead of my regular old human skills, but that day is not today.

Garrett has increased his speed as much as he can without getting us into a crash. He weaves his way around the tight turns of the garage with an expertise that is a little alarming. Clearly, this is not his first escape.

I'm sure it won't be long before the MED team regroups getting their own vehicles. A few of them were definitely down for the count, but not enough for any sort of ease.

"Brace yourselves, and maybe try to buckle in if you can."

Garrett's words have me glancing up, and I realize we're headed straight for the entrance rather than the exit. No entrance signs in screamy red letters warn us away from our impending doom.

"C'mon, Soph." Hands tighten on my upper arms before yanking me up and buckling me into the bench seat.

I brace myself for a crash as Garrett steers straight for the narrow way that leads in, shooting past the shouting guy in the tollbooth. The flimsy gate explodes in a colorful spray of red and white splinters that rain down on us like dangerous confetti at a demon's birthday party.

A car horn blasts my eardrums as Garrett veers around the vehicle heading in the correct direction then leaps the curb. My ears are really taking a beating today, and the day is not even over yet. Yay.

Traffic is heavy on the road, but there's no sign of a familiar MED van, so I assume they're all waiting for us at the exit. Good thinking on Garrett's part. I can look at it in a positive light now that we've managed not to end up dead. Yet. The way he's swerving around cars and driving in the bike lane doesn't leave me confident we're going to stay on the living side of the spectrum.

He makes a series of turns that leave my head spinning before slowing down to more of a blending in sort of speed. I guess he figures we're safe, and no one is following us. For the moment, at least.

Logan

My head is still reeling, and the adrenaline is coursing through my veins as we slow to a more reasonable pace to match the traffic around us. I give a scan of the road behind, but there doesn't appear to be anyone following.

The fabric of Sophia's shirt is soft under my hands as I run up and down her arms in a continuous loop. I think I'm doing it to reassure myself just as much as her. She tilts her head up and I can't resist dropping a handful of kisses on her forehead, cute little nose and a lingering one on her soft lips.

"Break it up. Remember, your sister is right beside you."

I pull away to check out our surroundings, including the thoroughly disgusted expression on my sister's face. You think she'd give me a bit of a break given I was just captured and tortured in the Nether Realm, but that's not her soft and fuzzy way. "Awww, sis, glad to hear how much you missed me." I reach over to ruffle her hair but pull back at the last second. "Guess I don't even need to do that. You look like you took a ride in the dryer."

"Well, you look like you got adopted by a family of bears and have been living in their cave for the last month or so." She wrinkled up her nose. "Smell like it too."

Sophia gives me a strange look when a laugh bursts out. Nothing like my sister to push away the trauma of what I've just been through.

"Really, guys?" Trey twists around in his seat with a look that matches Sophia's.

The worn light blue velour of the seat rasps at my palm when I run my hand over it.

"Wait a minute? Did you steal a mini van, Garrett?"

"Yeah. Older model. Easier to jack. Plus, there's enough room for everyone." His gaze doesn't veer from the road ahead at the straightforward statement of fact.

He goes up a notch on the respect tree for me at that. Stealing cars was not exactly one of the things I learned from the straight laced teachings of my father or the NAMC trainers. I tilt my head and give Liz an appraising look. My sister, on the other hand, might have learned the skill on her own. She worries me a little.

"Anyone happen to know where we're going from here? Ivy, Garrett?" We didn't exactly have time to catch up after they tore into the garage.

"Right. I got a hold of your parents. Things are…not good there…" I open my mouth as fear takes hold of me again at the thought of my family in danger, but she holds up a hand. "Everyone is fine. We figured out a rendezvous site on the outskirts of town. Just need to get there intact and they'll pick us up and get us away from here."

"Are we going home?" Liz's eyes are bright with hope.

Ivy looks apologetic. "I'm not sure. We're going to meet them and figure everything out from there."

Tall buildings gathered in tight clusters give way to houses sprawled further and further apart. Even when vast stretches of white blanketed grass separate the sparse buildings, my shoulders remain tense. I keep glancing back to make sure no one is following us. At this rate, my shoulders are going to be hunched in a permanent stoop and my teeth will be worn down from my permanently clenched jaw.

Sophia's hand slides into my rougher one and gives it a reassuring squeeze. "Hey, how are you doing?" She speaks in a low tone, leaning in until her lips almost brush my ears.

My eyelids drop and I take a deep breath to maintain some chill at her proximity. "I'm fine. How about you?"

Her look calls me out on my bullshit. She's right. I'm not fine, but I don't exactly have time to deal with that right now. Not when danger is still at our heels and even the good guys seem to be after us. I don't need her worrying more, too.

"Seriously, Logan? You know I can feel what you're feeling, right? I know you're not ok. I wish you'd talk to me about it." Her hand squeeze is a little sharper this time.

I tilt my head up to look at the hideous blue interior of the stolen van and release a huge breath while contemplating my words. "I'm not." It's hard to admit. I've learned to keep my emotions to myself and I've gotten pretty freaking good at it. The bond was faint and one sided for so long sometimes I forget she can delve into my head now too. "But, I think if I talk about it right now, I'll lose it and I can't afford to do that right now. You know?"

Warmth flows from her to me and a small smile edges up the corners of her mouth. "Thanks for the honesty. I get it, but know that I'm here for you when you're ready. When things are more settled."

I nod and pull her into my side where she belongs. A spark of fear flickers in my gut for a moment, but I try to focus on her soft body tucked in beside mine. Getting taken by her uncle, losing her friend. The pursuit on all sides. None of these things are helping ease my mind. All I want is to give her back a little of the peace and normalcy of her old life, but I'm wondering if that's ever going to be possible.

"It's going to be ok, Logan. It has to be."

Sophia

Something I said must have reassured Logan, or maybe he finally gave in to the exhaustion that must have been riding him after his ordeal. I can't comprehend what he went through and I really want him to talk to me about it, but I know what he means. Not exactly the time to get into a deep and existential conversation.

His chest is rumbling with soft snores under my hand while I run my fingers through the tangled mess of his dark hair resting on my lap. Even in sleep, there's a slight edge of anxiety to his thoughts, but at least he's finally getting a decent rest. I have no idea how much sleep he got while trapped in a cell.

"We're here," Garrett calls from the front seat as we pull into an old gas station hanging out all lonely in the middle of a barren stretch of field. The pumps look like they've been around for a few decades, but the place is still open.

He eases around the building to a small lot in the back dotted with a few stray cars. I don't see any that look like they belong to the Armstrongs, but they're probably going incognito.

"Logan." I call softly, not eager to wake him up from his much-needed sleep. He doesn't even stir, so I try a gentle shake of his shoulder. Still nothing.

Liz twists around in her seat, and I'm leery of the evil arch of her brow. "Hey, Bro! Wake up!"

He startles awake with a kinda adorable snort. "Was that necessary, Liz?" I get it the whole brother-sister dynamic they have going on, but he's been through a lot.

"What? It's not like he hasn't done that to me a million times. I'm gonna get out and see if our parents are lurking around anywhere," she says, already swinging her legs out the big sliding door of the ugly van.

"Be careful," Ivy calls back. "Maybe I should go with her, keep her out of trouble."

"Good luck." Logan is still rubbing the sleep out of his eyes, but he's upright and tense again.

The two girls take a quick stroll around the few other cars in the lot before heading to the small convenience store with the faded sign.

"Do you have any idea of a timeline?" I call up to Garrett. His fingers are still drumming on the steering wheel.

"No clue." His response is curt, cutting off further conversation.

He seems off. In fact, he's been off for a while. I haven't exactly had time to analyze anything, but he's barely spoken to any of us since he found out his crystal was stolen. He did offer to help Ivy, though, at the mall, and he stole a car for us. Just like with Logan's issues, that's something I can hopefully talk to him about later.

I perk up when a dark gray van with tinted windows pulls into the lot. It's newer than the one we've commandeered. That's gotta be them. I snap my seatbelt off and lean forward before changing my mind and turning to Logan.

"Do you think that's them?"

"Not sure. We should wait here until we know." I nod, but instead of settling back in my seat, I lean forward with my elbows propped on my knees. It wouldn't be good to get caught off guard if it turns out to be an enemy. Especially not while we're separated from Ivy and Liz.

The van pulls up right beside us and I hold my breath as the window slides down, only relaxing when Mr. Armstrong's face appears. The creases that line his face have deepened with worry, but it's an immense relief to see him. I push up off my seat and scramble to get out.

A firm hand closes on my shoulder, pulling me back.

"What are you doing?"

"It could be a trick. An illusion."

Right. Magic. "How do we tell?"

Logan crouches down to ease out of the sliding door. "I've got this." Helpful as usual.

"Where are you headed?" My nose wrinkles in confusion at the first words out of Logan's dad's mouth. Maybe it's not him?

"Truth or Consequences." I do a double take at Logan's odd response. "How about you?"

"Soda Springs. Hurry up. Get in. Anyone could be following you, and that monstrosity wasn't exactly designed to blend in." He directs a nod at the van.

It might be ugly, but it helped us escape. I give the upholstery a last pat before creeping to the door. Logan reaches up to help me down as I'm about to hop.

"I can get out of a vehicle by myself, you know." His hands feel good wrapped around my waist, but I can't help the chastisement from escaping.

"I know," he whispers, brushing a stray strand of hair off my forehead. "I just can't seem to keep my hands off you."

The smile creeping up my face stops in its tracks at the barked order coming out of the other van. "Hurry it up. Where's your sister and Ivy?"

"They went in the shop. I think they were checking if you were in there."

"You let them go in by themselves?"

I'm taken aback by his father's tone. He was so helpful with our escape. I would have thought he'd be happy to have his son back safe. "You know Logan's been through a lot recently, not to mention Liz and Ivy are their own people." Logan's eyes widen at my words and I'm kind of surprised at them myself. I'm usually not confrontational with adults. But the way his dad treats him gets my defensive quills up.

Instead of taking offense, the stoic man seems to crumble before us. He steps down from the car to pull Logan into one of those half shoulder man hugs that involves some hearty back slaps. "I'm sorry. I was really worried about you, son."

Shock radiates through the bond and Logan raises tentative arms to return the sort of hug. "It's ok, Dad." His voice comes out gruff.

Not exactly a warm welcome home, but it's progress. The two men release each other and turn to watch as the girls round the corner of the shop.

"Dad!" Liz picks up her pace and zips up in a blur to give her father a big hug.

"Sweetie. I missed you." His tone warms up and his stoic expression even softens with a smile for his daughter.

Garrett doesn't move from his seat through the weird little family reunion, staring blankly ahead. He doesn't budge even as everyone climbs into the van.

I pull my hand free of Logan's and step over to the driver's side window, tapping on the glass. "Hey, you coming with us?"

Garrett swivels his head toward me, but it doesn't even feel like he's seeing me through his eyes that have gone a dull mud puddle color.

The door creaks as I yank it open when he makes no move to get out. "Garrett. Come on. We've gotta get out of here."

"Maybe I should stay. I don't really belong with you and the Armstrongs."

I don't know what's going on in that head of his, but I'm not going to leave him here alone. "You do. They helped rescue you. You're one of us."

His lips twist in a bitter parody of his usual smile, and he lets out a snort. "I'll never be one of you. I'm a Witch. You're all Mages."

"We're all magic users. Just different flavors." Pain shoots through me when he flinches away from my touch.

"That's what you think. I doubt any of your other Mage friends would agree." He turns away from me.

"They wouldn't have helped get you out of there if they didn't. Heck. You're even growing on Logan, and I never thought I'd catch him looking at you with anything other than daggers in his eyes. C'mon, Garrett. You're my friend. And friends don't let each other get left behind."

His face hardens, and a flash of steel darkens his irises. "Not necessarily what I've seen from your friends." I stumble back, hand flying up to my chest at the stab of pain that pierces my heart, opening up the wound that hasn't had time to heal over. He's right. How could I forget about Xavier, even for a second. Things don't end well for my friends. I have no right to expect him to stay with me.

The roil of Logan's tumultuous rage hits me before he storms up. "What did you do to her?" He directs the words at Garrett before turning to scan me for injury.

"Nothing. I'm fine." My words come out all soft like a wounded animal.

"Get your ass over there." He reaches in, tugging at Garrett, who is still trapped in place by his seatbelt.

"Nah, man. I'll find my way from here." He struggles away from Logan's insistent yanks.

"No, you won't. You're getting in that van and coming with us. I might not care what happens to you, but apparently she still cares, so I won't have you hurting her any more. Not to mention I know there's no way she'll leave unless you come with us, and we don't have time to mess around."

Garrett's eyes flick to me once more and I could swear I catch the barest hint of guilt before he shuts down again. "Fine." He shoves Logan off and gets himself out of the stolen van.

Normally, I'd roll my eyes at the way my boyfriend can't resist getting in one last shove as Garrett climbs into the nicer van that Mr. Armstrong traveled in. He shoots a dirty look over his shoulder, but doesn't retaliate.

"That wasn't nice." Liz flips her hair over her shoulder. Catching sight of the faded teal painting the bottom of her dark locks reminds me how long we've been at this for. On the run, or the chase. Seems like even when we start out on the offensive, like when we tried to lure Zeus into a trap, we still end up on the defensive. We need to change that. We need to get through this so we can make some sort of attempt to get our lives back.

Logan let Garrett take the back bench this time, so we settle into the middle. Before his dad has started the engine, Logan is leaning forward between the front seats. "What's going on? Ivy didn't seem to think things were good. Is Mom ok? Mrs. Tennant? What's happening?"

Mr. Armstrong runs a hand over his chin, and I notice the stubble for the first time. I've never seen him anything other than clean shaven and polished. Now that I'm doing a double take, I realize he's not wearing a tie and his blue striped button down is wrinkled and only half tucked in. Something is definitely wrong.

"Your mother and Sophia's are both fine, but we're going to meet up with them, and then we can talk about what's happening. It's not a conversation for the car."

Well, that can't be good.

Logan

The only thing that held me together during the car ride was Sophia's calming presence. She's on edge too, but I always feel better when she's near me. Must be a bond thing.

I know things are really not good when we pull into the long curving driveway of Houston's house rather than our house. The manager of the magical council's training center has always been a bit of a loner. He hasn't lived at the training center since he was in training himself and his house is completely off the grid.

My soul temporarily leaves my body as the heavy ward hits me halfway up the curving road. I know for a fact there are all kinds of traps and security cameras that he can activate from the comfort of his house, in addition to the magical barrier.

It's become a bit of a challenge for new recruits and kids who live at the NAMC compound to try to break in. No one has ever done it. I would never have been stupid enough to try. Not gonna happen, not to mention my father would have had my head for making him look bad. I've done some stupid things to piss him off, but I have too much respect for Houston to try that one.

His neat little gray stone house with the tidy garden is at odds with the rest of his image. It's all the work of Flora. His young daughter is a Bio Mage, and she tends to the place to the point it looks like it belongs to a fairy tale character rather than the tough Mage.

Obviously, he's expecting us, since no nails come shooting up from the road to derail our progress.

The butter yellow curtain in the front window twitches and relief floods me at the sight of Mom peeking out with a huge smile on her face.

She's at the door waiting with arms open wide as I'm helping Sophia out of the van. I know she thinks I have to help her for some manly help the little woman nonsense, but it's not that. It's really just an excuse to get my hands on her in a publicly acceptable way. We weren't separated for too long, but any length of time has me restless and crawling out of my skin.

"Logan, I'm so glad you're safe." Her arms are around me before I even get up the little wooden stairway to the front porch.

All the tension Sophia was still holding onto washes away as her mom comes out to join us. Everyone shares hugs and greetings, except Garrett who hangs back leaning against the van. He looks bored, but he's probably leaning more toward the uncomfortable side, seeing as how he isn't part of the family.

His presence pisses me off sometimes. I recognize that's more of a me problem and I'm not gonna try to dictate who Sophia is friends with. However, I'm really not happy about how he was upsetting Sophia before. She wouldn't tell me what he did, but it couldn't have been good for that intense pain to hit me through our connection. I do feel sorry for the guy, though. He lost his whole family in one go. That's gotta mess you up. I can't even imagine what that's like. Sophia has some idea.

"Garrett, come on up here." Mom gestures at him to join us up on the porch and he reluctantly forces himself up the stairs.

His body stiffens when Mom pulls him in for a hug, but after she doesn't let go, he makes an effort easing his arms around her in a half hug back.

"Logan." Sophia's mom gives me a nod, but doesn't welcome me back with an embrace the way my mom does to Sophia. I suspect she blames me for putting her daughter in more danger than she was already in.

"Mrs. Tennant." I hold my hand out for a shake in a compromise. She accepts it with grace, sliding a smooth hand into mine.

"Reunion all over? Come on in. We've got some things to talk about." Houston's booming voice brings a smile to my face. I've known the guy since I was a kid, and if we're going to be safe anywhere, it's going to be at his house.

After everyone has hit the bathroom and gotten drinks, we settle onto the delicate furniture. I can't think of a better word for it. There's an ivory couch with a delicate pink and green floral pattern, and assorted armchairs in various matching hues. This is clearly all the work of Flora. She's taken over as the head of the household since her mother died a few years ago.

"Where's Flora?" I'm curious. She's close to my age, but she's always been a quiet, shy girl. Since she graduated, she doesn't socialize much with the other mages in our cohort, preferring to stay here and tend to the house and look after her dad.

"Oh, you know how shy she is. Plus, there's no way I'm letting her get involved in this. She's not a warrior."

His face generally looks like it's chiseled out of stone, but it hardens to marble when he talks about his daughter getting involved in the mess we're in. "Tell her I said hi." I don't know her that well, but she was always sweet to everyone.

Houston dips his head in a curt nod that lets me know the subject of his daughter is closed. "Anyway, Robert, did you want to get started?" He turns to my father with the deference everyone shows him.

Dad leans his bristly chin on steepled hands before sweeping his gaze over the room. Even with the out of character scruff, he commands the room. "We've lost control of the council."

Our small group turns to each other with startled expressions and mutters. "What? How? It's only been a few days, right? A week?" Have I been gone longer than I thought? I had zero concept of time down in that dungeon.

The conversation stills as he holds up his hands, palms out to quiet us, as if he's the teacher to our group of third graders, but we all comply. "You've been gone a week, son, but apparently this plan has been in motion for a while. It turns out Lawrence has been working with Sophia's uncle behind the scenes. I knew Lawrence was up to something, but had no idea he'd gotten involved with that criminal. Your mother has been working with a team to discover who is working against us. They had identified a few of the instigators, and were building a case against them when Tobias showed up and announced he was in control of HQ now. Things have gotten bad out there. Both Mages and Witches who have defied them are in prison and they've even killed some who refused to come quietly. It's a mess."

"That explains why the MED team was pursuing us. They really weren't on our side." Ivy's got a strand of hair tucked in the corner of her mouth and a thoughtful look in her dark eyes.

"What about the humans?" Sophia asks from her tense position perched on the edge of the couch. "Do they know? Have they been affected?" She tilts her head up to turn to her mother, brows drawn together.

Trust my girl to care about the innocents in the situation. I think that may be the first time I've heard her refer to humans as a separate group. It's been tough for her to accept herself as a true member of the magical community.

Mom pipes in on this one. "So far they're still maintaining the secrecy of the magic world from the mundanes, but if they keep up this war on Mages something's going to give way. Someone's going to record something, or too many people will bear witness to an event. And since they've diverted most of the MED resources to capturing dissenters, they're not keeping track or fixing leaks." The warm feeling I got seeing my mother again blurred my vision. Now that I'm really getting a good look at her, I can see the worry lines around her mouth have deepened and there are dark circles bruising her eyes. I want to wrap my arms around her, but now is not the time.

"And what about the other NAMC locations?" I ask. There are offices in several regions of the country and a few other compounds like ours, but this one is by far the largest. It is the headquarters, after all. We'll definitely need support from the other branches, because if you take out the head, the whole body is going to collapse.

"There hasn't been a complete takeover yet, so we have reached out for aid. They are trying to maintain their own control as well at the moment. This is a well-calculated move, and I suspect they've also infiltrated some of the smaller branches to a lesser extent."

"So what's the plan?" Liz's foot is tapping on the ground in a staccato beat, and she looks about ready to leap out of her seat to storm HQ all on her own. I wouldn't put it past her. "When are we going in?"

"You're not going anywhere. You're still underage and not at your full power." My lips twitch at the futile order from Mom. I get where she's coming from, but she's never gonna keep Liz out of this.

She jumps to her feet. "No way, Mom. You're gonna need me, and there's no way I'm getting left out of this."

Ivy pulls at Liz's tattered shirt. We really need to change into some fresh clothes.

Mom turns to Dad with a beseeching look. "Robert? A little help?"

A shade of guilt passes behind his eyes. "Name@? I know she's young, but we're going to need all the help we can get." He turns to me. "Logan, what do you think? You've been working and training with your sister this year. Do you think she's ready for this?"

I school my face into a blank mask to hide the shock that punches me in the gut. My father is asking for my opinion? I don't even know what to do with that.

"Logan." Liz hisses at me through clenched teeth. There's a murderous look in her blue-green eyes. I know she'll follow through on the threat behind them if I let her down. That's not the decisive factor for me, though.

I nod. " She can do it. You should have seen her fighting blank@ at the farmhouse after she got kidnapped. And you've already trusted her once to break into the compound to rescue Garrett." I wave a hand at the guy who has been awfully silent during the proceedings. He's leaning against the wall, arms crossed over his chest.

"Ok, I trust your judgment, son." He nods.

"Gee, thanks. Glad the men got to decide that all neat and tidy for me." Liz rolls her eyes, something my father would never let me get away with.

I get where she's coming from, but it's not really a male/female thing and more of a she's-still-underage thing. We all know how strong and fast she is, but she's still not an adult. I know Sophia's mom is probably going to try to pull the same thing on her. While I'd love to stop Sophia from coming, I'm not foolish enough to think there's any chance of keeping her out of the action.

A sharp smack jolts me out of my head as Dad claps his hands together. "That's it for business right now. I imagine you all want to clean yourselves up and maybe get some rest in. We can catch up later. I would like to hear about how you got Logan out of there, and any information you have on the Nether Realm or Tobias' plans would be helpful."

There he is. That's the dad I know. All business. Mom's mouth falls open to protest the abrupt departure, but he's already standing up.

"It's ok, Mom." I walk over to her to, pulling her into a hug. "We can talk later."

I sway on my feet a little, leaning into her. A wave of exhaustion is ready to knock me flat any second. For the first time since Zeus dragged me down into his creepy little underground lair, I'm able to relax.

I turn away, reaching for Sophia, only to find her in her mom's arms. There are tears streaking down both of their faces. Right. Have to remember she's not all mine. Her mom must have been frantic with her gone and completely out of contact. I should give them some alone time.

I walk over, dropping a light kiss on the top of her golden head, as I can't seem to resist one more touch to remind myself that she's really here and we're both safe. For the moment.

Sophia

Houston's house is bigger than it looks. There are four bedrooms upstairs and two in the basement. Mom wanted me to stay with her, but she understood that we all wanted to stick together, so us "kids" are all in the basement and the adults are upstairs. Apparently, he has a few more small outbuildings that the other Mages can use when they start to arrive over the next few days. We didn't really talk about any details of who is coming or when, but we're going to get into that more tomorrow.

The guy's door clicks shut and I settle on one of the twin beds in the room I'm sharing with Liz and Ivy. Liz slides a pull out from under one of the white wooden daybeds. Convenient. I got the impression Houston was more of a stay at home kind of guy based on the fact that he lives off the compound and keeps his daughter to himself here. All the places he's got for guests to stay tell a different story. I guess he doesn't actually mind the company as much as he implies.

It feels good to be in my own pajamas. Our parents brought us small bags of clothes. I guess we're staying here for the foreseeable future. At least until we can get things sorted out and back to some semblance of normalcy with the magical council.

I brush some strands of damp hair behind my shoulder and prop my hands on my knees. "How are you two doing?" I look up at my friends, searching for some truth in this madness.

This is all just beyond anything," Ivy says. Her legs are curled under her on the top of the bed. Liz perches beside her on the pullout, legs folded under her chin. "I came back here to help Logan and make sure you were safe. I never expected to be getting involved in some terrifying war. This is unheard of. The council has been stable for decades.

"You don't have to stay." The words sound kind of wrong as they come out of my mouth. "I don't mean like I'm trying to chase you away, but you have your grandparents back in Japan, right? You can go back to them. This isn't really your battle. No one would judge you for it."

Her eyes glitter with a hard resolve. "I'm not the kind of person who turns away from my friends. I learned my lesson. I ran once, and it was a mistake. Sure, it was fantastic to spend time with my grandparents and I learned a lot from them, but that's over. I'm back here. You guys are my other family, and this is where I grew up. My home. I always thought it wouldn't be the same without my parents here. Like it's not really my home without them. But I was wrong. This will always be home for me, and I'm not afraid to fight for it."

I admire her loyalty. I've been a little lost and wandering since my dad died. Following a path that was never meant for me. It was his path. Now I need to find my own way. If we survive this. My eyes keep straying to the door and I reach down deep for that strand that connects me to Logan. It's a soft hum right now. I think he's probably sleeping.

"You can go to him," Liz says. "We won't judge."

"Wouldn't that be weird?" Staying in a room full of guys seems weird.

Ivy shrugs. "Send Trey over here. He won't mind."

Should I? With my mom upstairs? I only hesitate for a fraction of a moment more before I make up my mind. It's not like we're going to do anything. Just sleep. Heck knows how badly we both need a good sleep, anyway. I'll sleep better with him beside me. Just this one night. I need to know he's there beside me. I know I'm rationalizing it to myself and I don't care.

Liz pulls me into a last hug before I leave. Pretty sure she cracks a rib, just a little. "Behave."

I shove her off, padding over to the door that leads into the guy's room. It takes a moment to psych myself up. This feels significant. Like I'm making a choice. Sure, I've slept in the same bed as Logan before, but after all we've been through, I want more. I want to fully show him how much he means to me. I need to tell him in words and more than words how much he means to me.

Trey looks up from the book in his hand when I walk in. He's leaned back against the headboard. They have the same beds as in our room only in a dark brown wood. "Hey, Soph."

I give him a tentative smile that spreads on my face when I catch sight of the other bed. Logan is softly snoring, blankets pulled right up to his chin. His dark hair is sticking out all over the place, standing out in stark contrast to the white pillowcase.

"Hi, Trey." I narrow my eyes when I notice something is missing. "Where's Garrett?"

"He went for a walk. Said he deeded some fresh air. He's been weird all day."

"I know. I feel bad for him. We're all going home to our families and he's all alone, stuck in the middle of that. It must be hard for him."

"I'm sure he'll be ok." He gives me a weird look. "did you need something? Or did you just come in to see Logan?"

I pause and look and my feet "Um, I was wondering....."

"Did you want to swap rooms?" He chuckles under his breath, unfolding himself from the bed. "I don't mind as long as the girls are ok with it. I'm sure Garrett won't care either when he shows up."

"Thanks Trey." I give his arm a squeeze as he passes by. "Thanks for everything. You've been a good friend to all of us and we barely even met a few weeks ago.

"It's all good, Soph. Friends do that for you. Even if they're new friends."

I wait until he's going before I pull the covers gently back and look down at Logan. He's wearing a pair of black and blue plaid flannel pants and a gray t-shirt that's a little too snug. Or maybe just the right amount of snug, judging by the way the shirt clings just a little to his sculpted chest and biceps. I love those arms.

He mutters something under his breath as I slide in next to him as gently as I can. I don't want to wake him up. He needs his sleep. I just want to be with him.

Once I'm settled in the tight space beside him, I slide an arm around his torso, happy to feel his solid bulk beneath my hand. I curl into his back, basking in the heat he gives off. I'll probably overheat in exactly two minutes, but I can't say that I care. I'm just happy to have him close and in my arms again.

I curl into the comfort of a strong hand stroking circles over my back, blinking at the sliver of light falling on my cheek. As the fog clears from my vision, I look up to meet Logan's turquoise eyes. They look like the ocean on a sunny day today. Takes me right to the Caribbean. My parents took me and Scott on a cruise when we were still in middle school. We spent most of the day in the kids' club there, but it was so much fun. Bright, shiny, happy. Back before things fell apart. Logan is my future happiness. The eyes are just a reminder of everything we might have together in the future. If the dream doesn't slip away like the smoke from a campfire slipping through your fingers.

"Morning, gorgeous." He smiles down at me before pressing soft lips to mine. His lips are so contrary to the rest of him. So soft while the rest of him is hard, toned muscle. I could get lost in those lips. "I love you." I mumble the words into his mouth in between kisses without even thinking about it.

He pulls away. Oops. Should I have done that? Yes. I regretted not telling him before we went off to face my uncle the last time. I'm not going to let the chance slip away again. I hold my breath, waiting for his reaction. What if he doesn't feel the same way? Don't be stupid, Sophia. I scold myself. You can tell how he feels through the bond. He feels it too. It's real.

Despite my mental gymnastics, I still relax when a huge grin spreads across his face. "I love you too."

I tangle my hands in his air and pull him back into me, searching, exploring, delving into him. Heat flares between us and I squirm to press myself closer. My hands slide down to his chest to feel his heart beating for me, but then I freeze. We're not alone. He was staying in here with Garrett.

I roll away the inch I can in the tight space of the single bed and prop myself up to peer over his broad shoulder. The other bed is empty and still made. Did Garrett not come back last night? Did he leave because I was here? Crap, I shouldn't have stayed here without at least telling him.

"Where's Garrett?"

"Who cares?" Logan moans and leans back in, nipping at my exposed collarbone. Heat shoots through me, disrupting my concentration.

I lean into his nibbles for a moment.

"Wait. No, I care. He's my friend."

Logan groans and rolls onto his back. "Trust that guy to ruin everything. It is his specialty."

"Hey, that guy risked his life to help rescue you, you jerk." My hand lands a gentle slap on his shoulder.

His brow arches toward his hairline and the grin he levels at me is downright wicked with a side of tease. "You didn't think I was a jerk a moment ago."

I roll my eyes at him. "Not the point. We need to make sure he's ok. Not to mention we can't risk any of the grownups finding us down here together."

He gives a careless shrug. "Let them find us. We didn't do anything wrong."

"I mean, if you want to risk the wrath of my mom, go ahead shout it to the rooftops. Ok. I'm going to see if I can find him. You." I jab a finger in his chest that's taunting me to run a hand down its ridges. "You should stay here."

He grabs my hand, twining his fingers in mine to pull me back onto his chest as I try to force myself into a sitting position.

His lips are less than an inch from mine as he says, "Are you sure?" His heated breath sends a shiver through me.

It takes all my willpower to get away from the magnetic pull that he has over me. "Yes, I'm sure."

"Fine. You go on up and I'll join you a suitable time later, mi'lady." He ducks his head in mockery of a bow.

* * * ★ ★ ★ ★ ★ ★ * *

Ivy and I emerged from the top of the stairway into the hallway of Houston's house. We left Liz as always snoozing late in her bed. She's like the definition of a night owl. Pretty sure you'd find a picture of her in the dictionary beside the term. The place is adorable. Nothing at all like I would have expected from the stern trainer I'd worked with for a brief time at the NAMC training facility. Pastel watercolors of flowers and trees dot the walls and a there's a sunshine yellow throw rug by the front door.

We walk in the kitchen to find Trey catching up with Houston. They're like two peas in a pd. Serious, hardworking warriors. There's no sign of anyone else as we pass through the quiet house. When I catch sight of the time, I realize why. It's only six am. I guess we went to bed pretty early last night for some much needed sleep.

"Morning, Houston, Trey." I dip my head at Houston with a shy smile. It's kind of weird crashing at someone's house that I hardly know. My smile stretches all the way up my face by the time it reaches Trey. Ivy gives a wave.

"Morning, ladies," Trey replies.

"Come on in, get yourselves settled. I can grab you some breakfast or you're welcome to help yourself to anything in the fridge or cupboards. I knew we'd be having guests, so I stocked up."

I stretched my neck to peer out the window over Houston's shoulder. "Maybe soon. Have either of you seen Garrett?"

The frown that pulls Trey's brows together worries me. "That's actually what we were just talking about. He seems to have... left."

Alarm triples my heart rate, and I spin around searching for the unseen danger. "Did someone get on the property?"

Houston's stoic look doesn't give away anything, but he shakes his head. "No, looks like he left on his own steam, Sophia. I'm sorry."

Right. Obviously Trey and Houston wouldn't be sitting all chill at the kitchen table if there was danger in the house. My brain knows that in theory, but the constant threat of danger we've been under seems to have short circuited my higher reasoning skills.

The reality comes crashing in on me and I don't even know what to think. Sadness, guilt and betrayal are all swirling around in there, but underneath it all, I understand. Of course he left. This isn't his war, and he's helped us more than enough. That nagging little voice at the back of my head tells me I deserve this. Look what happens to my friends because of me?

Logan

A jolt of panic shoots through me and I'm racing up the stairs, leaving the shirt I was about to put on fluttering to the ground behind me. Something's wrong. Sophia.

I follow the feeling into the kitchen, only to find Sophia and Ivy casually leaning on the cupboards, talking to Trey and Houston.

"What's the matter? What happened?" I skid to a stop and bend my knees into a ready stance. I wish I had one of my knives with me, but I haven't acquired any weaponry since we got here. I'll have to rectify that today. As soon as I figure out what's going on in here.

Sophia turns to me, her face crumpled and eyes bright with the tears she's fighting. The panic is gone. Now there's a mixed assortment of feelings of sadness and anger roiling around in her.

"Garrett left."

"What do you mean, he left?" I turn to Houston and Trey, but their faces don't reveal any secrets.

"I don't know. We were just getting to that." She's got her hand rubbing at her chest again as she turns to Houston. "Anything else? Did he take a car? Get a ride. Leave a note?"

Houston sighs, and Trey cuts in. "We checked out Houston's security camera. He just walked out of here. Didn't meet anyone. Didn't leave a note. Just gone."

"Do you think we can catch up to him? I don't want him leaving like this." I really don't want to extinguish the hopeful look in her eyes, but I don't have a choice. We can't leave the safety of the compound. And he must have had his reasons for leaving. That's his choice. It's the wrong one, obviously. After all they did for him, but it was his choice.

Watching the last bit of hope draining out of her expression as I shake my head has me wincing. The departure leaves her bright eyes dull again.

She straightens her spine and hardens her resolve again, not wasting any time to wallow in the blow of losing another friend. "What's the plan for the day?" Houston pushes up from his chair to stroll over to the fridge, answering over his shoulder. "I thought the lot of you could use a break after the week you've had. I imagine you need a bit of a rest. Your parents and I have some planning to do. Make contact, and the first of our out-of-town guests will arrive this evening."

That's a new side of Houston. He's always been the one to push me harder and work us all to the point of exhaustion. We could definitely use the break, though.

Sophia looks a little agitated at his statement. "Shouldn't we be training, getting ready, strategizing? Something, anything."

I grab her hand and am hit with a wave of restless energy. I get it. I'm usually the one who needs calming down, but I can see she needs something today. I think we need a little catch up time. We haven't been alone together since the cottage. We had some moments there. Good and bad. God, what would I give for just a bit of peace to enjoy each other's company? We've been running from one fight to the next since we met.

"I just feel like I need to do something. Anything."

She pulls away from me to check out the view out the large window. There's lots to explore around Houston's house. I used to come here with my parents when they had meetings with Houston. I'm familiar with his grounds, and there's a perfect place to spend some time together in those woods to our right. I slide up behind her. She freezes for a moment before relaxing into me. Her soft curves settling against me. She tilts her head back to gaze up at me under her long lashes.

I lean down close to whisper in her ear. "We will. But can we take today to appreciate each other? I've been worried about you nonstop since I got taken and I need some time with you. Is that ok? We could even sneak in a mini one-on-one training later if that would make you feel better."

Her lips curve up in my favorite smile. The one that's meant for me and me alone. "That would be nice. Thank you."

The snow out back is a soft layer of white coating the grounds. The house is modest for the size of the property. But various outbuildings, sheds and a garage he's converted into a training area fill up some of the space. Trey and Ivy might make use of those today, but I imagine my sister will take advantage of the permission to slack off for the day. As she should. She needs the rest as much as the rest of us.

We're leaving a trail of footprints behind us, but I'm not worried that anyone will come after us here. They'll be busy looking after their own stuff.

"Where are we going?" Her hand is in a borrowed purple mitten that she slides into mine.

"You'll see. You're going to like it, I promise."

Our walk takes us through a series of green needled trees that smell like Christmas. The top of the building peeks out over a small hill before the rest of it makes its appearance slowly. Sophia's squinched her eyes in curiosity as she assesses the small wood building that appears in front of us. The tiny place is fancier than the actual house, with curlicues hanging from the peaked room and pink curtains fluttering in the little front windows. It's like a real house only in miniature.

"What is this place?" She releases my hand to run up to the tiny front porch, complete with a little rocking chair. "It looks like it belongs in a fairy tale. I'm not going to find a wolf in there, am I?"

I lift an eyebrow and curl my lip in a snarl. "No telling."

A warm contentment seeps into my core at the burst of laughter that explodes out of her. This is what we needed.

I hope I didn't misjudge this place. I have to duck my head way down to get through the miniature door. We used to come here when we were kids and therefore much smaller. It's not as much of a problem for Sophia. I make it through the door without smacking my head but can't even straighten up when I make it inside.

The place really is like a dollhouse. A tiny table for two with matching little chairs sits in a pink play kitchen that has a sink and pretend oven and everything. The living room area has pink flowered couches that are more like chairs to us, but I try my luck flopping down on one, pulling Sophia down into my lap after me.

She squeals as she tumbles down. "This place is so adorable. Floras I guess? She won't mind if we use it, will she?"

"I highly doubt she still comes down here. She's my age or a year younger, maybe. I'm sure she's got other places to go."

"Maybe, but it is rather clean and well looked after for a place that no one uses anymore." Observant as always. I sweep the room and note the lack of dust and the clean scent of pine floor cleaner.

"You're right. I'm sure she won't mind though, even if she does still come here."

"Now. Tell me everything I missed while I was gone."

She twists in my arms and a dark shadow has passed over her face.

"Scratch that. How about we don't talk about any of the bad things that are after us and just enjoy each other's company? Let's pretend for one day that our world isn't about to collapse all around us and just talk."

She brushes her hair over her shoulder and I can't resist grabbing a lock of the gold stuff to twist around my finger. Now that we've had a time to shower and clean up, it's back to its soft, silky usual state. She shivers a little at my touch, leaning back.

"That sounds good. Let's forget that the rest of the world exists. We can face reality again tomorrow. Or maybe not. Maybe we can move into this perfect little doll house and stay here. Let the adults deal with the big problems."

"You can. I'm sure your mom would be delighted if you stayed at home and out of danger. Me too, to be honest." The thought of her going willingly into danger again sets me on edge.

"Thats the thing, though? You won't stay back. You'll go running off to fight my uncle and take back the council and I'd have to sit back at home worrying about you and all my other friends, even though this is all on me. Not going to happen."

Her head tilts up to meet my gaze when I place a finger under it. "This is not on you. I don't know how many times I or anything else has to tell you, but you are not responsible for the actions of your uncle our anyone else. You didn't take over the council. You didn't choose to hurt and killing other Mages. It is not your fault, and you have to stop blaming yourself."

"I'll try, but after Xavier and now with Garrett disappearing. It feels like I'm to blame."

"You're not. I don't know what's up with Garrett, but if we ever see that snake again, I'll make him pay for hurting you." My words come out in a rasp. Nobody hurts my girl.

I drop a kiss on her nose and then her eyelids, one after the other. "Now, can we forget about this and pretend the rest of the world doesn't exist?"

My mouth moves to her softly rounded cheek and the crevice just below her ear before making its way down her neck. Her warm skin heats further wherever my lips land.

"Mmmm. I think we can do that." She spins around, sliding a leg over mine so that she's straddling my lap and we're face to face.

She ducks her head down, pressing her lips to mine, and I sink into the tiny couch, trying to get comfortable. She presses into me.

"I missed you." Her heated breath matches the look in her eyes, sending all kinds of tingles through me.

"I missed you too, lovebug."

She pulls back for a minute, giving me a hell no look. "Nope. I can't even believe you tried that one."

"Hey, I'll try anything once." My fingers tangle through her hair, pulling her back in to me.

I delve into her soft mouth, exploring. It's like she's my reason for breathing and I need to be as close as possible to her to take advantage of my source of oxygen. She's like my sunshine. Necessary for survival.

Her hands explore my chest tentatively, getting bolder as she reaches my shoulders. The kiss goes on in a never ending connection of joy.

I keep one on her waist and one at the back of her head. They're itching to search deeper, to slide under her shirt, to feel her soft skin under mine, but I keep them under control.

She doesn't exercise the same restraint. It's not long before her hands are sliding under my shirt. I gasp the moment her hands touch my bare skin.

She pulls them back immediately. "Oh, sorry. My hands are cold."

I almost growl, pulling her hand back to my side. "They're perfect."

She replies, but I cut it off with a kiss, needing to feel her lips against mine once again. "There you are." I mumble against her lips.

I give her free rein of my torso, letting her explore each curve of muscle that I've worked hard to hone. A sweet agony grips me. Her touch is the best thing I've ever felt and I want more. I want all of it.

She seems to have the same idea because her hands creep lower to meet my waistband. She slides an inch or two underneath my waistband and there's nothing I want more than to let her slide my pants the rest of the way off. It takes everything in me to still her hand.

She opens her eyes, looking up at me under her lashes with a questioning look in her milk chocolate eyes that have gone hazy with lust. "No?"

"Not today, Sophia." I use the last of my reserves to grab her by the hips and slide her sideways so she's not quite so close to my need.

I land a soft kiss on her lips again, gripping her face between my palms. "Not today, not here."

Her eyes wander around the excessively pink playhouse taking in the miniature furniture. "Right. But soon. I'm ready."

The words ignite a fire deep in my core that I shove down. Not yet. She deserves more than this for her first time. More than a hurried encounter in a borrowed playhouse.

Her hands slide back up to my shoulders and she pulls me back to her lips with surprising strength. "But this is ok, right?" She mumbles against my lips.

I return the kiss and time and space fade away in the moment that's ours and ours alone. Who knows when we'll get alone time like this again?

Sophia

The kitchen was a crowded mass of people this morning, so I sneaked out to the living room to spend some alone time with my mom. It feels like forever since we've had time to just sit and chat.

She's got her phone on speaker and its ring breaks the silence of the quiet room.

"Hello." My heart warms at the sound of my brother's sleepy voice coming through her phone.

"Hey, Scott!"

"L'il sis. How's it going?" He clears some of the sleep grit out of his voice.

"And your mother. We wanted to talk to you since you couldn't come home for Christmas this year. I'm so sorry about that."

"It's fine. I still don't think I quite understand your reason, but it was fine. I went to stay with my friend Tyler's family. They were pretty cool. A little weird, but aren't all families." He has no idea. "How about my favorite girls? How was your holiday?"

I glance at mom momentarily stumped. We can't exactly tell him what actually went on over the last few weeks, or months.

"It was nice, honey. Didn't do anything too special, just some quiet time at home."

The lie slips from my mother's mouth surprisingly easily, and I give her a shocked look. Really? I mouth at her and she shrugs back.

"Glad to hear it. Listen, I hate to do this. We don't talk nearly enough anymore, but I have a practice in 45 minutes and I'm going to be late if I don't get my butt out of bed and dressed right now. Can I call you back later?"

"It's ok, Hon. You can call us later. Have a good practice." My mom's tone is wistful but understanding.

"Bye, bro. Look after yourself." One of the constant worries I've had is that Zeus somehow gets to my brother, so I'm happy we had time to speak to him. It's bad enough my mom has to be involved in all of this.

"Bye, dork. Love ya." Even the nickname doesn't hold any weight to me anymore.

Her face falls out of the cheery smile she was maintaining while talking to my brother. Almost as if she had to smile on the outside in order to sound happy while we were talking. I know how she feels.

"It was nice to talk to him. Even if only for a moment." I muse.

"Yes, it was. I really wish he could have come home for Christmas." The vines of guilt that have twisted around my heart tighten.

"I know. I'm sorry." I drop my eyes to stare at my hands wringing in my lap.

"Oh, honey." She stands up out of the high-backed chair she's sitting in to settle onto the couch next to me. I lean into the comfort of the warm arm she slides around my shoulders. "This is not your fault."

"But wouldn't your life be so much easier without me and my supernatural problems?"

"Life isn't supposed to be easy, my love. Life is a series of trials that help you grow stronger. Your problems are just a little bigger than most peoples. But you'll get through it. I raised you to be strong, and I know you're capable of handling these trials. And I'll always love you and be there for you. No matter what."

I settle into the crook of her neck, laying my head on her shoulder to inhale her soft floral@ scent. It soothes my mind for the moment, at least.

"Now, Houston said the first of our guests were arriving soon, so maybe we should actually get out of our pajamas." She looks down at the fuzzy flannel pants she's wearing with snowmen scattered all over them. It's weird to see her dressed like this in a houseful of strangers. Sure, she loves her weekend PJ mornings at home, but she's always collected and ready to go before she goes out in public. Not like me. I'd wear my PJs all day if I could.

"Right." I wrap my arms around her in one more fierce hug before pushing up off the couch.

"Hurry up." She shoos me with a wave of her slender fingers.

My brow wrinkles and a yawn stretches my mouth wide. "What's the hurry?" Not like we need to get to know these people or anything. I'll probably just be going off to train, anyway. I don't need to be part of this meeting. And there's no way I'll remember all their names.

"Just go."

I give her a suspicious look but head downstairs to see if I can snag the shower I'm sharing with the rest of the younger crowd.

Someone's already in the shower when I get down there, so I settle onto the bed I'm supposed to be using. I've got a random book I grabbed off the bookshelf in the living room. It's some serial murder mystery. Not my usual genre of choice, but the selection here was pretty much mysteries and non-fiction books about physical exercise.

I've gotten so engrossed in my reading, I don't lift my head at the sound of the door opening or the murmur of voices. I haven't even gotten myself cleaned up when Liz comes bounding down the stairs.

"Come on!"

Liz grabs my hands and yanks me so hard off the bed that I stumble as I land on feet tangled underneath me.

"What is going on?" I ask Liz, not even trying to hide the irritation in my voice.

"You have to come upstairs like yesterday. There's something you need to see."

"I was about to have a shower and get dressed. Can it wait until whoever is done hogging the shower?"

Her eyes flit to the door of the bathroom. "That would be your boyfriend." Figures. "No time though. Come on."

I sigh but end up straightening myself out to follow her. If I know one thing about Liz, it's that once she has an idea in her head, you're not going to get her to give it up. At least not without a massive fight. That would just be a waste of both of our time.

"Fine. I'm coming. Stop pulling at me."

My entire body tenses when something hard barrels into me at the top of the stairs, almost knocking me over.

"Sophia!" Shock shoots through me at the familiar voice and I swipe at the mass of black curls that have engulfed me.

"Charlotte? What are you doing here?"

"Nice to see you, too." Her smile is so big all of her teeth are on display and I catch a view of her elusive grandmother over her shoulder.

"You know that's not what I meant. Of course it's good to see you. I'm just a little surprised to see you here, of all places. And with your entire family." I wave at the family of Witches behind her.

"I was teasing you. But yeah, we're here to help. Clearly you Mages are doing a crap job of running things in the magical community so the Witches are stepping in." She cocks a hip with a confident smirk that's all Charlotte.

Makes sense. "Gotcha. So you're going to be staying here with us?"

"Sure am. Somebody's gotta look out for you and make sure you don't get in to any more trouble."

"That's probably a lost cause, but I'm glad you're here." A nagging sense of worry eats at me, but I try to ignore it. I worry about every single one of my friends that's getting involved in this mess, but she's here with her family. They wouldn't have brought her if they didn't think she could look after herself.

"Are you the only Witches getting involved?"

She scoffs at me. "Of course not. Us Witches are tight. We look after our own. If my grandmother can get the Mages on board with some reform of the NAMC including the inclusion of Witches on the council, we're coming out in force."

"That's great. The more fighters we have on our side, the better."

"Exactly. Now there are some Witches who have joined with your uncle and his minions, but they're in the minority. It's hard to believe that any of them have gotten involved with that lot, to be honest. They've been persecuting Witches and capturing them with lame excuses like in the bad old days."

"Right, like Garrett." An idea sparks in my brain at the thought of him. Charlotte was the one who dragged him out of hiding to help rescue me after Zeus caught me when we went to rescue Liz.

"Yeah, but you got him out, right?" She looks over my shoulder as if she's expecting to see him lurking there.

"We did, but…" I gnaw on the corner of my lip. "He left. Do you think there's any way you could…"

She throws her hands up at me. "No way. I'm not getting involved with him again. Did he betray you at last? I knew it was coming."

"No. He just left, and I'm worried about him. He was really upset when he lost his family tracking crystal, but he still stayed with us to help get Logan from the Nether, and he even stole a car to help us escape. There's no way he would have done any of that if he was just going to turn around and betray us, right?" I don't think I'm trying to convince myself.

"I don't know. Doesn't sound like it. But he's always been one to look after his own hide. Maybe the danger was just getting to be too much for him."

I nod at her. Something's not sitting quite right, but I can't quite put my finger on it. He's been through so much with us already. Why would he leave now?

"Ok, we're going to figure out where we're staying and get settled. Then maybe we can get in some training after lunch?"

"Definitely. It sounds like it's going to continue to get more crowded in here over the next few days. We may as well take advantage of Houston's training area before it gets too busy. Why don't you stay with us down in the basement?" We've still got another pullout bed underneath mine that she can have.

"I'll have to check with the fam."

While we were catching up, her family made their way into the kitchen, so we head into the now overflowing room.

Charlotte's Gran is in a spirited conversation with Mrs. Armstrong, and her parents are chatting with Houston and Mr. Armstrong.

"Mom, Dad, can I stay downstairs with Sophia? If it's ok with you." She gives a nod to Houston as well. It is his house after I guess she's acknowledging his right to a say in the decision.

"Fine by me. Welcome to my house, Charlotte. I'm Houston. Your family is going to stay in one cottage, but you can certainly stay in here with your friends if it's ok with your parents."

The ultimate decision seems to rest with her grandmother. Her parents turn to her before answering. She gives a tight nod, but it's still a yes. "If that's what you all want, it's ok with us." Her mom is like an older version of her, but she's got her pulled back in a tight bun and she's wearing more makeup than I think I've ever seen Charlotte wear. She's actually got an intimidating glamor to her. From her sleek hair to her expensive looking clothes.

"Perfect. How about you show me to my new room?"

I lead the way to the basement, dropping onto the bed I didn't make use of last night.

Charlotte's nose wrinkles. "Who is staying in this room?"

"Umm, Liz, Ivy, and I," I reply. Charlotte hasn't met Ivy yet. She's heard all about her, though. I hope she doesn't go all defensive friend on her. Ivy and I have formed a friendship since she first reappeared in our Logan's life.

"Smells like man stank. Have you been sneaking Logan in here with you?

Realization hits me. "What are you, some kind of bloodhound, or werewolf? Wait, are you part werewolf?"

"There's no such thing as werewolves. Don't be ridiculous. Also, don't try to change the subject."

I forgot how hard it is to hide something from the friends who you've known forever. I can still get away with some secrets around Liz, Ivy, and Trey. Not so much with Logan, but that's a bond thing. "No." I leave it at that. It is true he didn't stay in here with me.

"But..." Her look lets me know she isn't buying my avoidance.

"I stayed in his room last night, and Trey stayed here."

She smiles triumphantly. "There it is. Are you two..." She bobs her eyebrows a couple of times.

"No." I reply again, keeping it short and sweet, but the heat that creeps up my neck to my cheeks gives me away.

"I see. When you're ready to talk boys, let me know. I'm glad you two are getting along. Now tell me what else you've been up to."

She plops down cross-legged on my bed, and I realize I'm not going to get a chance to shower and change out of my PJs. Not until I've filled her in on everything that I've been through since I talked to her last. I settle in for a long chat, leaning against the headboard with a pillow in my lap.

Logan

A slam between my shoulder blades knocks me to my knees. The fog of mist around me is disorienting and I gasp as it feels like I'm falling off the edge of the cliff that's immediately in front of my feet. Instead of hurtling to my death, a shock of pain vibrates through my knees.

"Gotcha." The mist clears away to revealing Sophia's friend Charlotte standing over me with a triumphant smile on her face. "Again."

She reaches down to help me up and I give a Sophia a dirty look at the giggle that escapes her. She was the one who slammed me in the back. While I appreciate that she's been honing her skills enough to take me down, she maybe could have pulled back a bit on the super strength.

"No fair. You teamed up on me again."

"That's your problem. You Mages don't work together enough. You're arrogant and you think you can do anything on your own. Us Witches, we're all about the teamwork. Weaving joint spells, sharing potion recipes over decades. We've got a ton of old knowledge and we're a tight community. You should try it sometime."

She's right. They've bested me using Charlotte's illusion spell and Sophia's various powers multiple times now.

"I'm just glad we're working together on this one."

"As long you your Mages keep their word."

My parents and the council members, who are still on our side, agree to give the Witches an equal share of positions on the new council once we're able to take it back. It's a smart move, and I can't believe we've never gotten to this place before. But I guess it's better to work together than against each other when we're all under threat. My parents raised me to treat Witches as useful members of the magic community, not like some Mages. But after working with them, I realize that I've never really treated their magic with the respect that it deserves. Foolish and arrogant of me, as it was.

"Oh, I'll make sure of it." There's no way I would let the older Mages go back on their word on this one.

"Ready to go again?" She folds her hands in a come-and-get-me gesture.

I wince, rubbing at the sore spot between my shoulder blades. "I think it's time for a lunch break."

"If you need a break, I get it." Charlotte laughs at me again.

"Not what I said," I mutter under my breath.

Sophia moves into my back, pressing herself close enough that her lips tickle my neck when she speaks. "You ok?"

I get a flash of concern through the bond. "I'm fine. Let's get out of here." I spin around in her arms until I'm able to lift her up and plant a huge smack on her lips.

She laughs and her concern drifts away. We're going to be fine.

Lunch has become this huge raucous affair with all the new Mages that have come from out of town to stay at Houston's place. Not to mention the rotating handful that have been stopping by every day to train and plan. It's strange to see Houston's house like this. Full of people. I've always known him as the workaholic trainer at the gym. I think he used to be more socially active when his wife was alive.

I've reconnected with a lot of old classmates that I lost touch with after Ivy's "death." She's been super popular with everyone, wanting to talk to her to find out all about her time in Japan with her grandparents.

The younger group of us have formed our own area for meals in Houston's living room, crowding on the couches and perched on the arms of chairs to fit us all in. It's nice to be around a group like this again. I never thought I'd miss it, but looks like I did. It's been nice introducing Sophia to them as well. It's good for her to be around other Mages her age. She didn't have a chance to socialize with them when she was staying on the compound before since we were still hiding her Archimage secret.

She's a bit on the shy side, so she usually keeps close to one of us, but she's getting to know a few more people. The cat is out of the bag now as well. Everyone knows she's an Archimage, so she's become just as popular as Ivy for them. I have to force myself to not glare at some of the guys who eye her up, though. She is mine, but I know she wouldn't appreciate me staking a claim like a wild animal.

I pulled her onto my lap for lunch, though under the guise of saving space. She's perched sideways on my lap with a plate of food talking to Charlotte. That little crease that forms between her brows when she's thinking hard has appeared and her sandwich is sitting uneaten on her plate.

"Sophia, eat your lunch. Gotta regenerate those Archimage powers, remember?"

She waves off my concern. "Yeah, yeah, but listen to this. Tell him Charlotte." Her head bobs at her friend.

Charlotte leans forward on her knees. "So I've been thinking about your bond thingy, and you Mages that don't know how to work together properly."

"Hey, we can work together." I gesture at the roomful of other Mages all chatting and planning a massive attack on the council compound. Obviously, we can work together. The MED teams, the council.

"Yes, maybe strategically and physically. Not with your magic." Her dark curls bounce as she shakes her head at me, rolling her eyes.

"Like the Witches do with spells?" I'm curious where her line of thought is going on this one.

"Well, maybe. I'm sure you'd be better off if you learned more spells and maybe made your own potions instead of relying on us all the time." A mischievous light glints in her brown eyes. "Of course you'd never do it as well as us, but it wouldn't hurt to put in the effort."

"She means with our Mage magic though." Sophia cuts in to help her friend get to the point. Mages have innate magic inside of us. Not like the Witches who use external objects of power, spells, and potions to do their magic.

"Exactly." Charlotte takes back control of the conversation. "You Mages don't work together to combine or layer your magic. Some could probably multiply their magic by using it together.

But more specifically I'm talking about you and Sophia. You have something special with that protection bond connection."

"So you think we could use the protection bond to amplify our magic somehow?" It's an interesting thought, and she's right that I've never heard anyone even suggest the idea before.

"I think it's worth a shot."

I look up at the ceiling, considering. I'd try anything once in the pursuit of keeping Sophia safe.

"So, can we try it?" Sophia twists around to look at me.

"Only if you eat your lunch, Baby Bird."

She gives me a weird look. "You're not calling me baby bird. That might be one of your weirdest ones yet."

I shrug. I'm running out of ridiculous nicknames to call her. Maybe one day I'll find the perfect one, but we'll have to see how that goes.

"Finish up and then we'll see what we can do after lunch. Maybe focus on that with our psychic blocking session. Now that you've started picking up on more of the thoughts coming from everyone, you need to master that."

The younger Mages in the crowd have taken over the old barn as our dedicated training space. Less to destroy than in Houston's super swanky training gym. As soon as we get to the dusty space, I try to creep through Sophia's defenses through the bond to read her thoughts. She slams her wall up before I get even a small snippet. She arches a brow at me.

"Did you actually think that would work?"

"I was kinda hoping, but I'm also glad you're getting so good at the blocking. When we face up with your uncle next, it's a very real possibility that he'll have someone's stolen psychic powers, so it'll ease my mind to know you can block him."

She really is getting scary good at this. The last week has been a blur of physical and magical training in the mornings and psychic blocking and strategizing in the afternoons. Every day she gets a little better. It's easy for us to practice since we've got that connection through the bond. But it's better to test her skills with someone she's not attached to, so one of my old classmates, Brent, has been testing all of us on our skills. He's a pretty powerful Psyche. I realized I have gotten a little rusty without practicing. I shouldn't have gotten so careless.

"Since I'm getting so good at this..." She pauses for a moment and I can tell from the look in her eyes that I'm probably not going to like where she's going. "How about we test out that bond thing that Charlotte suggested?"

The air stills around us and I realize everyone has stopped what they're doing to stare at us. Great, now we're going to have an audience for this... whatever this turns out to be. I have no clue what we're even trying to do, and while I like an audience as much as the next guy. I don't love it when I'm trying something totally new and will probably look foolish failing at.

"Yeah. I guess. How are we planning on doing that?"

I scan past a few sets of gawking eyes to land on Charlotte's. "Any brilliant ideas, Witch? This was your idea."

Her loose necked t shirt slips off her shoulder as she shrugs at me. "Hey, I came up with the idea. I've served my purpose. I don't know how your fancy Magey powers work."

"Great. Anyone else? If you're all going to stare at us, you may as well make yourselves useful."

There's a general shuffling of feet and resumption of conversation as they pretend to go back to whatever they were working on.

Ivy is the only one to respond with a tentative raise of her hand. "I have a thought."

"Sure, go for it. I'm open to anything."

"Well, my grandparents are all about weaving our magic in to whatever we're doing. So if we're doing, say a sword training session, we concentrate not only on our body and mind but on our magic. I use my personal flavor of magic to weave it into my movements. You can all do the same. Psyche, Elemental, whatever."

Interesting thought and definitely not something that's ever been taught by my father or any of the council trainers. I've noticed Ivy has a remarkably fluid connection with her sword. Even more so than she did before she left. So maybe she's got something here.

"How does that work? You're a Bio Mage after all. How does that tie in with swordplay?"

Her narrowed eyes swing back and forth as she considers her words. "As a Bio I have a connection with nature right? So I can feel the trees and plants and animals around me. So if I focus on my magic. You know how you can feel it whispering inside you all the time. I concentrate on pulling it out. Just a thread so as not to waste it." She pauses, waving her fingers in the air as if she can feel it speaking to her. "And then I use it to feel changes in the air. Subtle clues to where my opponent is. Where to put my feet, etc. I use it all the time, so it's almost like second nature. Like an extra sense."

Sounds like she knows what she's talking about, but I'm an Elemental, not a Bio, so I'm wondering how that fits for my magic. And with the bond not for like a sword fight or whatever.

Sophia takes a moment to process Ivy's words.

With a shake of her head, Ivy dismisses her idea. "That probably doesn't make sense."

"No, no, it does." Sophia turns to me. "We just have to make contact with each others' magic and then maybe share it through the bond. See if we can use or amplify each other's powers. Weave them together."

I have helped to pull her magic out before when she couldn't access it. "Like when we first started training. Like with the pillows and stuff."

A strand of hair escapes her ponytail as Sophia nods her head with excitement. "Right? We did used to do that. But then when I mastered accessing my powers on my own, we stopped."

I wonder if we could have become even more powerful if we'd kept up with that practice. "Ok. I think we can do that. What should we try it with first?"

"Maybe not fire. I've had enough traumatic experiences with fire magic for like the rest of eternity." I laugh, remembering how she burned a great black hole in the bleachers at her old high school when she first tried working on her magic. She barely believed in it at all then.

"No, definitely not fire. Come here." I hold out a hand to her. "And focus on your powers."

I focus on my magic before she even makes contact. I feel the electrical current that runs through me in a continuous flow. It tingles awake, reaching out as if it's sentient and wants to be used. It uncurls with a little zap and responds to my focus. A small shock jolts it up as soon as Sophia's soft hand slips into mine. It recognizes her.

Once we've made contact, I follow the thread of the protection bond from my chest across to her. It thins out to a fragile thread in the space between us before increasing in power as it enters her. I follow it all the way to the glow of her powers. I see them as a pinkish glow emanating from her in a powerful wave of energy.

I send some of my magic through the bond. It swirls and mingles with hers and then I draw it back all the way through the bond and the thin exterior thread to pull it back in with mine. Our two flavors of magic swirl around each other.

I meet her eyes. "Can you feel that?"

Her eyes are shining with the thrill of discovery. "I totally can. It's like you pulled some of my magic into you. Let me try to do it back?"

More of her magic creeps through the bond, and she's a bit more tentative, searching around until she has a grasp on some wispy strands of my power. She twines her glow around mine and steadily pulls it back through the bond with her own.

It's a little strange at first. I've had my powers my entire life, so even a small chunk missing leaves me a little off balance, but I know I'll adjust quickly.

"What now?" She's staring at me expectantly, as if I have any clue.

Since she got dragged into the magical world, she's relied on me to be her first source of information for anything magical. Of course when she's reached the limit of my knowledge the first place she turns to is books. Somehow, I don't think she's going to find any useful information about this. Like Charlotte said, us

Mages aren't exactly known for sharing and combining their powers like this.

A shrug is the best I've got. Trey steps forward. "I volunteer. Try to take me down as a team."

Sounds like fun. "That doesn't sound like much of a challenge. Two against one."

Liz is jumping up and down. "Me, me! I'm in." That's a little more like it.

"Oh, now you're in for it. How about you take on all three of us?" Ivy suggests.

I know this is going to be good when Charlotte steps forward. "Make it four. I think that'll even the playing field."

I know Charlotte hasn't trained in combat much. She relies on her illusions and various spells to get her through, but with all of them combined, we should be in for a good fight.

I turn to Sophia, give her a nod, and send a small jolt of energy at her. "You ready?"

I love all of her smiles, but the one she sends back at me is my favorite. A hint of mischief, a little swagger, and a hefty dose of determination curl her lips.

"We got this!

Sophia

My magic is thrumming deep inside me, coming closer and closer to the surface, begging to come out and play. It's like it knows that it's about to be released.

Our friends nod at each other and quickly spread out into a loose arc around Logan and I. We've formed quite the little tight-knit group of weirdos since this all began. Charlotte hasn't spent as much time with us, but she settles into an easy rhythm with everyone else as if she's been with us the whole time.

My heart throbs for an instant with the ache of a missing member. I keep trying to tell myself that Garrett has every right to leave, and it's probably for the best, but that doesn't stop the ache.

I reach into Logan's mind for a hint of his plan and a flash of wind fluttering the leaves of a willow tree shows up in my mind. Got it. I focus on the elemental wind power we both share. Good idea to start with something we both possess. See if we can amplify that before we start sharing powers that only I possess with my Archimage abilities.

We both send out a burst of our unique flavor of magic. It twists together like a strand of rope, getting ever tighter and tighter the longer we focus on it. A powerful gust of wind knocks all our friends to the ground except Liz, who zips out of the way appearing behind us.

She slams a foot into Logan's back, taking him to his knees. It doesn't break the connection we're currently sharing, so I pull more of his power and spin around so fast that I become a little disoriented. Liz lunges at me, but Logan has sprung up and sweeps his sister's feet from underneath her.

Something quickly snakes around my legs, tightening until I topple to the ground, helpless to save myself. While we focused on her attack, the others recovered and Ivy grew some vines to trap me. Logan is still engaged in a physical fight with his sister.

I target the vines around my ankles with a small burst of lightning that cuts them off from their source. They fall limp around my ankles and I scramble to release them so I can stand up. Trey throws spiral of wind at me while I'm getting myself together, but I throw up an automatic shield in the form of another gust. Our wind powers collide in a spiral that shoots wildly off to the side.

Meanwhile, Ivy has come at me with her hands and feet. She pulls me back down and tries to lock her arm around my neck. I spark up a small ball of fire and hold it near my neck so she can't close her arm around me without burning herself.

I leap up in the move that Logan had me practice over and over until I was ready to murder him in his sleep. Glad I didn't. I've gotten kind of fond of him. It was good practice though and I can now deftly jump to my feet from the ground with ease. Not something I'd ever have pictured myself doing in my previous life.

Charlotte has been casually leaning against the wall, watching the action. Is she planning on participating? I thought she was all about this.

And that's when six Treys come at me. Right. I spin around and sweep a hand through one of them, only to stumble when my hand meets nothing but air and the image of Trey shivers before snapping back into place. While I'm trying to figure out which one is the real Trey, Ivy traps my arms behind my back in a circle of vines, and the real Trey closes in with a dagger to my throat.

Matching vines wrap around my ankles until I'm completely immobilized and at their mercy.

I send more power Logan's way as he continues to battle with his sister. They know each other so well it's not a surprise they can predict each other's moves and keep the fight going for a sustained amount of time.

Excitement pricks at me as I watch Logan's movements increase in speed. He's zipping around and trading blows with Liz almost as fast as she moves. It's gorgeous and terrifying to watch all at the same time.

He fumbles for a minute, swinging around as if he's searching for his opponent. I swing back to catch Charlotte laughing. The crystal she uses to perform her illusion magic is glowing as bright as a star in the night sky. She's definitely got something going on and it's for sure working.

Logan stumbles. Hits out at an invisible opponent and falls to his knees. Liz lands a blow between his shoulder blades and he falls gracelessly forward. She plants a booted foot on his back.

"We win!" Her smile is as gleeful as her tone of voice.

"You did." I concede, but she doesn't move from her power position above her brother. "Could you maybe let us go now?"

The vines keeping me trapped loosen and Trey moves his dagger away from my throat, but Liz keeps standing there. "Liz, can you let Logan go, please?"

She sighs. "Fine, spoil all my fun." She steps off her brother and reaches a hand down to help him up.

He ignores her offer of help, springing to his feet on his own steam before turning to me.

I can't resist the urge to rub the smudge of dirt off his cheek that the floor so kindly painted him with and straighten out his hair that got ruffled up.

He pulls me to him in a hug, looking way too excited for someone that just suffered a defeat. "We may have lost, but it worked! Did you see me moving there?"

"I did. That was amazing. You actually used my Phys powers. How did we never figure this out before?"

His arms tighten around me. "I don't know, and it doesn't really matter. Now that we know it's possible, we can practice and we've got one more massive advantage over your uncle."

Ideas spiral in my head. Of all the ways we can use this in a battle. Some ways I probably can't even imagine.

"Tobias. His name is Tobias. I don't want to be associated with him as a family member. He's not family. Then there's the ridiculous code name he gave himself. That makes him seem more like the unseen enemy that was hunting us down before we knew his identity. His name is Tobias, and he's just a man. A dangerous man who steals people's powers, but just a man."

I nod. "I did. You were amazing. You were actually using my powers."

Liz can't resist jumping in. "Might I point out hat I still beat you even when you were moving with Phys level speed?" She smirks at her brother.

He lifts a brow at her. "Maybe so, but Charlotte over there messed me up with her illusion. It was not exactly a fair fight."

"Get used to it. Do you think Zeus is going to make sure we have a fair fight? You know he's going to use every tool in his arsenal to beat us. If that's six Mages on one welp." her faded ends brush her shoulders with her shrug.

"I know. I'm just saying you can't claim the tile of better than me based on that fight."

"Whatever I won. You lost. Too bad."

Sophia

The buzz of Liz's voice in the background is getting dimmer and dimmer as sleep tries to pull me under. I gave the bed to Charlotte after she showed up, so I'm sleeping on the slide out mattress thing beside her. I don't know how Liz still has the energy for any kind of conversation. Since our session yesterday morning when we figured out how to weave our powers together, we've been training non stop.

I used to think that Liz's almost manic energy was a Phys Mage thing, But I have Phys powers. Shouldn't it affect me too if that's the case? Maybe it's because I'm not a full on Phys. I've got all those other powers fighting for contention. Something to think about. Maybe tomorrow.

I'm walking in a dark field. It's the woods out back on Houston's property. The adorable little doll house appears where I shared the last moment of peace with Logan appears. A flash of blinding light snuffs out the darkness, and suddenly… Tobias appears. I freeze looking around for help, but I'm all alone.

"Sophia." The voice is a whisper in my ear. Insistent and way more vivid than any dreams I've ever had before. "Come on, Sophia. Wake up. I just want to talk."

I'm torn. Struggling to make sense of the lifelike sway of the trees in the breeze and the bright colors of the curtains in the playhouse window. Is this real?

"It is real, Sophia. I'm here and I just want to talk."

Call for help. I have to sound the alarm and call for help.

"Now don't do that. I only wan to talk. If you come out here. Alone. I won't cause any trouble. Tonight. Call it a truce."

He's lying. Obviously.

"I'm not lying. I won't hurt anyone if you come out. I haven't had the chance to get to know my niece."

I debate his words. Sending out magical feelers. Do I trust him? Why would I listen to him? I should just call Logan and his parents.

"If you sound the alarm, I'll be out of here faster than you can blink, but I won't go alone. I know everything. I know where your brother is. I know where all of your friends and former friends are. I can target anyone I want. But if you come for a friendly chat, I'll be out of here no harm. I won't target anyone else for now."

It piques my interest when he mentions former friends. Is he talking about Garrett? Does he know where he is? Has he captured him?

A mirthless laugh comes out of him. "I know where your little friend is, but I haven't hurt him either. Come on. What do you say, Sophia? A little conversation in exchange for the safety of all your friends and family. At least for the moment."

IS that even a choice? Not really. If it means my friends stay safe, I'd do anything, and he seems to know it. I don't like that he's in my head.

"Fine. I'll come."

"Excellent. You know where to find me." He waves his arm behind him to encompass the area before disappearing into the playhouse. I hate that he's in the special place I shared with Logan.

My eyes snap open. I'm wide awake. No slow easing out of sleep. It's like someone snapped their fingers and woke me up. I take a moment, listening to the sounds of deep breathing that indicate my friends are all asleep before I swing my legs to the side. I shiver as my bare fee hit the cool wooden floor of the basement room.

I ease out the door with one last glance at my friends to make sure they're sleeping soundly and walk up the stairs.

The third one for the top has a distinct creak, which I avoid with ease. Wouldn't do to wake anyone else in the house. That would only end badly. I'm not sure why I believe him. Why should I take him at his word? But I do. I don't think he'll hurt anyone tonight. He probably couldn't get into the house if he tried. It's warded up the wazoo, not to mention the technology. How did he even get onto the property? It's well protected too.

The boots I slid on crunch through the ice that's formed a crust on top of the snow with the overnight drop in temperature, and I clutch my coat closer around myself.

My heart sinks a little when I spot lights on through the small windows of the playhouse. I was kind of hoping this was really a dream. But somehow I knew it was real.

I slip up the stairs and the door opens as I'm reaching my hand up to turn the knob.

Tobias is standing there, looking oddly elegant in the middle of the tiny room of the house.

"You showed. I knew you were smart, niece." Sure, smart people slog out alone to face their evil uncle alone in an isolated playhouse.

"How did you even get on the property?" Is the first question that pops out of my mouth.

"Does it matter?" he asks. "That's not what we're here to talk about."

It does matter. The flash of light from my dream?—if that's what it was—pops into my head. A portal. He opened a portal right on to Houston's property. Audacious. That is a serious security flaw when facing this particular enemy. We know he's been traveling through portals in the Nether Realm. "You opened a portal?"

"There are those brains again. Looks like I was correct. Still doesn't matter. Come on in. Sit down. Make yourself comfortable." He gestures to the tiny couch.

Bile rises in my throat at seeing him settle down on the cute little couch where I… my cheeks heat as I think of the kisses I shared with Logan on that very couch. A red rage replaces the sick feeling as he crosses one leg over the other in a studiously casual pose, as if he belongs.

He gives the spot on the tiny couch a pat, but I ignore the invitation to sit next to him. As if I'd put myself that close to him. I instead perch on a puffy pink cotton candy pink chair with unicorns on it that sits across from him and closer to the exit. I appreciate the unicorn aesthetic and the chance of a quick escape if need be. You can't say I haven't learned anything since I entered this world of magic.

I give a tentative feel of my powers. They're there. A slight sleepy hum in my core. I've been stretching them to their limits during my stay here to maximize my practice time, but not enough so they don't regenerate over night. I'm not completely back to full power, but I'm getting there.

"How have you been since I last saw you, niece?"

"That isn't what we're here to talk about, is it?" I spit his words back to him. I know he has, like, zero concern for my wellbeing, so there's no use in trying to pretend differently.

A brief laugh escapes. "Delightful. I like you. If things were different, we could be friends."

"Unlikely."

"You want to get to the point? Well, here it is. I need your powers, and I want you to give them to me willingly." He pauses for dramatic effect or something. I don't know.

My mouth drops open. "And why exactly do you think I'd just hand my powers over like that?"

He leans forward, propping his clean-shaven chin on his hands. "Like I told you before. I know where all your friends and family are. I could grab your brother, Scott. That's his name, correct? Like that." I wince as the snap of his fingers echoes through the tiny space.

Scott. He knows where Scott is and he's threatening him. I've been worried about my mom and my friends around here this whole time and it's really my brother I should have been worried about. This man, if you can call him that, knows where my brother is and has no problem casually threatening his life. A sick roil twists my stomach, and I swallow hard.

As much as it pains me, I know I can't act rash just to save my brother. "And if I hand over my powers to you, you're going to go on with your merry life and everyone I know will be safe?" I tilt my head at him. He's saying he thinks I'm smart while seriously underestimating my powers of reasoning.

"I won't hurt anyone you care about." His lips turn up in a small smile.

I notice the missing information behind his words. "And all the other Witches sand Mages?"

"Ahhh, I can't promise anything there. If they choose to defy me, I'll make no promises as to their safety."

I nod. "I see. I guess you're out of luck then. You're seriously underestimating me if you think I'm the person who would sacrifice the rest of the world to save her own friends and family."

"I thought that might be the case. But the point you're missing is that. When you Mages and Witches come to take back your precious council headquarters, a lot of lives are going to be lost." He raises his head from his hands to steeple his fingers in a picture perfect villain pose. Yeah, he's a hundred percent the problem. "Now that's not how I want to do things, but I will if I have to."

I stare at him for a minute, gathering my thoughts. "I don't know if you think you're fooling me or you're trying to fool yourself, but cut it out with the benevolent I-wouldn't-do-this-if-I-didn't-have-to villain shtick. If you don't want to do something than you don't do it. Normal, well-balanced people don't go around kidnapping people and hurting them."

"Touche. Fine then. I'm going to hurt people, but if you sacrifice your powers to me, then the damage will be minimal. If I have your powers permanently, then I need to kidnap any other Mages. It's rather a bore hunting them down and draining them, anyway. So if you think about it like that. You'll be saving a lot of people in the long run."

These words are like a punch to the gut, something I was unfamiliar with until recently. Now that I've been through a bunch of fight training, I'm quite familiar with it the sick feeling.

His words steal my breath. Now the guilt is resting heavily on my heart. I really could save a lot of people by just giving in to his demands, but… then what happens? "And then what? You're not sacrificing any other Mages, but you've got this wild power now? You're telling me you're going to take over the council and rule all the Witches and Mages benevolently. You're not going to punish those who opposed you?"

A dark look passes behind his eyes. "There ares some who will need to be punished for their past actions. That can't be helped. And after that, I'm going to dismantle that stifling council brick by brick. There'll be nothing left. Mages and Witches will be free to do as we please. If they want to reveal themselves to Mundanes? Not my concern. I don't want to lead that sorry group. I can do what I please and so can everyone else." The fiery bright light of a zealot glazes his eyes. He won't stop. No matter what choice I make, he's going to do as he pleases.

I still am not sure why he expects me to believe him. "Who are you planning on punishing, anyway? What are these past wrongs?"

"That's the other piece that might, in fact, convince you to come over to my side. You don't know what it was like when those people stole my powers as a child. It's like having your insides ripped out. Being seared from the within and leaving a hole that still aches like a phantom limb. I was just a child. They made me like this. These precious council members of yours were the ones responsible and they need to pay."

It does sound horrible, but those people aren't even on the council anymore. Right? Those kinds of barbaric practices aren't allowed anymore. I mean, everyone was worried about my safety when they found out I was an Archimage, but they wouldn't have done that. I don't think.

"I can see you faltering. You know I'm right. You know, if you hadn't had the protection of you precious Logan and his powerful family, you might be in the same position as I am now. You'd be just like me." He puts a little extra emphasis on each word in his last sentence and that shakes me out of it.

I shake my head. "I could never be like you. I don't care what they've done to you. There's no excuse for murder and torture. I will never be like you, no matter what happens. Sure, the council might need some updates, but this is not the way." I know my pleas are futile. He's not going to just come over to my way of thinking after these years of stewing in his own anger and hatred.

He unfolds his legs and goes to stand up. "So then. Are we at an impasse? Are you going to let me continue to take Mages to sustain my powers? Going to let all your Mage friends come at me in a battle that won't end well for anyone?"

He brushes some invisible lint off his tailored black pants and looks back up to meet me in the eyes. "Or are you going to hand over your powers peacefully? The choice is yours."

He's got me and he knows it, but I'm not giving up that easily. The thing he hasn't factored in is that there's no way they won't come to rescue me. Going to him willingly won't prevent the coming battle. People will still die. But it's up to me if the people I love most stay safe. If he leaves my completely innocent Mundane brother out of it. Plus, I might gain our side an advantage with some inside information.

"I'll tell you what, Sophia. I'll give you three days to consider my offer. After that.. no one you love will be safe. No one."

His words send a shiver up my spine. "Fine. I'll think about your offer." A gentle nudge pokes at me inside my head. He's trying to read my thoughts to figure out what I'm actually thinking. I slam up the wall I've been carefully reinforcing lately to keep out unwanted psychic invasions.

"I see you're learning things. Three days. If you don't show up at the compound. Alone. By, let's say, noon, three days from now, I'll assume you're not coming and I'll pay your brother a visit. That's only where I'll start, mind you."

"Fine." The glare I level at him doesn't do anything except make me feel better.

"Excellent. Very productive chat." He turns his back on me to walk toward the door as if I'm no threat.

I pull my power up and unleash it in a flickering ball of crimson and yellow flames.

He's out the door in a blur, leaving behind only his grating laugh. Pain sparks in the palm of my hands as I tighten my fists so hard my nails break the skin.

I rush out the door to see a portal snapping shut. I guess psychic powers aren't the only stolen powers he's got at the moment.

I make my way back to the house, stealing in as quietly as I can.

I breathe a sigh of relief when I make down the stairs without getting caught, but I pause at the door to the guy's room. The handle turns noiselessly at my touch and I poke my head through the doorway. My eyes land on Logan's sleeping figure. Moonlight shining through the window kisses his cheek. He looks younger and more vulnerable in sleep, with his dark lashes resting on the dark smudges under his eyes. He hasn't been getting enough sleep, so I leave him be, backing slowly out the door to return to my room. Any hope I had of getting a good night's sleep is gone.

Two days until my birthday. Three days until Tobias' impossible deadline.

Logan

My dad pulled me into an office for a chat and I can't stop staring at the door and tapping my knee, anxious to get out and back to Sophia. She's not big on crowds of strangers and this house is now overflowing with them. Most of them are nice, but I know she's an introvert at heart and really just wants to curl up in a corner with a book.

"Son, are you paying attention to me?" I swing my gaze back to my father's finding his eyes have gone hard. New gray hairs have popped up around his temples over the last few months. I know there's been a lot of stress on him, but we've been the ones constantly putting ourselves in danger.

"Yeah. I'm listening." I guess the quicker we get this little talk over with, the faster I can get back to Sophia. She was weird this morning. Rushed off to breakfast before I could even sneak a kiss. She looked tired. Even more so than usual.

"I wanted to talk to you about potentially leading a team into the fight. We're down to five days away, so we're formalizing all the teams."

Wait, did I hear that right? He wants me to lead a team in this fight? He's never trusted me with that kind of responsibility.

"Don't you mean, Trey?" I ask, letting my confusion show on my face as much as he won't love me showing emotion of any kind.

He sighs and folds his arms on the table in front of him. "I know maybe I haven't exactly shown a level of trust in you in the past. But I can see how much you've changed since you took on the role of protecting Sophia, and I think that you're ready for this." I study his face for any hint of sarcasm. Maybe even a 'just messing with you'. If it was anyone other than my dad, maybe. But that's not exactly his style.

"Ok." I'm not sure what else to say. I know I can do this. We've all been taking turns heading up various things, but I have taken on a leadership role within our little group.

"Excellent." He seems to pull his regular personality back on, sliding it over the hint of emotion he showed. "I'll include you in the evening planning session tonight and we'll figure out where everyone's place will be. I know you've become quite familiar with the strengths and weaknesses of your friends, so you can help with that." He reaches down to pull a folder out of his desk, dismissing me.

"Is that it?"

He looks up from the papers. "Yes. You're free to go back to your training. Don't push Sophia too hard, though. We want to conserve her powers."

"I won't. I would never pout her in a vulnerable position."

"I know that," he replies.

I walk away and then turn back, one more question nagging at me. "But you're ok with that too now? With me and Sophia together? You were pretty against that in the beginning. You don't think I'm going to compromise my duty now?"

"You seem to have done a solid job of protecting her, other than getting yourself kidnapped, but no. I've talked to your mother and I've seen the two of you together."

"Ok then. I'll see you later." I lift my hand in an awkward wave, and he drops his chin in a brief nod of dismissal.

Well, that was beyond weird, but I'll take it.

Liz catches my arm on my way down the hall to find Sophia. "What was that all about? You in trouble, big brother?"

"No, dear sister, I'm not in trouble. Not this time, at least. Dad was actually kind of..." nice is the wrong word "respectful. It was strange."

"Well then. Look at you. All grown up now." My younger sister has the audacity to ruffle my hair before darting away in a blur. She really needs to stop wasting her energy with the constant use of her powers. Not that I expect her to listen to my advice.

I head for the kitchen where I last spotted Sophia chatting with her mom.

"What do you want to do for your birthday tomorrow?" The knife that was about to leave her hand flies wildly off to the side, landing with a thud after it bounces harmlessly off a hay bale.

"Don't creep up on me like that. That could have ended up in your foot, or worse, someone else's." Her brows close up in a cute scowl.

"It would be worse if it was someone else? Wow! Glad to know how deep your love runs." I let one corner of my mouth pull up in a smirk.

"Yeah." She punctuates the word with a nod. "It would have been your fault if anyone got hurt, thus it would have served you right if it were you. Buffoon."

"She's right." Trey crosses his arms, watching the show with amusement.

"On the other hand, if you hadn't snuck off to train with him," I tilt my head at Trey, " rather than me, I wouldn't have to sneak up on my girlfriend for a little friendly conversation."

"He's better at the daggers." Her eyes scan me from head to toe. "Not to mention, you're way too distracting."

The small smirk grows into a cocky smile, and I tilt my chin. "I get it. My stunning good looks are too much for you. Fair."

"Nope. It's your mouth that's the problem."

Her words do nothing to wipe the smile off my face. "In front of all these people? I never took you for an exhibitionist."

The force behind the answering smack she lands on my shoulder has me rocking back on my heels. "Not what I meant, and you know it."

"Do I?"

"Yes."

Trey's got a hand covering his mouth to hide the laughter that's trying to escape, but he can't hide it from his eyes.

"You didn't answer my question. What do you want to do for your birthday? It's your eighteenth. I suggest a huge blowout before we have to go off and save the world."

She pulls away from me, staring at the ground under her lashes. "I wouldn't want to inconvenience Houston. This is his house. Kinda rude to just throw a party."

I scoff. "Do you doubt my pull?" She rolls her eyes at me. "He won't mind. His house is stuffed full of random Mages and

Witches already. We can figure something out. Get some food delivered."

"I don't know." I don't love the way she's fully turned away from me now. I reach out to grab her hand and send out a little feeler to see if I can catch a glimpse of what's up in that head of hers. I'm not trying to pry, but I worry about her pretty much constantly and this is kind of a big deal. I don't want her blowing off her eighteenth birthday. Her wall is already up, and she doesn't let me in. Fair enough. She deserves her privacy.

"Come on, Sophia, you deserve to celebrate. Look at it this way. You survived to your eighteenth birthday in spite of everyone trying to kidnap and murder you." I throw my hands up in the air, unable to express the size of the obstacles that have been working against us, and her in particular.

"Exactly. When I think of the people who didn't make it, and those that have bailed out. Not to mention the danger we're about to put all these other people in. I don't know. Doesn't feel right. You know?" She turns her head enough to flick her eyes back up to me.

Xavier... and Garrett. Well, that one's all on him. I don't want her feeling any responsibility for his cowardice. "It's bigger than you now, Sophia." I reach out slowly as if I might spook her and when she doesn't protest, I tilt her chin up with my fingers. "None of us want your uncle or Lawrence or any of those other hooligans running the show. They're all doing this for themselves and their families as much as you. And you can't stop living because other people have. I know how much you're hurting." Empathy might not normally be one of my strong suits, but having actually felt her pain through the bond, there's truth in my words. "And if I could take any of it away from you, I would, but I can't. So let's go out with a bang. Don't let Tobias or anyone else stop you from living your life or enjoying the moments of peace you have. Not to mention I wanna spoil my girl on her birthday."

My words finally drag a small smile to her face. "Ok. I guess we can do a small thing. My mother would probably kill me if I she couldn't do something for me anyway, no matter how much she's dreading my eighteenth."

I lay a loud smack on her lips, only pulling back a little to whisper. "I knew I'd win."

Sophia

My bloodcurdling shriek does nothing to deter the face pressed right up into mine.

"Happy Birthday!" Liz yells in my face.

"Wha…" Charlotte's sleep muddled voice comes from behind me.

"Liz. What time is it?"

"I don't know. Way earlier than I would normally ever get up. You should consider yourself lucky to have a friend like me."

"Lucky? What exactly is it about you shrieking in my face this early in the morning that makes you think I'm lucky?"

"There aren't many people I would get up this early for. You. My friend are very special."

Trust Liz to think that her presence is a privilege even this early in the morning. I fumble around beside the bed until my hand closes on the smooth surface of the temporary burner phone I've been given to keep in touch with anyone here. That's the limit. No outside contact.

"Whatever you say, Liz. Can I go back to sleep now? It's going to be a long day after a series of long days and I'm not really interested in spending my birthday exhausted.

"Nope. Come on. I made you breakfast."

I finally check the face of the phone and see that it's six o'clock in the morning. I do a double take at her words. "Wait. You made breakfast?" I drag my eyelids open a little wider to give her a skeptical look.

"Yes. I can cook."

"Really? I did not think that was one of your many skills."

"I can make Poptarts and open a can of fruit salad."

"Got it." Everything clicks into place. Liz is amazing and bad ass and capable of many incredible and dangerous things, which is why she's fast become one of my closest friends. I don't believe cooking is one of those things. I really don't know how they were surviving alone when I first met them, since Logan isn't much of a chef either.

"Can I at least shower before I have to face the light of day?" My question is more of a plea than an ask.

"I guess. But hurry. I don't want the pop tarts getting cold."

Right, cause molten artificial fruit filing in a sugary crust is going to go bad with a little neglect.

"I will." I turn my head to see Charlotte's eyes open a mere crack. Her hair has fluffed out all around her face in an amazing halo.

"Happy Birthday." She smiles at me. "I'm going back to sleep now."

"Come on. You're my bestie. You can't leave me to her mercy on my birthday."

"Sorry, babe. I'll catch you after a few more zees."

I look over to the other side of the bed, but Ivy's spot is already neat and made next to the mess of sheets tossed in a heap all over Liz's bed. At least I'll have someone sane to keep me company, even if she doesn't get up unreasonably early for fun.

True to her word, there's a small plate with two white frosting covered pop tarts sitting next to an open can of fruit salad and a spoon. She didn't even pour it into a bowl. Her mother would be ashamed of her.

There's another plate across the table with nothing but a few crumbs sitting on it. Liz didn't' waste any time before digging in to her breakfast. She hops out of her seat and pulls my chair out when I arrive. "Milady."

"You're so weird."

"Why thank you." She bows down deep, drops into a seat for a millisecond before popping up again to prowl the kitchen like a cougar stalking her prey. Am I her prey?

"Can you sit down for a few minutes? You're making me nervous." Well, more nervous than I already was. Everything that faded away while I was sleeping comes rushing back to me. What I'm planning on doing today. That this might be the last time I see her like this. "Or not. Do what makes you comfortable."

"No, it's fine. I'm sorry. I don't usually get up this early, but now that I'm up, I have all this energy, and I'm not sure what to do with it."

"I get it. Do you know what the plan for the day is?" Logan didn't share anything further after I told him he could do something for my eighteenth. I know the only thing I want to do, but that's for later.

She jumps up again. "I don't know. Logan doesn't trust me to keep secrets, so he didn't tell me anything. That's why I made breakfast for you. I wanted to do something just from me, you know, and I knew my brother would monopolize you for the rest of the day."

That's kinda sweet. "Got it." She's not wrong. I'm sure he will be a little on the possessive side today. I'll have to be careful to guard my thoughts from him. If he catches even a hint of what I'm planning, he'll have me on lock down like a werewolf who can't control herself on the full moon. Silver chains and all. If they existed. They don't, right???

Despite my worry, a genuine smile crosses my face when the man himself shows up. He's still wearing flannel sleep pants and a soft gray shirt that begs to be cuddled. He looks happy. Like, really happy. Like, way too happy for this time of the morning, but unlike his sister, I know he generally is an early riser.

"What's this?" He snags a Poptart off my plate, wrinkling his nose at it.

Liz bounces over with a proud smile. "A Poptart! I made Sophia a birthday breakfast." She gestures at the spread.

Logan sighs dramatically. "I'm sorry you had to suffer my sister's excuse for cooking. And on your birthday, no less. I really didn't expect the brat to get up so early. That's unheard of."

"Hey. There's nothing wrong with my meal, right Sophia?" She turns to me and I'm pinned in between the siblings.

"It's kind of fun. Mom never buys junk food like that."

"See."

Logan ruffles her hair. "One day you're going to have to learn to cook. You're not always going to have Mom to look after you."

"Not like you're a master chef yourself. Besides. We live in the twenty-first century. I don't need to learn how to cook. I can get takeout, or delivery."

"What's up today? Training this morning?"

"On your birthday? No way. You get to chillax today."

Liz's mouth falls open, and he swats away the hand she reaches over to feel his forehead. "Are you ok? Should I call a doctor, maybe get a potion or something?"

He glares at her. "Enough. I can relax."

"Could have fooled me."

"Can I steal you away for some mother daughter time this morning?" The kitchen's been filling up so fast I didn't notice Mom sneak in.

My eyes soften, and sorrow twists my gut. I definitely owe her a little time today. "Of course, Mom."

"Happy Birthday, darling. I love you so much."

"I love you too." I feel so guilty that all this magic stuff has completely uprooted her life. She even had to take a sabbatical from work and hand off her research to one of the other professors. She's still keeping in touch remotely, but it's not her research anymore. But my decision will fix that. She can go back to her old life.

I can't resist the urge to slide my arms around Logan's coziness, pressing my cheek against the warmth of his soft shirt. He buries his face in my hair for a kiss, and everyone else disappears.

"Go on with your mom. I'll see you soon."

The out of town Mages have been staying at a nearby hotel only coming by during the day to train and plan, so Mom kept this room all to herself. I plop right onto the plush, sunny yellow duvet that covers her bed, crossing my legs under me She settles into the little white bucket chair covered in yellow daisies across from me.

"Room's nice."

"You could have stayed in here with me, but I know you want to be with your friends. You're all grown up now. I can't believe it. I remember when you were just a tiny little thing. So gorgeous. You're still gorgeous. I'm so lucky I got to be your mom. I'm sorry I never told you about being adopted before. I just wanted you to be mine. It was wrong, though. I should have told you when you were younger."

"It's fine, Mom. I don't think I would have been any the wiser as to all this Mage stuff. They still wouldn't have come for me until they had to."

"I know, but I'm still sorry." She shifts in the seat, clasping her hands in her lap and spinning her wedding ring around her finger like she does when she's nervous.

"I'm sorry, too."

"What for?" she looks up from her hands with a question in her eyes.

"For all of this stuff. The magic. Upturning your life, opening your eyes to all this madness."

"Oh, honey. You're my daughter, and I will always love you and be there for you. I don't regret anything. It's kind of interesting to find out all this stuff exists. Your father would have loved it. He would have loved learning about Mages and magic, and most of all he would have loved seeing you all grown up." There's a complex array of emotions warring in her eyes. Soul deep pain, pride, longing, and happiness are all engaged in a never ending battle. Her words resonate straight through to the hole in my life that losing my dad left behind. I know it'll always be there. Part of me.

"I know, Mom." I reach over and grab her hand. "He would have been proud of you, too."

"I don't know, hon. I spent too many lost years when I should have been looking after you and your brother."

"I think we turned out all right in the end, so I think you did all right." I wink at her, trying to bring some light to the conversation that's grown so heavy it's dragging my shoulders down like an overloaded backpack.

"You turned out more than all right. I know your life has taken a turn you never expected and maybe things don't look so good right now, but you'll find your way. A new path in this magical world. A new role to fill. I've always told you that you can do whatever you want with your life. I know that goal used to be to follow in your dad's footsteps, but I think the world has something spectacular planned for you."

"Thanks, Mom."

"Speaking of that. I bought you something a few months ago to prepare for your eighteenth, and it might not be the right thing anymore, but I want you to have it. It'll be a memory of your father and your past rather than your future, I think."

She reaches into the drawer of the white bedside table. "Somehow I brought this with me when we moved to the Armstrong's house and now here. It's been through a lot. Just like you."

The long, narrow blue velvet box piques my curiosity as she places it in my hand. I hesitate over the little button that will snap it open. She nods at me. "Go on."

I press down on the latch and the box springs open, revealing a silver chain with a shiny caduceus pendant dangling from it. A deep red stone is inset at the top of the staff. Heat burns behind my eyes. "Garnet?" I ask.

"Yes. For your birthday…and your fathers." Her eyes are bright now with tears, so I let mine escape as well.

She slides onto the bed beside me, pulling me into an embrace I never want to end.

"Thank you so much, Mom. It's beautiful."

"Just like you. In all the most important ways. Inside and out."

I slide the cool metal around my neck, struggling to do up the clasp behind my head. "Can you…" I look at her.

She smiles through her tears and helps me do it up before pulling me back into her.

When she's finally ready to let go, she pulls back and gives me a shaky smile. "Now go on and get back that boyfriend of yours. He doesn't exactly seem like the most patient, but then what man is?"

I laugh, giving her a last hug. "Thanks, Mom. For everything."

"I love you. Just do one thing for me?"

"What's that?"

"Stay safe." Her face hardens in its intensity.

"I'll do my best."

"No. Do better than your best. Make sure you come back to me. I couldn't take it if I lost you, too."

"You won't." I whisper the words, but I don't make any promises. I'm not in the habit of making promises I can't keep. That's one thing she definitely taught me.

Logan

The door slams shut behind me as my heel makes contact. Finally, a moment of peace. I haven't been able to get Sophia alone all day. Everyone has wanted a piece of her. Can't say as how I blame them, but I really have been wanting to carve out a splinter of her time all to myself.

"So." Her golden hair is down today, hanging in a long wave of over her shoulders until I tilt her chin up and it slides to her back. My fingers are itching to run through it, but my mouth is also begging to land on hers. When her little pink tongue darts out to lick her lower lip, that settles it. I descend on her lips with a light nip, followed by a crushing kiss.

"Happy Birthday. Party Girl."

She laughs through the kiss, but it doesn't last long when I delve in deeper. She returns my insistent need, pressing me back up against the door. Man, that's hot. I let her take control for a little longer, exploring until we're both breathless. Then I pick her up and spin her around, crowding her toward the bed I've been staying in. I only got that one night with her in it. Unfortunately, there's an obnoxiously loud knock on the door just as the back of her knees hit the soft mattress.

"Go away!" I get out between breathless inhales.

"Sorry, dude, but dinners here and everyone is waiting for you, Sophia." Trey's deep rumble sounds sheepish even through the door. He knows what's going on, but if he knows, then he's not the only one. I really don't want to think about what her mom might do to me if she catches me in here alone with her daughter, eighteen or not.

Sophia pulls herself together to answer before I can. "We're coming, Trey." I'm happy to hear that her voice at least is a little breathless, too.

"We can get back to this later." She pokes me in the chest.

I groan. "Can we?" I wave at the door. The chances of avoiding another interruption in this full house are slim.

"Yes. I promise. I got this." I've never been one to doubt Sophia's powers of getting things done. If she says she's got this, then I guess she does.

"Fine. You hungry?"

"You have no idea," she replies, and I can tell she means that in more than one way.

I run my hands down her hair as if it needs straightening, because I just need to touch her, then close her smooth hand in mine.

"Should we go up separately or something?" she asks.

"No way."

She seems a little hesitant, pausing when we get to the top of the stairs and looking at me. I know she's a little shy with all these people in the house, especially when there's so much focus on her today. Like the Archimage thing wasn't enough, now it's her birthday too.

She shivers as I slide my hand out of hers, trailing my fingers along her lower back to close around her hip, pulling her in close. "We got this," I whisper in her ear.

She nods and pushes through the door.

"Happy Birthday!!" The discordant chorus of voices hits us in a wave and a blush creeps up her neck at the attention.

All our friends are there in addition to our parents, Houston, and the assortment of Mages that have been in and out hanging around the place over the last week. I've known all of them for most of my life. Some are better than others depending on where they're coming from, but they're mostly new to Sophia, so I get why it's kinda awkward for her.

"Thanks." Sophia smiles.

The notably missing component is the rest of Charlotte's family. "Char, where's your family at?" I know they didn't have a lot of dealings with Sophia over the years before they found out she was a Mage, but she is Sophia's best friend. I'd expect they'd at least hang around for her party.

She turns from her friend. "They went to batch cook some potions for the upcoming battle." She gives Sophia a wink, and a sly smile creeps up her face. Some sort of girly secret going on there that I'm not privy to, I guess.

"What's for dinner?" The smell coming from the rectangular cardboard boxes that she's eyeing is mouthwatering.

Mrs. Tennant steps forward, lifting the lid of one box to reveal a deep-dish pizza. "We ordered your favorite. Moon Pai."

Sophia moans, stepping forward. "Dill Pickle?"

"Of course, and their special was Garlic All the Way."

"Amazing." She turns to me. "Have you tried this before?"

"Nope, but I recall you raving about their pizzas. They don't deliver, so we had to send out the brigade to pick them up. I'm sure it will be worth it from the look of it."

"You go first, Birthday Girl." I kiss her on the nose before I send her off.

"Oh, I will." She piles her plate high with some amazing looking slices and waffle fries covered in Parmesan cheese. Once she's all set, I head for the meatiest pie I can find.

* * * ★ ★ ★ ★ ★ ★ * *

"That was amazing." Trey's sprawled out on an armchair, groaning as he rubs his stomach.

The door clicks shut on the last of the visiting Mages heading back to wherever they're staying for the night. Now it's just us and Sophia's mom lingering in the living room space.

She rises with a stretch and a yawn, walking over to pull her daughter up from her cozy spot, curled up next to me on the couch. "Ok, sweetie. I'm exhausted and I have to do some online work tomorrow, so I'm heading off to bed. Happy birthday, I hope it was a good one in spite of everything that's going on right now."

"It was amazing, Mom. Thank you so much for making my birthday special, even in this strange house."

"Always sweetie, and when thins are back to normal we can throw you a huge bash at our house." A shadow passes over Sophias face as if she knows they might never get to live that normal life again. I'm determined, though. Even if she can't go back to her family's house, she's going to be living without fear soon. Very soon. If I have to kill her uncle with my own hands.

I've spent my entire life training to fight, but murder is not something I've ever contemplated before. After everything he's put her through, death is probably a kinder punishment than he deserves.

She hugs her Mom back so tight her mom laughs. "Can't breathe, sweetie."

"Sorry, Mom. Remember, I love you. No matter what."

"Of course." Her mom looks down at her with a strange look on her face before pulling back and lifting her daughter's chin. "I know you're off to put yourself in danger, and I also know that nothing I can say will stop you from going, but please don't do anything you don't have to do. Don't put yourself in more danger than you need to."

A small smile turns up the corner of Sophia's lips. "You know me, Mom. I'm nothing if not logical."

That seems to satisfy her mom, who heads up to her room after one more hug, but it doesn't satisfy me. I don't like the look in Sophia's eyes or the tone of her voice. It's like she's apologizing to her mom in advance for something. She better not be planning anything. I grab her hand and try to peek in her mind just a little, but find I'm still blocked. I helped her build this wall to prevent psychic invasions and now she's using it against me. Great, I've created a monster.

"You're not hiding anything from me, are you? I hope you're not planning anything that's gonna get you in trouble."

My parents come back in from the front hall and she turns to face them before I get the answer I'm looking for.

"Ok, kids. We're off to bed as well. Remember, we're only a few days away from the battle, so we're back to some serious training tomorrow. And I'm going to need you, Logan, in on the team lead meeting." Dad gives me a brief nod.

"Got it." I reply.

"What he means is. Don't stay up too late." Mom gives all of us hugs.

"We won't. After all that food, I'll be lucky to make it to my bed," Trey says. He's always so restrained with everything. What he eats and how he trains, so it was good to see him let loose for the first time in a long time.

"Don't worry, Mrs. Armstrong. We'll be good." Sophia returns the warm hug Mom gives her. A wrinkle pops up between her eyes in a look I recognize as her probing someone's thoughts. She's not one to invade other people's minds without a good reason. I wonder if she thinks Sophia is up to something too, but she pulls away after a moment. Looks like she might not have been able to breach Sophia's shield either. I've got mixed feelings on that one. On the one hand, I'm glad Sophia is holding her wall up against a Psychic Mage as powerful as Mom. I'm not sure if she's put that wall up unconsciously or if she really is trying to hide something from us.

The conversation turns to a random assortment of video games, science, and fighting techniques after the parental units leave. We're having so much fun I don't realize the time until I glance at my watch. It's almost midnight. The so-called grown-ups left us over an hour ago. I try to stifle the yawn that's trying to escape.

Ivy's mouth stretches open in response to my almost yawn. "I need some sleep." She rises from her seat before pulling Trey up out of his chair despite all his groaning and complaining. "Come on. I know how you get when you don't get enough sleep. Nobody wants to deal with that hot mess tomorrow." She teases him.

I raise an eyebrow at my sister after they're gone. "What?" She asks. Oblivious as always, or more likely just messing with me.

Charlotte laughs. "Have fun, kids. Don't do anything I wouldn't do? Come on, Liz. I think they want some alone time."

Liz shudders, then she's gone in a flash without even a good night.

"Good night." I call to the space where my sister disappeared.

"Night, you two," Charlotte waves.

Sophia jumps up off the couch before Charlotte disappears through the basement door.

"I love you, Char." She wraps her arms around her friend with a tight squeeze. "Thanks for being here, and for everything else."

"Of course. Love you too. Be safe." They pull apart and Charlotte turns to me. "You too. Be good to my girl."

I give her a puzzled look. "Aren't I always?"

"Not good enough. No one is good enough for my bestie. She deserves the entire world. Are you prepared to give it to her? Cause if not, I'll get my grandmother to hex you."

"The world? Sure, I can do that. No problem." I wink. "Why not the entire universe while I'm at it? Go big or go home, right?"

"I'm holding you to that." I flinch away when she shakes a finger at me. I wouldn't put it past her to hex me preemptively in case I hurt her friend. I didn't fully appreciate how scary Witches could be until recently. Don't underestimate them.

"Get out of here, Char." Sophia scolds her friend.

"Fine. Nighty night."

"Good night." I barely get the words out before Sophia has bounced back to me and flung her legs over mine to straddle my lap.

"Finally, some alone time." She ducks her head in for a quick peck on the lips.

"As alone as we can be in this house jammed full of our parents and friends." I tell her between soft kisses.

"I have a solution for that." She grins at me.

I try to pull her back in for another kiss, missing the fiery connection between us when our lips are touching.

"What are you doing? Get back over here." I try to tug her back to me.

"Nope." She slides back off my lap. "Come on."

I'm still in a bit of a stupor from all the food and now the kisses. Why is she getting farther away rather than closer?

"Where are you going?"

"Not me. Us."

"Still confused here. As much as I'd like you to come to my bed with me, I don't think that's a particularly good idea with all our parents upstairs."

"I've got somewhere for us to go. Trust me."

I push up off the couch. I trust her, but also kinda need to get some details. We can't be heading off the property or anything.

"Where?"

She bobs her eyebrows with a smile. "You know the cabin Charlotte's family has been staying in?"

"Yeah."

"They went home to stay the next few nights there while they brew up some potions. The place is ours."

"Really? Did you arrange this?"

"Well, I had a little help from Charlotte, but yeah. I love you, Logan. And I really want to show you how much." Her word steal my ability to breathe.

Sophia

I have to slap my hand over my mouth to stifle the giggle that tries to escape as a stray lock of hair tickles my neck when Logan trails a line of kisses down my neck.

"Stop it." I hiss at him. "You're going to get us caught."

I hate the emotionless stone face he used to wear all the time. It's been making less and less of an appearance lately, but it slides back into place now as he tries to control himself. He adds a brief salute, though, that almost sets me off again.

"I can't even look at you. Let's just get out of here before I give us away."

"Your wish is my command." He folds at the waist in a bow.

A rush of icy winter wind tries to steal my breath, and he has to grab the door to make sure it doesn't get ripped from his grasp.

A thud and rustle of papers behind us has me wincing. The gust of wind whipping through must have knocked over a small lamp and sheaf of papers that's sitting on a small table in the hallway. I hold my breath, waiting for his parents or Mom to appear.

"We're good," Logan says, pulling me out the front door with one backward glance that tells me he's not waiting another second to risk getting caught.

The walk to the little cabin takes far too long and at the same time, we're there a little too fast. The butterflies in my stomach seem to have mutated into bats, judging by the incessant twirling of them. Pretty sure they're fighting for dominance in there.

The cold air has frozen my cheeks, but it's the nerves that are freezing my feet in place. They're refusing to cross the threshold past the maple leaf spattered door mat. Logan's already through the door, but swivels his head around when I make no move to follow him.

"You coming?" I nod at his words, but it's the hand he's holding out that finally jolts me out of my state. This is Logan. This is what I want, what I need. This may be the last time I see him after all if things don't work out, and I can't destroy Tobias and break down his organization from the inside.

I wish our hands weren't separated by the thick fabric of our warm gloves. The reassuring heat of his palm would definitely help me along right now. It's like we're already disconnected by all these layers of winter clothes. Necessary, but annoying.

His arm slides over my shoulder to push the door shut as I make it through.

A sliver of moonlight gleaming through the couple of inches between the open front curtains highlights his sharply cut cheekbones as he looks down at me. "You know, Sophia. I'm not expecting anything. All I need is you. We've hardly had any alone time together since you found me in the Nether." A haunted shadow darkens his eyes. "We don't need to do anything other than talk."

Right, he's trying to be all noble. I get it, but this is what I want. I see maybe I'm going to have to do some convincing here. "What if I want to do something…everything. I never expected to find you. I wasn't looking for love and to be honest, if I had been, there's no way it would have looked like you."

The snort that escapes him doesn't take away from the mood. "What? Not a fan of tall, dark, handsome, and buff?"

I laugh, but then school my face back into seriousness. He has to know that I mean this. I have to make him understand that no matter what happens, he's it for me. "You know what I mean. What I'm trying to say is that I wasn't looking for you and then you appeared in my life all snarky, and strong, and magical, like literally magical, and it worked. I love you, Logan. You're it for me. I want you to know that. I want you to know that I choose you for now and forever. No matter what happens."

He presses a finger to my mouth. "Nothing is going to happen. We're going to get through this and we're going to make things right again. With the council, with the magical world. I'm going to make sure you're safe. No matter what I have to do. I would do anything for you. You're it for me too."

His lips replace his finger in a desperate promise of a kiss. I lean into it, trying to express all of my feelings for him in this one kiss. It's not enough. Our puffy jackets are in the way and I claw at mine until I get it unzipped, letting it fall to the floor in an uncharacteristic move.

His lands on top of mine a moment later even as we remain connected at the mouth, heat flowing back and forth in waves of increasing intensity.

Hats, gloves and boots all follow until we're down to the comfy clothes we spent the evening in. Even the thin cotton of my t-shirt feels like too much distance. I pull myself back from the heat of his mouth for a moment, curling my fingers around the hem of the shirt. He stills my hand as I start to drag it up.

"Wait." I almost growl in my frustration. "Can I?"

My mind is already clouded with all of the intense feels, so my brain isn't quite processing his request. "Can you what?"

"If this is what you want. If you're sure." His eyes are almost shining in their intensity.

"I'm sure. A hundred percent sure. I want you to be my first. Tonight." I want to be perfectly clear in case he gets any ideas that he's taking advantage of me or something.

"Ok. Then I'd really like to take my time. I'd like to make sure you know how much you're worshiped. I love you more than I ever thought it was possible to love someone. Let's not rush this."

My fingers uncurl from the hem of my shirt and I look up at him, trying to let my love shine through for him to see.

"What are you thinking? I can't catch any of your thoughts. You're blocking me."

I was kind of hoping he wouldn't question the mental wall I've thrown up. "Practice," I mumble. "I'm thinking, let's get on with this. I've waited long enough. Don't keep me waiting any longer."

I throw my arms around his neck and crash into him with my need, not giving him any more time to question it.

It's like the last of his reserves crumble under my passion. The floor disappears beneath my feet as he scoops an arm under my knees, lifting me up. He trails fervent kisses down my neck even as we're moving through the small space.

My entire body is alight with need by the time we make it through the door into the bedroom, and I don't even have time to look around the room as he carries me in.

I throw my arms around his neck and crash into him with my need, not giving him any more time to question it.

It's like the last of his reserves crumble under my passion. The floor disappears beneath my feet as he scoops an arm under my knees lifting me up. He trails hot kisses down my neck even as we're moving through the small space.

My entire body is alight with need by the time we make it through the door into the bedroom and I don't even have time to look around the room as he carries me in.

Sophia

Bliss.

I'm not sure I've ever experienced such utter contentment as I lean into the solid warmth supporting my head. My lips curl up in a smile at the familiar fresh woodsy scent of the arm I'm resting on. The perfect memories of last night flood back to me in a rush of heat that has me turning my head to lean in for another kiss. Everything else comes rushing back like a freak rainstorm hitting to douse the fire. The gray light of dawn creeping through the window is a warning rather than a promise. I have to go. Before Logan wakes up. I won't get another chance at this.

My head feels like it weighs a thousand pounds as I lift it off his arm as carefully as I can. He mumbles something and turns toward me while I'm sliding away from him inch by agonizing inch.

I keep my wide eyes locked on him the entire time I'm slipping out from under the covers. I even reach out through the bond to make sure he's not stirring from his slumber. Disjointed thoughts and flashes of last night are cycling through his mind, heating my cheeks. Still asleep, definitely.

I slip into the soft heather gray yoga pants I wore to the cabin last night and get my first glimpse of the place. We didn't see much in the darkness last night, but the soft light of the morning shows off the pale yellow walls and patchwork quilt that covers the bed.

This is my favorite Logan. The soft vulnerability of sleep softens his hard edges out and his lashes lay inky on his golden skin. My heart wrenches as it's not even safe to lean in for the one final kiss I'm dying to plant on his forehead. I can't risk waking him, though.

I turn away, pulling on my shirt as I head out the door without looking back again. I feel like if I do, I won't be strong enough to leave. I'll stay here with him forever and I can't do that. Not to my family, friends. The other Witches and Mages. Despite what he said, I know Tobias is doing this all to get his hands on me. I'm the only one that can stop him before he hurts anyone else.

My hand closes on the hard edges of the car key I grabbed off the hook by the door. Sorry, Houston. I'm sure you can get your car back.

The air outside feels like it has even more bite on my already numb cheeks. I had to tuck my feelings down so deep that they wouldn't stop me from leaving, so the air matches my soul.

"I'm sorry." The words are a whisper in the air of the little cabin as I walk out. I have zero regrets about what happened last night. I knew it would be amazing with Logan. He was kind, considerate, but so full of passion. He was perfect. At least I have the memory to live off after I turn myself in. I know he'll be angry, but I hope it doesn't ruin his memory of the night. I hope he understands why I'm doing this. It's for his family and friends and the entire magic community.

The fresh coating of snow that fell overnight leaves the ground and the trees a wonderland of white. The kind I'd normally revel in, but today it feels cold, like me. I'm walking toward what may well be my doom and this beautiful fresh world has no part in it.

A different kind of heat has taken over my body now. That sick feeling you get before you throw up. I'm driving at a snail's pace down the long driveway without the headlights on to avoid notice. If anyone catches me leaving, they'll sound the alert and Logan or rather Liz will be on me faster than you can say Psych.

The thrumming of my heart eases the slightest bit as I reach the road. The beam from the headlights is now lighting up my path, showing me the way for my grim journey.

After that, the world speeds up as if it's been set to triple speed. Very few cars are out this early in the morning, so it's an easy drive even for someone like me driving a strange car and not super fond of driving. I'm pulling up to the gated entrance of the NAMC headquarters before I know it. That's when my heart kicks into overtime, and my head is spinning so fast I'm almost dizzy. I pull to the side of the road for one moment before I turn up to the gate, not knowing exactly what I'll find here. I need to pull myself together or I'm never going to get through this.

The last time I left his place, we were kind of in a hurry, bursting through the front gates in a shower of broken metal. Now I'm returning willingly to hand myself over to the occupants who have taken over here. The bad guys may have won, but it's only temporary. We're going to take this place back and make it better. No matter what, I have to sacrifice even if it's myself.

I have to force myself to ease off the brake and step on the gas to turn into the drive. The imposing black metal gates have been repaired and the guards' gate is sitting there the same as before.

I've never been this nervous pulling in here, even when I was leaving my home and my mom and everything behind to embark on my new life as a wanted Archimage. What a messed up few months it's been. There's been a lot of good too, though. All the fights and hurts, losses and pains, but out of it I got a whole new world. I got Logan and Liz, a second family, really. I steel myself before pulling up to the speaker. That's why I'm doing this. For them. I'd do anything for them. And Scott. I shudder at the thought of him getting yanked into the magic world against his will.

"Password?" The voice crackling through the speaker is unfamiliar. Figures. I don't imagine most of the Mages I've gotten to know would be a party to this madness, but I haven't met a fraction of the magical community. I'm sure I'll see some familiar and disappointing faces supporting Tobias and Lawrence.

"I'm here for Tobias. It's Sophia. Tennant. Sophia Tennant." He didn't give me a password to enter, but I'm sure he's warned them I might be coming.

"And you came alone?" The voice is raspy with suspicion.

"Yes."

"Open your trunk." I guess I could hide someone back there. Clearly, I'm not that stupid.

As per the request, I slide out of the black car and pop the trunk. A black clad guard emerges from the booth holding with a rather large gun pointed at me. This one doesn't look like a tranquilizer. Looks like they've upgraded their armory. See, I'm already learning important information to pass on.

I raise my hands by instinct until the guard has circled around the car to check out my trunk.

I don't recognize the person at the gate, but I send out a little magic feeler. My skills at identifying magic aren't amazing yet, but he feels human. Figures. Tobias has probably enlisted an entire army of mercenary humans with big guns to protect him. His Mage numbers might not be up to what he needs for protection. It seems risky though to have so many Mundanes close the heart of the magic community in the area. Surely they won't keep silent about what they see, no matter how well he's paying them.

A thought dawns. Maybe he doesn't care. Maybe he's planning on taking over the human world after he conquers the magic one. That would make sense. Power over the magic community is probably not enough to satisfy someone as grasping as him. The humans did nothing to him, though. I guess that makes it doubly important to make sure he never gets the chance. Once that cat is out of the bag, there's no going back. I know humans have persecuted Witches and Mages in the past and I'd hate to see a repeat of that. Mages might have access to powers that humans could never dream of, but they definitely win in the numbers department. Billions to our millions worldwide from what I've read. Not to mention they've got all kinds of advanced weapons now. Magic is great and all, but I don't know what it can do against an unseen sniper. My eyes slide to the upper windows of the main office building onsite. Are there snipers hidden up there?

A dark car catches my eye, pulling out to follow my slow progress up the drive. The trees lining the way are now fittingly barren of life, with the leaves long gone in the winter chill. The car follows me up the entire driveway until I reach the main building that houses the offices of the council members and staff. Where the Armstrongs used to work.

The magnificent ivy covered building looks different now, darker somehow. The villain effect. It's like there's something inside the building radiating evil. The shadows under the window seem deeper and the welcoming facade is forbidding. I'm pretty certain it's all in my head, though. The mind is a tricky thing, sensing patterns where there are none and instilling meaning into randomness.

I swing my legs out of the car, walking toward the imposing front doors. I act like I don't know about the two men who have gotten out of the car behind me, but I'm fully aware that they're following me. They're wearing all-black outfits with stern expressions and guns held in front of their chests at the ready in case I decide to make a break for it. I was the one who came here alone to turn myself in. What would be the point of running now? I don't bother to knock on the large front door that leads into the headquarters of the NAMC. I don't even use caution when I push the door open. My presence was requested, and here I am.

I forgot how big this place is with its huge sweeping ceilings making me feel insignificant like a tiny ant crashing a human picnic. The formal front desk is like some sort of hotel lobby mixed with a government building and fancy corporate office all in one. It's lacking the life it was the last time I was here. There were always people bustling and lounging around the vast lobby like space. To be fair, the sun has barely breached the sky, so I guess most people are still in bed. That drags me back to where I left Logan sleeping peacefully after our magical night together. Our first and maybe last.

This time it's just my uncle, Tobias. I eye him, searching for any trace of humanity left behind in his blank eyes. My heart aches for the boy he was, and the Mage he could have been, but that doesn't change anything. He's hurt and killed too many people to be deserving of my sympathy.

He's wearing a crisp navy blue suit with a subtle check pattern on it this time. Tan shoes polished to a high shine, and a neatly trimmed beard speckled with gray hairs complete the trendy executive look he's got going on. I'm not fooled by his appearance. A knife stabs through my heart at the memory of what he's truly capable of, but I shove the thoughts of Xavier down deep. They're the fuel that's going to help me destroy Tobias, but it won't help to become incapacitated by grief.

He holds out his arms to me in welcome, as if I'm going to run into them with a hug. "Sophia," he says with a smile. I guess he is happy to see me, although I'm definitely not flowing on the same wavelength. "I was worried you wouldn't come, and I'd have to cause you further pain."

"You don't have to do anything. Any pain you're causing me or anyone else is your choice. Don't forget that." I'm not letting him get away with blaming anyone else for what he's done.

The short laugh that bursts out of him has a bitter and rusty quality to it. I'm not at all surprised. I doubt that he's the type to goof off with his friends, if he even has any of those. "I like that sass niece of mine. Shame you won't come over to my side of your own will."

"Yeah, that's never going to happen. I'm not like you." I'm insulted he thinks that I could actually act the way he does, treat people the way he does. The dark thoughts running through my head at what I'd like to do to him might not show it, but I'm not a murderer.

"Enough of this chitter chatter. It's time to come with me. I've got something to show you."

I reluctantly trail after the unfamiliar halls. I didn't spend a lot of time in this building during my stay here. It's where the offices are and I didn't have much of a reason to spend time here.

The sweeping staircase looks more like a mountain to my tired eyes. Every footfall takes more effort as he takes me up toward the unknown. When we reach the top, it opens up into a long hallway lined with wooden doors. Brass plaques hang on the rich wood doors like in any other office building. The decor is a richer than your typical corporate bland style. Rich burgundy carpeting lines the floor, and detailed pictures line the walls. When I peer a little closer at one, it's a magical battle scene. Mages are facing off with fire magic, and giant vines snake around immobilizing foes. Very dramatic.

Not sure where we're heading, but we passed by the offices of both the Armstrongs next door to each other. I wonder if they have an interconnecting door, so they can visit each other during the day. That would be a nice way to spend time as a married couple. You wouldn't have to work together all the time, but you could visit throughout the day. Logan's parents seem like a bit of an odd match to me. Mrs. Armstrong is so warm and welcoming, and Mr. Armstrong comes across as stern and standoffish, but I know that deep down, he loves his family. He did everything he could to help us escape. He gave us all the tools we needed to break into this very compound to rescue a Witch he barely knows. That's how I know.

After we've passed through the quiet hallway, we get to a door that has no plaque on it. I'm still curious about where we're going. I thought he'd end up just taking me away to the prison area where I was before with the stark white rooms.

I don't even know if I was aware of what was going on at that time. I was so out of it. After losing Xavier, and destroying that building after Logan got taken away, I was numb and in shock when they locked me up. That's how I know what kind of people Laurence and these other Mages are. The kind of people that would lock up a traumatized girl after watching her friend die. That's my reason. That's why I have to keep pushing on, working to save my friends, save my family, save the rest of the magical community. I know the council wasn't perfect, but they never would have done something like that.

A wave of fear and panic rolls through me, buckling my knees and threatening to bring me to the ground. I whip my head around looking for the danger and I don't see anything. What's going on? What's happening? It hits me in a rush as I realize that everything is fine here. As fine as it can be under the circumstances. It's Logan. It's his pain and fear. He's woken up and realized that I left. My eyes drop closed, and I clutched my aching chest at the rage and sorrow he's feeling right now. That pain is all on me. I did that to him.

"What are you doing back there? Hurry up, we don't have all day."

The annoyed look on his face says it all. I force myself to keep moving. It's not your pain. You can keep doing this. I'm trying to convince myself, but I'm kind of doing a terrible job of it. The ache is as real as if it was my pain. That's how strong the bond has become. I'm not sure if it's the genuine feelings we've developed for each other, the connection we shared last night, or the way we were working together to combine our magic.

Whatever it is, though, his feelings are more intense and real than any I've felt before.

Tobias swings open a door and I look into a lush bedroom, as if this place is really a fancy hotel. I didn't know there were bedrooms in this part of the compound. I thought they were all in the dorm area. I guess when I think about it now, the dorm area is more for students and younger people. Maybe this is for visiting Mages or Mages who live off the compound, but need to stay over occasionally.

The elegant decor is the first thing that catches my eye until I spot something I never expected. Logan's terror is still coursing through me, trying to drag me to my knees when my shock joins it as my eyes land on Garrett sitting in an armchair in the corner. His eyes flick to mine, a shadow darkening the hazel to the color of the mossy undergrowth of a forest at twilight.

"Garrett! Are you Ok?" I rush over to him when a snide laugh from Tobias halts me in my tracks as awareness dawns on me.

Garrett's got one leg swung over the other in a casual posture. He's sitting there in this fancy room with no restraints, and his eyes dark with guilt. They have a clarity to them that tells me he's not under the influence of any kind of drugs. A flash of anger rips through me, following on the heels of sadness.

His eyes drop to his feet and he hunches in on himself. That, combined with his words, tells me everything. "I'm sorry."

Logan

I wake up to a feeling of contentment more pure than anything I've ever felt in my life. It's not like it was my first time like it was for Sophia, but for me, it was the best night of my life. Never knew it was possible to be so happy. And it's just not just the bond, although that's part of it. The connection we have and the love I feel for her are beyond intense. So as I drag my eyes open to face the day ahead, I reach out for her only for my arm to fall on emptiness. I was so looking forward to a morning together. Just the chance to hold her in my arms for a little longer before we have to face everyone else.

She must have gotten up early. I'm not surprised. She's a planner and we've got a busy few days ahead of us before we head to the compound. We're going to take down her uncle, Lawrence and everyone else that's squatting at HQ right now. Not to mention she probably didn't want to broadcast our activities from last night to this house full of everyone we know, including our parents. It was smart of her to sneak off early, not something I would have thought of doing. I don't really care who knows.

It's funny though because usually I'm the one up first. I get up and exercise, get ready for the day, but since I've been with her, I've been taking it a little more slowly, taking my time and enjoying moments.

I push myself into a sitting position, swinging my legs off the bed. My mouth stretches into a yawn as light filters in through the blinds. I don't panic until I walk into the other room and she's not there. I hope she's not upset. I hope she doesn't regret what we did. Nah, there's no way, and I'm not being my usual cocky self. I know it's true. I may not have been able to read her thoughts with that mile thick wall she's got built up, but I can still sense her feelings through the bond. I know she was every bit as happy last night as I was. Well, maybe not quite as much. I don't think that would be possible.

So where did she go off to so early in the morning? Library. I bet that's what she is. That's always where she is. Once this is all over, when the time is right, I'm gonna give her an entire room for her books. Heck, I'll give her bookshelves in every room if I get to keep her.

It's not until I'm about to walk out the front door that I pause when I spot a post it note stuck to the front door. Covered in Sophie's neat handwriting. I pull it off the wall and the innocent-looking thing shatters me.

I'm sorry, Logan. I had to go. This is best for everybody. Don't try to come after me. I've got this. Last night was amazing. You are amazing. I love you so much. Sophia.

The shock freezes me momentarily, as if my legs don't quite believe what my mind is telling them. When I recover, I'm tearing out the front door, following her footsteps through the snow until I get to a spot in the driveway where a car obviously pulled away. She took one of Houston's cars. She's gone. She's really gone. There's no way I'm going to catch up to her. Judging by the look of her footsteps, the light snow that's been falling, she's been gone for a while. How did I not notice? I should have realized that she left me. I should have known, right?

I rush through the door of the main house, slamming the door with a force that leaves the frame rattling behind me with. I don't care if it wakes up everyone in this house. I hope it wakes them all up. I don't know who to go to first, my dad, Houston, Trey.

My feet decide for me, taking me down the stairs three at a time. Liz. My sister is the one I go for first. As strong as the urge to protect her is, it's eclipsed by the need to get Sophia back, and I know Liz is the least likely to oppose my plan.

I stop myself before barging in. She's not alone in there after all. "Liz!," I call out even as my fist slams into the door. It's not Liz that opens the door, though it's Ivy. Her inky hair looks like it's already been brushed smooth and her eyes are bright and alert. She's always been an early riser, just like me. In theory, we should have worked out we're so similar. It's Sophia for me, though I think it always has been even before I knew her. I know she doesn't believe in fate, but I can't help thinking that we were always meant to be together. The protection bond that was put in place when we were mere children just solidified that fate.

"What's the matter, Logan?" Her legs are slightly spread in an alert stance and the light from the hallway glints off a dagger clutched in her right hand.

"I need to talk to Liz." It's not a stretch to peer over Ivy's shoulders to see if I can catch sight of my sister. Of course, she's still in bed. I have no idea what time it is, but the gray light outside let me know it was still early.

"What's the matter?" she repeats her words, and places a small hand over mine that's gripping the door so tightly I'm going to leave indents in the wood. Her touch should be a comfort, but I can't get myself to loosen my hold on the door even to ease the ache straining my knuckles with the tight grip.

"Sophia. She's gone." I can't keep the tremble out of my voice, and I'm sure my eyes are wild with panic. It's not like me to let myself get out of control, but everything about Sophia makes me lose my cool. I never knew love could make you like this. Although that's probably why I avoided it for all those years. Or maybe I was just waiting, waiting for her, because despite the constant fear she's caused me, I wouldn't change our relationship for anything.

Ivy's dark eyes immediately go wide with fear. "She's gone? Zeus took her? We have to go now." She looks over her shoulder. "Liz, Charlotte get up!"

Liz just turns over in bed, yanking a pillow over her messy head. I don't know how she's still capable of this after the training we got as kids. Our father wasn't afraid to wake us in the middle of the night now and again to train. He used to say he had to make sure we could be ready in any emergency. I always thought he was full of it. The Mage community has been relatively peaceful for years, but maybe he was getting us ready for this. He did always know about Sophia's powers. Maybe he always knew it would come to this, and I'm pretty grateful I'm capable of waking up alert and ready to go. Somehow, Liz seems to have avoided absorbing that lesson. Charlotte rises, blinking the sleep in her eyes away. At least someone gets the seriousness of the situation. "What's happening?"

I let Ivy know my intent with a new look in my eyes before I push through the door, heading over to my sister and yanking the pillow off of her head. I can't even keep the growl out of my voice. I know it's not her fault, but doesn't she understand how urgent this is? "Liz, you need to get up." I shake her slim shoulders a little harder than necessary. "Sophia is gone."

"Whaaa…" Finally, my sister blinks up at me, sleepy eyes adjusting to the light.

"Sophia left. I think she's gone off to do something stupid and brave. I think she turned herself over to Zeus."

Those are the words that finally jolt my sister into action. She pops out of bed in a flash. "She's gone? How do you know she hasn't been taken.?"

I tear my fingers through my hair. "She left a note. On a freaking pink Postit. She just left." I grab my sister's hand, dragging her all the way up. "We gotta go. Now."

"Hold up. Wait one second. We can't go rushing off like this."

I didn't even hear Ivy sneak up behind me, but the calm reassurance of her hand on my shoulder alerts me to her presence. "She's right. We have to tell your father. And Sophie's mom. It's bad enough that she's gone. What would happen if we all just left?"

I look at them in surprise. "We'd get her back. That's what would happen. There's no other option. Hurry up. Don't you understand? Time is of the essence."

"She's right, Logan. You can't just go rushing off like this. We have to make a plan." Charlotte's sleep husky voice has joined in now and I realize all three girls are against me.

I turn to leave. I'll go myself if I have to. "Well, I'm going. You guys can stay here if you want, but I don't think you understand the urgency. If she's turned herself over to put Tobias, who knows what his plans for her are?" I rub my chest… "She's not…" I can't even say the word. If she died, it would destroy me. "She's still alive. I can tell, but who knows how long that will last if we just leave her there. I thought you guys cared. That's why I came to you first. I knew the parents would try to stop me, but you're her friends, too. I thought you'd help."

Liz zips around me and she's blocking the doorway by the time I storm over to it. I'm already halfway out the front door in my mind. "I'm not gonna let you leave like this. I know you think it's your job to protect me, but I'm your sister. It's just as much my job to protect you as it is for you to protect me. This isn't what Sophia would want. You running off going to get yourself killed? She must have a plan."

Something nudges at my brain. Does she have a plan? Is she planning on taking down Tobias all on her own? I wouldn't put it past her, but she can't seriously think she's capable of taking him down all on her own. She's smarter than that. Smart, but also caring. She cares deeply for the ones she loves and she'd do anything to protect them.

"She shouldn't have run off then. She knew what I do. Of course I'm going to come for her. I'm always going to come for her. Haven't I always? Even before I knew her. Even before I fell in love with her. Even before we… " I let those words die in the air. Probably not the best idea to let them know what we did last night. I might not care, but it's her secret as much as it is mine, and she'll tell everyone when she's good and ready.

"I'm not saying we won't come with you. We need to do this right. We need to talk to the adults. We need to plan this. Then we can go in there with all of our vengeance, and I'll be happy to do it. Because how dare he take someone like that from us?"

My sister is definitely not usually the logical one out of our pair. She's impulsive. She'll go running off half cocked into doing anything. So the fact that she's the one who's cautioning me. That gives me pause. Dragging a deep breath, I say, "OK. Let's do this."

Liz eyes me with suspicion for another moment before moving aside to let me pass. The thought of telling my father that I've lost Sophia again, and the look of devastation I know is going to be all over her mom's face, is daunting, but at least I've got my team backing me up.

Sophia

Black-clad guards lurking in the shadows mar the peace and beauty of the snow-covered terrain outside my window. They're on top of roofs, behind trees, and guarding the entrances to all the buildings. The place has become more of a prison than a training headquarters. On the way in, I was so focused on my destination, I didn't notice how many of them patrolled the grounds. I spent the drive clutching the steering wheel with white knuckles, hoping that Logan wasn't immediately chasing after me in a rage.

I scan the area, running through everything Trey and the others have taught me about strategy. After Tobias threw Garrett's betrayal in my face, I kind of thought he'd lock me up in a cell. Instead, he's left me in this beautiful room with no lock on the door, as if I'm an honored guest. Is he underestimating me so badly? Does he think I won't do whatever it takes to stop him? No, I know better than that. He must have eyes on me. The thought has my eyes darting to all corners of the room. There could be cameras anywhere. The alarm clock on the bedside table, hidden in a picture on the wall, or the black and white patterned vase on the mahogany dresser.

This room offers the illusion of safety. But that's all it is. An illusion like one of Charlotte's fantastic creations. The best thing I can do right now is a poke around the building. It's always been the heart of operations for the NAMC. I bet that's one thing that hasn't changed too much. I pad across the plush carpet to the fancy wooden door and ease it open, peering out. There is a guard outside the door, but just one. Pretty sure he's human too, by the feel of him.

"Excuse me," I say, dropping my voice to a decibel barely above a whisper. I even add a little tremble at the end of the sentence.

"You're not allowed out of there." There's trepidation in his eyes, and if I'm being honest with myself, I kind of like it.

"Oh, I'm so sorry. I was just kind of hungry and I didn't know I wasn't allowed to leave." I play up the innocent young girl image as best I can to ease his fears. See if maybe I can trick him into misjudging me. Someone has warned him I'm dangerous, but it shouldn't be hard to make him doubt that fact.

He lifts his gun just a little with a slight twitch that makes me uneasy. I take a step back and pretend to trip in the doorway. Not that hard, given I've never been the most coordinated of individuals.

His reflexes kick in and he reaches out to catch me. It's freeing to grab hold of the energy flowing through my body, sending it down my arm as easily as if I've been harnessing it my whole life. I have a split second to decide what to do with it and settle for giving him just the tiniest zap. Not enough to cause him any serious damage. Just enough to incapacitate him for a little while. I wince at the thud of his large body hitting the floor. The thick carpeting dulls the sound a little, but the noise could still raise some alarms. When no one appears, I step carefully over his prone body and sneak down the hallway.

I eye the room where I saw Garrett was, pausing for a moment. I can't believe he did that to us. We've been through so much together between rescuing each other, working on spells, training. Something is off about the whole thing. If I look back, I can pinpoint the moment he disconnected with me. When we were in the Nether and he lost his family tracking crystal. That's when I lost him. He may have been there in body for the rest of the journey. He may have fought beside us and stolen a freaking car for us, but he was never really with us after that.

We haven't really known each other that long, but that time has been so intense it's created what I thought was a close connection. Logan never thought I could trust him, but I always pinned that on his jealousy. Maybe there was more to it. Maybe I never should have trusted Garrett. The pain of betrayal goes deep, leaving a hollow anger inside of me, but I don't have time to worry about my false friends or their betrayals right now. I need to gather as much information as I can to take down Tobias. There's no way he's going to make it this easy for me.

I can't believe he's going to let me freely roam his territory. He wouldn't have left a guard at the door if he was ok with that. He's going to stop me eventually, but anything I learn could be useful. The original plan to invade HQ and take it back will stand, and any information I can pass on will be useful for the coming battle.

Tobias isn't going to stop just because I turned myself over. I know that. But this is the best chance I can give myself and everyone else. There's a real possibility he might completely abandon this battle now that he has me. I'm sure Lawrence Kingston would take up the helm to maintain control of the NAMC. I think my uncle has been the one pulling the strings through this entire endeavor. Without him, we might stand a better chance of a faster victory.

His greatest desire seems to be to take my powers. If I knew that would be the end of it, I'd hand them over. I'd give up anything to ensure the safety of my friends and family. I never asked for these powers or to be part of this world. Now that I'm a part of it, the thought of that piece of myself being ripped out has my stomach churning, but I'd do it to keep my loved one's safe. But I don't think it's that simple. I don't think my powers alone will satisfy him.

I'm stuck staring at the door to Garrett's room. I shouldn't even bother talking to him. He's not worth my time. I tell myself, but I can't make myself move forward. I need to know. Why he betrayed us. What he was thinking. He's in the room right next-door to where my uncle left me. I don't know if that was on purpose or a coincidence.

Is he even still here? Who knows, but it's worth a try. I don't bother knocking. He doesn't deserve that. I'm a little surprised when the smooth handle turns easily, leaving me wondering if he was hoping I would visit. Maybe that's wishful thinking.

He hasn't moved from the chair where I saw him last, but now a sweep of his sandy hair spills over the tight fists propping up his bowed head. He doesn't look up when I enter. Not sure he's so lost in his own thoughts that he doesn't hear me or if I'm not even worth his time anymore.

"Why?" I can't find any more words than that single question.

His head slowly rises from his hands, hazel eyes brimming with something… I want to believe it's guilt, but if he felt guilty, he wouldn't have betrayed us like this at all. "Sofia, you shouldn't be here."

"Well, I am here, so can you just tell me why? Why'd you come here? What were you thinking?" I rub at the ache of pain lodged near my heart.

He reaches a trembling hand to slide under his shirt collar as if reaching for his crystal. When he comes up empty, his hand slides to his neck, massaging his throat. "It's not personal, Sophia. This isn't about you. I just saw my chance, and I took it."

"Your chance for what? You chance to betray us all? Your chance to lose all the friends you have in this world? I don't get it. I just don't understand why you would do that. I thought…I thought we were friends." I know the words sound pathetic, but I just can't wrap my head around why he'd do this to us.

His face twists with a bitterness I can't reach. "Of course you don't understand. You never understood. I know you think we have something in common because you lost your father. But I lost my entire family. The only thing I had left in this world was that crystal, and now that's gone too, thanks to you. So I guess what I'm saying is maybe it is personal."

His words send me rocking back on my heels like a physical blow. "You're right. I'm sorry. I never meant for any of this stuff to happen. I never wanted to hurt anybody. I know that doesn't make it any better, but I am sorry. I'll get out of here. You never need to see me again."

With those words, I stumble backwards, wincing as my hip slams into the door. I reach back and fumble with the handle, trying to get myself out of there as fast as I can.

I'm sorry. The words sound foreign in my head, like they don't belong to me, so I shove them away.

The hard lines of his face soften for a moment as he holds up his hand before pulling it back, shaking his head. I turn and run from the room, stumbling down the hall. I'm not sure where I'm going and even if I did, the haze of hot tears is blinding.

I don't know how long I stand there leaning against the wall trying to pull myself together before I pull myself back together. There's no time for tears. My life is in danger. Other people's lives are in danger. Garrett made his choice, and even if I'm responsible for his pain, there's nothing I can do about it now.

The hallway comes back into focus as I push off the wall. What's my next move? I need to see what's going on here. I need to figure out what Tobias is up to and how many minions he's got working for him. Information is my specialty, after all. Although I never thought I'd be using my skills to research battle strategy, it's a transferable skill.

I've learned that Mages are much more high-tech than I would have initially expected. They love their magic, but it's a finite resource, so they've learned to rely on modern conveniences to supplement their powers. I know they'll have a video surveillance room in here somewhere. That'll be my best bet for finding out the details of this place.

My biggest advantage right now is how early it is. Nobody seems to be out and about yet. But that won't last long. We're nearing the start of the business day and I'm sure there will be many people, both mundane and magical, buzzing about. I need to explore this place while I still can.

I keep to the edges of the wall, slipping along as quiet as I'm able. I'm straining my regular human senses. I'm worried I'll set off a giant beacon of Archimage magic if I use my magic, not to mention I don't want to waste my power. I'm sure I'll be needing it soon. But I might be able to infuse just a hint of magic into my hearing. Not enough to catch notice, just enough to get me through here safely. Problem is, I don't know how to use super hearing if I even have it. We've been so focused on my elemental powers and psychic blocking that I haven't been able to test out my potentially heightened senses.

It's just another phys power like any other though, right? How do I make that work? When I try to activate the extra speed, I send the magic into my leg muscles, so it stands to reason that if I send it into my ears, I'll be able to hear better. I focus on the magic coursing through my veins, grasping the thinnest strand of it and dragging it up through my body to my ears. By some miracle, it seems to work. I hear footsteps and spin around, expecting to see someone right behind me. But there's nobody there. They must still be a safe distance. This might be helpful as long as I don't get overwhelmed and I can actually figure out where the noises are coming from.

As expected, there's another stairway at the end of the long hall. It's a little less ornate than the grand main staircase. An industrial beige carpet and basic wooden banister greet me. I reach out with my senses, listening as hard as I can. There's a continuous buzzing sound in my ears that's overwhelming my senses. I scan the area, searching for the source of the noise, and my eyes land on the fluorescent lights flickering from the ceiling. No way. I can't be hearing those lights, can I? The ceilings are probably ten feet, and I definitely never noticed that sound until now.

It's not like I have time to investigate, so I walk down the stairway, trying to filter out the distracting noises. My heart is pumping so hard in my chest, it wouldn't surprise me if any Phys Mages on guard can hear it.

After what feels like about a century, I make it to the end, peering through the small window into the hall. This hall is as devoid of people as the others. Why is there nobody around? The hair on the back of my neck prickles with unease.

I ignore the alarm ringing in the back of my head and keep pushing forward. This place is an endless row of halls that lead to nowhere interesting. More offices, meeting rooms, a small kitchen. I duck out of there before the two people waiting for coffee to finish brewing spot me. I'm sad to leave behind the tempting smell of the roasted beans, but I keep going. I don't think I'd be welcome to stop by for a coffee break.

After a few more near misses and way too many rooms, I hit the jackpot. This room has a small silver plaque labeled Security. I'm sure there are security staff on duty, but if I can get even a quick glimpse, it should help.

I push through the door, poking myself through the narrow opening little by little. There's only one man in here and his back is to me. Perfect. I make it all the way through and try to hold the door so it doesn't alert him to my presence. Magic tingles in the air and a force slams it shut on me.

The voice causes my heart to sink to my toes. "Niece. Welcome. I've been expecting you." Tobias spins around in the large black leather chair, pulling off the black baseball cap that was covering his head.

"This isn't the kitchen?"

He laughs. "We both know you weren't looking for the kitchen. Would you like to come see what I've got going on here? I'm happy to show you."

Of course, he was expecting me. I knew something was wrong when no one tried to stop me. But he's here alone. Why can't I take him out quietly and be done with all this now? I nod and step forward to look at the array of screens. I recognize the dorms and the training center from my brief stay here, but the sight knocks the air out of me. There are so many soldiers. Hundreds, probably. He's really been hard at work, amassing an army. My hands grow cold. There are so many of them compared to our numbers. My friends are going to get destroyed.

"You look a little pale. Is something wrong?" He kicks a foot up on the wide control panel.

"No. Everything is fine." Anger and desperation spur me on and I focus on the energy that's simmering beneath the surface of my skin. It's always there now, waiting for me to take action.

He must notice the magic building in the air. It's so thick I think a mundane would notice, but he makes no move to stop me.

"You might want to reconsider that. If I die, your brother does too."

I douse the magic I was about to let loose. It's reluctant to respond, so I yank it back. "Scott? Where is he? You said if I came willingly, you'd leave him alone." My heart is racing out of control again and my entire body has gone hot. I should have known better to trust him.

"Oh, don't worry. He's safe." The *for now* is implied in his tone, as he points to one of the small screens clicking a couple of buttons. The picture is grainy, but it's clear enough for me to see the familiar face of my brother. He's sitting on a metal framed cot in a room I recognize from my brief stay in the prison building. His shoulders are sagging, but he's glaring at the door.

"Don't hurt him." I beg.

"Oh, I won't. I'm confident I have your cooperation now, so I won't need to. Stay in your room, behave, and he'll live. Try to escape or hurt me and his death will be on your hands."

That's it. He's got me. There's no way I'll try anything when he's dangling my brother's life over my head and the smile on his face tells me he knows.

Logan

The house is in chaos. There are Mages scattered about on every available surface of the kitchen, the living room, spilling out into the hall. Some of us are still in our pajamas and some have rushed over to Houston's for the emergency meeting. Our primary group is in the kitchen. All my family, our closest friends, Houston, and of course Sophia's mom, who is completely beside herself. It's hard to breathe past the tight lump in my chest. I promised I wouldn't let her daughter get hurt and I've let her down just like I let Sophia down. I should have guessed that she'd try to play the hero. I knew deep down she was hiding something from me. I should have tried harder to crumble the psychic wall I helped her build.

"We don't have a choice. We have to go in today. I know not everyone is here yet. I know we're not quite ready, but he's got Sophia. He could kill her before we get there. I know what he's capable of." A shiver runs through me at the memories from the Nether I've been keeping locked away. I was in his clutches for too long. The things he did to me... I don't ever want to relive the experience, but I wouldn't hesitate to trade myself for her life. That's not an option, though. He never cared about me other than as a tool to get to her. He covets her power and now she's walked right to him. Why? Why would she do that to me?

I'm weaving around everyone in the kitchen with every scenario of what he could do to her running through my head. Each one is worse than the one before. Spiraling into an increasingly dark space. At least I haven't felt anything through the bond other than a jolt of shock and sadness shortly after I found out she was gone. I don't know what that was about, but it doesn't feel like she's in any intense pain or suffering. Yet. Which means we're on a limited time budget to get to her before he does anything permanent. As foolish as it would have been to rush in, I regret letting Liz talk me into waiting.

"We can't go in today. We have more forces arriving. We have a plan. A good one. You need to calm down and think this through, son. You're letting your emotions control you." My father's voice is gentler than usual. It's more of a plea than a command.

"I don't care. She needs me. She needs us. This is my job, after all. You've been reminding me of that fact since I came home."

Houston steps up to my dad. "We can make a minor adjustment to the timeline. I think we can be ready to go in tomorrow if we contact everyone that's planning on coming with us. We might be short a few, but we can do it with those numbers. Tobias doesn't appear to have a significant amount of support from the magical community. From what we've seen, he likely has mundanes filling out his ranks, but we can handle them."

I appreciate Houston backing me up, but tomorrow is still agonizingly far away.

· ⋆ ★ ★ ★ ★ ★ ★ ⋆ · ·

I've been tearing my hair out all day. I wonder if Sophia will still love me if I show up bald.

We have spent too much of the day making phone calls, trying to get in contact with all the Mages and Witches who have signed on to help us break into the compound.

We've got multiple groups going in from multiple points of entrance. Lawrence and his crowd on the inside know the facilities as well as my parents do, so he has the advantage there, but this is the only shot we have. We need to take back the council and reinstate our rules before it's too late. If there's a widespread leak about the existence of magic to the mundanes, we might not be able to shove that knowledge back under a rock.

Would it be so bad if they found out about us? It's hard to say, but I have seen what horrors mundanes are capable of inflicting on each other. Especially those that they consider different. I have serious doubts that they'd embrace us Mages and Witches if the truth gets out. We're different enough they could classify us as a different species altogether. Not to mention they have a history of persecuting magic users.

Someone finally picks up the line I'm currently calling. I don't even remember who it is.

"Hello?"

"Hi, uhhhh.." I have to check the list in front of me to see who I checked off last. Sophia would be proud of my

organizational skills. *"Damian. How's it going? It's Logan Armstrong."*

"Good, what's up? Are we still good to go in on Friday?"

"Listen, we're planning on upping the timeline. We'll be going in tomorrow. Are you able to make it here in time? We've had to step it up due to the urgency of the situation."

No way I'm telling a bunch of random Mages that Sophia's gone. Most of them know about her Archimage status by now. That secret ripped through the community like a wildfire once a few people found out.

"I'm not sure if I'll be able to get down there on time, man."

"Damian. Come on. I don't think you understand the importance of this. We're going to need you. The entire magical community is depending on you. Lives are depending on you." My voice is ramping up to a hysterical level that I can't keep under control and my hand is shaking. Man, I'm losing it.

"I'll do my best. No promises, though. I'll get out as soon as I can. If I don't make it tomorrow, I'll see if I can help with anything after."

"Thanks." The word comes out sharp and sarcastic and I'm so frustrated at this point I pull my trembling hand back to hurl the damn phone across the room, but before I can launch it, a small hand closes on my biceps.

"Don't do it, brother."

I ease up my death grip on the poor cell phone before I grind it into a useless heap of metal, turning to find Liz behind me. I can't bear the sympathy on her face.

"Liz. This is killing me."

"I know, but you've got to be a little more patient. I'd loan you some of mine, but we all know that's not exactly my strong suit." True enough. "What exactly was Dad thinking, trusting you to make the phone calls?"

"I don't know. Temporary insanity. Maybe it was one of his tests."

Her eyes soften. "I don't think he's doing that. He's put a lot of trust in you on this mission. How about I help you finish up this list and then we go for a run? I feel like you need to burn off some of that tension."

"A run, with you?" My brow pulls up as I eye my sister. I could never even dream of keeping up with her super speed unless I was sharing with Sophia.

She laughs. "Don't worry. I'll go at your normal old boring speed for once. Now come on. Let's get these calls over with, and no more phone throwing. You're on your own if you destroy that thing."

Sophia

A heavy fog prevents me from pulling out of the restless sleep I've been trapped in. Wait, when did I fall asleep? The cold, rough surface pressed against my back has violent shivers ripping through my body. An oppressively sweet and smoky smell makes it hard to breathe. Where am I? I struggle to pull out of the haze that's slowing my brain down when I hear a laugh to my right.

Tobias. That's definitely his evil sneer. I struggle to drag my heavy eyelids open and sit up. Stiff leather cuffs cut into my wrists, thwarting my efforts. The realization that I'm tied down has me struggling to escape like a wild horse with a rope around its neck. My movements are frantic and my eyes flip wide open, but I don't see much at first.

The room is dark, with flickering candlelight casting weird shadows around me. When I adjust to the dim lighting and shake the last of the fog off, I spot my uncle off to my right. He's wearing a long dark robe like some sort of evil wizard in a movie. Dramatic much?

"What's going on?" My face comes out in a rasp.

"Ah, niece. Nice of you to wake up. We're about to start the ceremony." Extra fabric falls in a pool from his arms as he spreads them out to his sides, drawing my eyes to the ring of similarly dressed people around the perimeter of the room.

"What ceremony?" I ask, struggling once more against my bonds. I reach out for Logan and just find the constant chaos and worry that's swamped him since I left.

"The one where you hand over that magic to me. I've been waiting for this day for a long time."

Hand over my magic? I guess this shouldn't surprise me, but that doesn't stop my heart from sinking to my toes. Obviously that's why he wanted me, but I never imagined it would require all of this ceremony. The haze that was fogging me catches up. "Wait, did you drug me?"

"I'm sorry about that. It was necessary. Couldn't risk you trying to take off and save your brother and make your escape. I would have caught you, but it wasn't worth the hassle."

"I would have come willingly."

"I couldn't take the risk. I'm sure you understand."

I continue to struggle against the unforgiving leather pinning down my wrists and ankles, ignoring the burning sensation as the rough stone chafes my bare skin. Seriously. I'm lying on an actual stone table in the middle of a room that looks like something druids would have used to perform ritual sacrifices. Is this going to kill me? Is this it? Was that his plan all along?

Adrenaline shoots through me at the thought and my Phys powers course through my body in an uncontrollable burst. I rip my arms up from the table, tearing through the thick leather. My wrists are on fire as I reach down to tackle the thick cuffs around my ankles. They prove to be more of a problem, but I keep at it until I'm free, shaking out my numb limbs until the feeling returns in a painful prickling sensation.

"See what I mean? I couldn't trust you'd come willingly."

The hard stone floor jars my legs as I hop down. "Are you planning on killing me? Your own flesh and blood?" His hood is casting his face in eerie shadows as I stare him down. "And the rest of you?" I turn to look at the array of hooded figures circling the perimeter of the room. "You're all ok with this? The blood that's going to be on your hands."

"Relax, niece. The spell shouldn't kill you. It'll be worse the harder you fight it, but you should survive."

I snort. "How reassuring." I reach out an arm as I approach him, electricity coursing down my arm. The current shoots out in a blue flash, bouncing back at me. My instincts have me ducking out of the way.

"Circle. Sorry about that. Should have warned you." The twisted sneer on his lips says otherwise.

I didn't notice the chalk circle trapping me in its midst. No wonder he didn't seem overly concerned about my escape from the bonds. Now that I'm paying attention, I can feel the buzz of magic coming from it. It's overwhelming actually. I don't have an excuse for not noticing it before, other than I don't know. Drugged, tied down, etc., etc.

"Now that you're awake, it's time to get started. Everyone." He raises his hand in a gesture reminiscent of the orchestra's maestro and the room erupts into a creepy rhythmic chant. Now I really feel like I'm trapped in some monk's horrific ritual, which I guess I am. It's just that the monk is an evil Mage that I have the misfortune of being related to.

I can't decipher the words they're chanting. It's definitely not English.

Soon the shivers I was experiencing while tied to the table turn to sweat beads forming on my forehead. The temperature in the room is rising at a rapid rate as the candles edged around the chalk circle flicker and flare up higher. The heat in my body rises hotter and hotter until I'm gasping to catch my breath.

My core twists and turns with the chants and I can feel my magic moving through my body through no effort of my own. My magic has done some wild things and forced itself out of me on occasion, but this feels different, like it's being forced through my veins. It's painful, not like the magical dance when Logan's magic and mine mingle through the bond.

The pain intensifies, and the chanting gets louder. "Stop!" I can't help the weak cry that escapes my lips, but of course, no one pays me any attention.

My powers continue to build and rise, swelling inside me like a tsunami on the verge of breaking. Sparks are flying off my hands and wind whips my hair around my face. There's an inferno raging inside, burning me from the inside. I pull at the strands of my magic. I came here willingly. I offered to sacrifice myself to keep my brother safe, but it feels like my soul is being ripped out through my skin as my body rejects the theft. I pull on the threads in a vain attempt to do what? I don't know. Anything to ease the pain.

My trembling hands clutch at my temples, trying to tamp down the noise. There's a roaring buzz drowning out everything else, including the incessant chants. Sweat is pouring down my forehead in a river and my knees are trembling beneath me.

I struggle to stay standing, fighting the desire to collapse every second of the way. I won't fall to my knees for this man. He doesn't deserve to see me there.

I can almost see my magic swirling in the air as it's torn from my body in one final jerk that whips my head back as my back arches under the onslaught. With that final terrible wrench, it's gone. A dull, hollow ache replaces the torment as my powers travel toward my uncle, who has stepped through the magic barrier that separated us. I guess even my magic couldn't have passed through that barrier.

He throws his head back and his arms high, stumbling back as I my powers enter him. Regaining his stance, he flips his palm up toward the ceiling and I see the spark of a flame flicker to life, growing until a ball of fire sits on his palm. He cackles in his dark triumph.

I force myself forward on trembling legs, moving toward him. "This isn't over." A whisper is all I can get out as I stare at him in eyes that are eerily similar to my own. How can a person do something this terrible to another human? Someone related to them, no less.

"Oh, but it is niece. There's no turning back."

He turns his back to me as he steps toward the circle and I make one last effort to take him down, lunging at the man, and slamming him in the back. He spins around with malice in his eyes. "I'd say I'm sorry, but that would be a lie."

He touches my arm, causing a jolt of electricity to shoot up my body. My heart falters and my body convulses as I collapse to the floor into darkness.

Logan

An urgent shaking rips me awake, and I'm instantly alert. My eyes fly open to find Ivy staring at me. Worry creases her familiar face.

"We have to go. Now. Come on, Logan."

"What are you talking about? What's happening? Is it Sophia?" My feet are on the floor and I'm snatching clothes up, shoving on dirty socks and a t-shirt that I carelessly discarded last night.

"Yes. She's in trouble. Grab Trey, we're heading out now. Liz is waiting by the front door."

I don't ask any further questions. I know I can trust Ivy and she can fill us in on the car ride about what's going down.

I glance at Trey, considering for only a moment, before I shake him awake. Not too long ago, I might have hesitated to bring him along, thinking he'd tell Dad rather than blindly joining us on a half-cocked adventure. I know different now. He's loyal to us. He's loyal to me. He always has been. There was a time when I was too stupid to recognize it, but I'm long over that.

"What." His voice is a little loud as he startles awake, just as alert as I was. Years of training will do that to you.

"Keep your voice down. Get up and dressed. Get your weapons and we're out of here."

He pushes up off his bed, grabbing his neatly folded clothes off the small dresser slipping into them with ease.

I grab any weapons I can get my hands on, and we trip through the house quietly.

The agonizing drive down the long driveway has me drumming my fingers impatiently on the side of the car door. Liz shoots me an annoyed look, but she gets it.

Trey took the wheel. Probably for the best. I don't think I could have contained the rage and anxiety that's fighting for dominance in my brain. Not a great combination behind the wheel. See, I'm learning my limits.

"Ivy, tell me the details. You know I trust you, but where'd you get this top secret information that has us racing out of here? Well, crawling. Especially at this time of night?"

My eyes narrow when she pauses for a little too long. "I got some inside information from someone in there who is on our side."

"Really?" Ivy has been out of the country and out of touch with most of the Mages around here for years, given they thought she was dead and all. "Who's that?"

Her eyes dart away from mine as we hit the end of the driveway, and Trey can finally pick up some speed. "I promised I wouldn't tell, but believe me, it's a trustworthy source."

"Ok." I'm dying to pry further, but the closed off look in her eyes tells me she's not going to spill. Secrets are definitely something that Ivy has always been good at.

The light from streetlamps blinking in and out in a steady rhythm signals the passage of time. Not fast enough. "What's the plan? I'm sure we're not going to surprise them, and with only four of us, I'm not sure exactly how we're going to pull this off."

"My friend is going to clear the entrance and exit to the tunnels. We'll have to go in through the prison."

"Perfect, well at least I've got that down. Been there, done that," Liz says with a yawn.

"What about the alarms and other tech? Not to mention magic. After the last break in, they have to be expecting that we'll be coming, and beefed that up."

"It's fine. We've got it covered from the inside," Ivy says in a small voice.

I study her face as she avoids making eye contact, chewing on her lower lip. Alarms are ringing in my head. Even after all this time, I think I can tell when she's hiding something from me. Who is this inside source of hers and why won't she share their name? What kind of power do they wield in there, and how are they going to disable all those systems for us?

"We have one task in there before we get Sophia."

"What's that?" I'm not looking to delay this anymore than I have to. The longer he's got her, the more time he has to do the unthinkable.

"Tobias has captured Sophia's brother Scott. He's got him imprisoned there."

"You've got to be freaking kidding me!" There's no way Sophia will leave with us unless we get her brother out of danger. Fantastic.

"Yeah."

Trey pulls over to the side of the road, pulling far enough in the woods to provide the car with some concealing cover.

"We're here. This will get us to the outside entrance of the tunnels. Liz, wanna lead the way?"

"Happily," she says, practically bouncing out of the car. Impossible odds are no deterrent for my sister.

"Wait a minute." I grab her arm to stop her from taking off like the human rocket she is.

"I'm gonna call Dad and let him know where we are and what's going on. He can rally as many troops as possible to join us."

The light from the moon reflects in my sister's wide eyes. "You're calling Dad?"

"Yes. What we're doing is crazy. I know that, and I'm not willing to wait. That said, now that we're here and he can't stop us, I'm going to let him know we're here and he can bring the full force of our troops. At least as much force as he can get on the spot."

She pats me on the back with an incredulous look on her face. "That's very mature of you, brother."

"I know, right? Look at me being all responsible and what not." I give her a smirk.

"Not that responsible." Trey gives me a look. "This is, in fact, an insane thing to do."

"And yet you're here with us. You're one of us now, Trey. Irresponsible and impulsive. Deal with it." I clap him on the back.

"Sure. Be proud of the terrible influence you've had on me."

"Oh, I am. Now hold up a minute." I hold my finger in the air as the borrowed phone rings a few times.

"Who's this?"

"It's your son."

"Where are you? What's going on?"

"I don't have a lot of time. Sophia is in imminent danger. Ivy had a tip. We're all here ready to go in and get her out, but I wanted to let you know, so you can send back up."

"Have you lost your mind?" I pull the phone away from my ear, wincing at the roar that comes out of him. "Who did you take with you?"

"Ivy, Charlotte, Trey, Liz, and I. You're not going to stop us, but I wanted to let you know."

"So I can come in and scrape your dead bodies off the floor?" There's a tremble to his voice.

"So much faith. Look, we couldn't wait, and I knew you'd try to stop us. You're the one who bonded me to her. You put me in charge of her protection. I have to be here. I have to rescue her, but I respect you and I know you'll back us up. We're going. See you soon."

I click the phone off before he can protest further, nodding at my friends. "Let's do this."

The loudest sound in the snow-muffled forest is the crunches our booted feet make as we weave around the trees. Liz's black crocheted beanie has cat ears that wobble back and forth looking ridiculous when compared to her graceful movements. I'm glad she knows where she's going, because everything looks the same, all barren trees and snow-covered ground. The fresh, evergreen scented air is cleansing. I'm so thankful to be free and away from the sulfuric scent that pervaded everything in the Nether.

The trip through the forest takes entirely too long, despite the fast clip we've been traveling at. I'm scanning the area in a constant sweep, so I barely avoid hammering into Liz when she comes to a sudden stop. The area looks much like the rest of the woods. The only distinctive feature is a large rock to her left.

"A little warning wouldn't hurt." I grumble at her.

"Oops, sorry." The gleam in her eyes lets me know she did it on purpose to throw me off. Of course. "We're here."

I meet Trey's eyes with concern when we get to the other side of the rock to find the snow around the access hole in the ground cleared away. The round door is unlocked and ajar.

"Someone else has been here. We'll have to proceed with caution."

Trey folds his arms over his chest with an appraising look at the area. "Are you sure we should still go ahead with this? We could try to find another way in."

I turn to Ivy. "What do you think?"

She's nibbling on her lower lip, but she gives me a nod. "I think we'll be ok. This is where he said we should go in. Plus, there are no other tracks leading away. It had to be someone on the inside who opened it up." She's right on that one. The cleared patch of snow stands out in stark contrast to the pristine area surrounding it.

"He?" I lift a brow at her slip. So her contact is a male. I scan my mind to think of who might be in there, coming up blank. Could be anyone, really.

Agony courses through my body when I bend down to lift the lid of the access hole. I lose my hold on the door, doubling over with the pain. What's happening? Heat shoots through me in wave after searing, and it takes me a minute to catch my breath and figure out that the pain and fear ripping through me is not mine. It's Sophia. She's suffering. She's being tortured. Maybe killed. What's going on? The realization amplifies my distress rather than easing it.

"What's the matter, Logan?" Liz's hand lands on my biceps. I jerk my head up to meet the wild concern in her eyes.

"It's, Sophia." I drag the words out.

"What's happening to her?" Charlotte darts forward, throwing her hands up and twisting around as if she's ready to fight the unseen enemy.

"I don't know, but we have to go now." I shove her pain down as far as it will go, trying to compartmentalize it from my own feelings. Of course, now that I know she's not ok, adrenaline is pulsing in my veins, urging me forward and pushing me back to my feet.

All caution has deserted me as I rip the metal door off the sketchy dark hole in the ground and jump down.

"Logan!" I hear my name called out as the air whips around my face.

My feet land on something softer than the ground and give out, leaving me sprawling on top of…a body?

The tunnel is dimly lit, and it takes a moment for my eyes to adjust, especially after the bright brilliance of the sun reflecting off our snowy surroundings.

"We clear to come down?" Trey's deep voice echoes off the tunnel walls.

"One sec." I call back up.

I inspect the body I landed on. He's in a MED uniform, and he's got a gun at his side. Bingo. I pull it off him, then drag his body out of the way. He grunts as I move him so I know he's alive. Probably took a blow to the head. I scan the area to make sure he doesn't have any companions. None standing, but there are a few more downed guards near the tunnel walls.

Ok then. "All clear. Come on down." I back away from the hole so nobody slams into me before turning back to the downed guard.

My head tilts to the side as I stare at him. That'll work. I pause and swing around when there's a soft thump behind me. When

I spot Liz, I go back to my work, stripping the man of his uniform.

"Feeling frisky?"

"Shut up and help yourself. We should be able to slip through this place a little easier in uniforms to blend in."

"Right." She zips forward, using her speed to divest another guard of their clothes and swap her own out before Trey has landed.

She starts on another guard as Charlotte and Ivy make their appearances. It is handy having her around when she's not causing me unnecessary grief.

"Going incognito?" Charlotte asks, pulling on a pair of black tactical pants.

I shrug. "Seemed like a good idea. After all, someone did kindly leave all these downed guards for us. I'd hate to waste all that effort.

Liz is tapping her now black booted foot in impatience by the time the rest of us get dressed. Always a showoff. "Let's go, slowpokes."

As soon as the rest of has have gotten ourselves in some semblance of order, she's shooting off the long, dark tunnel. I'm after her just as fast. Normally I'd be advising her to be a little more cautious, but the escalating ache in my chest is a constant reminder that Sophia is in pain and she needs me.

My trip through the tunnel is a blur and I'm having trouble staying on my feet by the time Liz slides to a stop. Damp hair clings to my forehead and beads of sweat stream down my forehead. My vision is going blurry around the edges. With a final wrench that feels like my insides are getting torn out, the pain disappears into blackness and I stumble to my knees.

"Logan, crap. Are you ok?"

I blink up at my friends, not even sure who spoke. Movement snags the edge of my vision and I'm sure I must be hallucinating when I see who is leaning against the packed dirt wall next to a metal ladder.

Logan

"Garrett? What the hell are you doing here???"

My words come out in a roar and I stagger to my feet, winding up to punch the traitor in his smug face.

He throws his hands up. "Hold up."

"Logan, stop." Ivy grabs my arm, trying to restrain me, but there's no way she's gonna be able to hold me back from letting loose on this jerk. He hurt Sophia, and no one hurts my girl. "He's the one who tipped me off."

"What?" Her statement derails me. There's no way. He left. He went to Zeus of his own free will. After all we've done for him, he ditched us.

"It's true. I called Ivy. Somehow I didn't think you'd listen to me." I want to rip off the arm he waves carelessly at me.

"Uh, no. I would not have."

"I came here on purpose. I figured it wouldn't hurt to have someone on the inside. I've been scoping the place out and trying to figure out their plans."

"Why didn't you tell us?" Trey asks.

"I figured it would be better if I just left. I was in a shitty place in my head, but I always knew I'd help when the time came. Then when Sophia showed up." I don't trust the distress on his face as he tears a hand through his hair.

I shake my head. "How are we supposed to believe you? You ditched us. How do we know you're not still playing on his side? You're not gonna turn us in the first chance you get."

"If I was going to do that, I wouldn't have knocked out the guards at the end of the tunnel, would I?"

He has a point, and I don't really have a choice right now. I either believe him and get in there to get Sophia, or I don't believe him and do the same. Something nags at my brain. "Why did you wait until now? Why not as soon as Sophia got here?"

"She came here willingly. I wish I could have told her the truth, but I didn't want to show my hand yet. I figured she probably had her own plan. If I had known what Tobias had planned for her… but as soon as I figured it out, I called."

"Sophia." My hand flies up to my aching chest. The debilitating agony is gone, but there's still a hollow ache in my core. I can't feel her thoughts or feelings anymore, though, and it's freaking me out. My only reassurance is the weak thread of the protection bond, tying us together and letting me know she's alive. "Where is she? What has he done to her?"

I don't like the sad look in his eyes. They darken to a deep brown and he avoids meeting my gaze. "He took her power."

"What?" No, he can't have. It'll destroy her. "Why didn't you stop him?" The question is irrational, and I know it. What is he supposed to do as just one person? That wouldn't have stopped me if I were here. "Why didn't you call us sooner?"

He's wearing a haunted expression like a second skin. "I didn't know. I didn't know he'd moved her. I happened to overhear a couple of Mages talking about it and I found out where he was. It took me time to track down Ivy. I had to call Houston's house and talk to Flora. It was a whole thing. No way I could have stopped it on my own."

I slam a fist into my other palm, wishing it was his face. "You should have tried. Let's go. We need to get her out of there and figure out what to do." I don't even want to think about what her uncle will be capable of now that he has her Archimage powers. This. This is what all those idiots feared, and yet they helped create it. If they'd just left him be. Let him grow up in a happy house with family and taught him to control his powers. This would never have happened.

Garrett has the audacity to hold up a hand to stop me before I charge him in my haste to climb the ladder. "We need to do one thing before we get her."

"You think I'm going to help you out? Not a chance."

He shakes his head at me. "Not for me. Don't you get it. I'm on her side. I'll always be on Sophia's side. I love her too." Anger is uncoiling in my gut, turning my vision red again. I take a deep breath to keep it under control. Sophia, first. Then I can kick the shit out of this jerk. "Tobias took her brother. That's how he ensured her compliance."

My heart sinks. That makes sense. My little wildcat would have fought him tooth and nail if she had the chance. She would have taken him and this whole operation down from the inside. Or tried her very best. But if Zeus has her brother… she'll do anything to protect someone she loves.

My eyes drop closed, and I sigh. "Where is he?"

"He's locked up in here. Close to where I was. Minimum security. These Mages have very little respect for the capabilities of Witches and even less for those of mundanes. And now that he has what he wants, I doubt he even cares what happens to them."

"You can take us there?" Trey asks.

"I can. There is a rotation of guards patrolling up there." He points to the top of the ladder. "But we can take them out. Then it's a matter of getting to him and getting out. I've got a key card." The shiny rectangle of plastic glints in the lights of the tunnel. "We'll blend in so we shouldn't have too many problems getting through as long as we don't get recognized."

Liz reaches up to tuck her distinctive hair under the military style cap on her head while Trey and I pull ours down low over our eyes.

"I'll go up first. They're used to seeing me around here."

Everything in me wants to fight Garrett on it and go up first. I still don't trust him, but Ivy shakes her head at me.

"Fine. Hurry."

His legs move up the ladder with admirable ease, and I can't fault him on his speed, either. I'm halfway up though before he's made it to the top.

He pops the lid of the door, peering through the crack before shoving it open all the way. I pull myself up and out, spinning around, searching for the trap. But the hall is strangely empty.

"Is it normal for this place to be so empty? Where are the guards?" I whisper to Garrett. He replies with a shrug.

"I don't know. I only came in here once to scope it out and figure out where they're holding Scott. I think they're gathering their forces, so maybe they know what you guys are planning."

"Someone tipped them off?" It is possible. We've involved quite a lot of external Mages and Witches in the plan. Someone could have spilled. I'll be sure they get a slow death when I find out who it is.

"Maybe."

Great. That might actually give us an advantage for this mission if they're operating on minimal staff in the prison.

By the time everyone has made it up through the hole, I'm doubting our ability to remain inconspicuous. There's too many of us together. "Should we split up?"

Ivy shakes her head. "I don't think that's a good idea. We don't want to reduce our numbers in case we get caught in here."

"She's right. We're going to need all the Mage… and Witch power we've got if we're going to get through this place."

I'm itching to charge off, but Garrett is the only one who knows where we're going, so we exchange nods and he heads off. I follow close behind with Liz and the others drop back a bit, keeping a little distance, so we're not quite so conspicuous as a group.

* * * ★ ★ ★ ★ ★ * * *

"What about the cameras?" I ask Garrett after we've rounded another long white corridor without running into anyone else.

Each empty hallway we enter has the fluttery feeling in my stomach ramping up. I'm twitching out of my skin at the slightest noise. Everything about this place feels off, but I can't think of why he'd put so much effort into a trap. He's right. We would have put up a fight, but if he wanted to capture us, it would have been easy to surround us in that tunnel to take us down. No, something else is going on and it can't be good.

"I hacked their system and put the ones in this area on a loop. They won't even know Scott's gone. It'll look like he's still in the cell."

Impressive. I knew he was a thief, but I didn't realize he was so tech savvy. I guess that would be a necessary skill to be successful in this day and age. Everyone has cell phones and doorbell cameras. Not to mention the people he's been stealing are likely wealthy if they have valuable artifacts in their possession. A lot of them probably have expensive security systems to go along with their expensive possessions.

A couple of figures clad in the same black uniforms as us round the corner. I keep my head down and give them a return nod as they walk by. The illusion that we're in the clear shatters when the guy does a double take. It's a Mage and I've been clocked.

I spin back around before the walkie he has in his hand clears his belt. An unpleasant crunch sounds out as my fist makes contact.

"Murray? Really?" I kick him in the side after he hits the floor. I bend down to make sure he's out, then drag him off to the side of the hall so no one happens upon his body and realizes something is up.

Liz takes the other one down with a silent chokehold, easing him to the floor. I don't recognize that one. Mundane, I think.

Handles rattle as Ivy tries a few doors, finally landing on one that opens without undue force. Garrett took down the other guy, and Trey shimmied down the hall to keep watch in case anyone else was close by. The squeak of his boots on the polished floor grates my nerves as I drag him the rest of the way to the room. It turns out to be a maintenance closet with a shelf full of toilet paper and a wooden mop handle leaning against the wall.

I wipe my hand off on my pants in disgust, shaking out my fist as we shut the door on the downed guards.

After a few more turns, we end up in the hall where Garrett said Scott would be. It looks the same as all the other ones we've already passed through. He stops in front of a door with a nod.

I sidle up to peer through the window. There's a blond guy about my age doing pushups on the floor. Nice. At least he's not cowering in a corner. They're not related by blood, but it looks like Sophia and her brother share some of the same characteristics.

I snatch for the key card in Garrett's hand. He looks at me, then back at Charlotte. "Maybe it would be better if the first one through the door is someone he knows. We all look like the guards who took him. He has no reason to trust us."

He's right. It feels like I've known Sophia my whole life, and I've kept track of her and her family over the years. But in reality, it's only been a few months and her brother Scott has been across the country that entire time.

"Char." I dip my head at her and back away to let her grab the card from Garrett. I hold my breath until a soft snick sounds and the light on the door pad flashes green.

Scott pushes off the ground and springs to his feet as the door opens. Anger radiates from his tense posture and he's got his fists clenched at his sides.

Charlotte walks cautiously through the door and there's no immediate recognition in his expression. His knuckles go white as he clenches his fists tighter.

She holds her hands up. "Scott."

He squints, shaking his head until she whips the cap off her head, giving him a clear view of her familiar face.

"Charlotte?" He blinks a few times, as if he doesn't believe what he's seeing.

"Scott. Are you ok?"

His eyes are wide with shock. "Ummm." He looks around the tiny room he's been locked in.

"Right. Of course you're not ok, ok. Are you at least physically alright?"

His head dips in a quick nod. "What are you doing here? What's going on?"

"We came to spring you and then your sister." She takes another step toward him and he backs away until his long legs hit the small cot.

"Are you one of them? What's going on?" He peers over her shoulder, clocking the rest of us in our stolen gear.

She glances down. "No. Gross. We borrowed these outfits. This is a jailbreak."

"Wait. You said they have Sophia? Where is she? Is she ok?"

His question starts up the incessant ache again. I reach out for her, but it's still only blackness. I'd like to think she's just sleeping, but I imagine she's been knocked out.

"Yes. They have her and we need to get her now. We don't have any time to waste." I step into the cell. I know he's got a lot to process, but now is not the best time for that. We need to get to her. I don't have time to coddle him through it.

"Who are you?"

"Logan. I'm Sophia's bb…bodyguard?" I wince at the sharp look Liz sends my way, not to mention the guilt that tugs at my conscience. I almost dropped the b-word, but I don't think that'll help move him along.

"Why does she need a bodyguard? Who are these people? I've seen them do things. Things that aren't possible." He's obviously not ready to face the reality of magic. Maybe I should have gone with boyfriend.

"We can explain later. Your sister's in trouble. You can stay here if you want or you can come with us and get her. I don't care either way, but I'm pretty sure she's gonna want to see you."

I turn away. Not willing to delay any longer.

I step through the door and start walking, ignoring Liz's laser sharp glare. I can almost feel it slicing through me. "You could be a little more sympathetic."

"No time. We can go through the whole magic is real thing later. Now we need to get Sophia."

I eye the signs on the doors. They're all numbered in the 300s, so we're on the third floor. Now that I know where we are, I can get us out of the familiar place with no problem, so I aim for the stairwell at the end of the hall.

I'm not completely heartless, so I glance over my shoulder and spot Charlotte and Scott bringing up the rear. Good. I'm pretty sure Sophia will have my head if I let her brother get lost in the shuffle, no matter what I said.

Our boots squeak on the stairs as we pound our way down to the first floor. I lean against the wall and push the heavy metal door slightly ajar, scoping out the area. I chose the north stairwell since that lets us out down the hall from the main lobby area where everyone has to check in. That'll be our trouble spot. Getting out through there. No matter how empty the building has been, there will definitely be some guards near the entrance.

"Anyone have any ideas how we're going to get out the front doors unnoticed? Distraction maybe? How about that illusion of yours, Charlotte? Can you make us all invisible like that?"

"I don't know if I can hold that one up around the whole group. It's easier to make it look like something is there rather than concealing something. Especially when we're all moving. I knew I should have worked harder on that one like gran told me. I can try." Her springy curls explode from the borrowed black hat when she yanks it off her head, twisting it in her hands.

Garrett holds up a hand. "I got this one."

I'm shaking my head before he's even finished his sentence, but Ivy's hand lands on my forearm. "Wait, Logan, before you say no, hear him out."

Everything in me is screaming not to trust this guy. He took off. He came here. "How do we know this isn't some trick, and you're going to turn on us?"

"I'm not. I told you. I only came here to help." His eyes dart away and he folds his arms over his chest defensively. "Besides, like I said before. If I wanted to trap you, I could have already done it."

Trey steps forward. "I'll go with him. Keep him on the level."

The protest dies on my lips at Trey's offer. "Fine, but what exactly is the distraction you have planned?"

A hint of that annoying dimple makes an appearance with his grin while he's pulling something out of his pocket. I squint, trying to pin it down. Some sort of bluish liquid in a small bottle.

Charlotte takes a long stride forward, holding her hand out. "Ooh. A potion. What's in there?"

He pulls the bottle back out of reach of her grabby hands. "Careful. It's Fragrandor"

I look to my Mage friends to see if any of them have a clue. Ivy's almond-shaped eyes have widened to large circles. "Explosive. That stuff is dangerous. How'd you get a hold of that in here?"

"I picked a few things up on my way in. I've got some stashes around. This is a diluted version. Mostly makes a lot of smoke, not so much of the blowing things up."

Shady as I expected, but at least it's a useful sort of shady.

"How is this going down?" Trey asks not getting too close to Garrett and his explosive bottle.

"Keep it simple. You all head down this hall and wait." He nods to me and the ladies. "Trey and I can go around to the side entrance that opens up behind the reception desk, toss it through, and poof." He splays his fingers out to indicate an explosion. "You can sneak through under cover of the smoke. Just everybody cover your noses and mouths."

"And how are you two getting out?" I ask as I'm patting myself down, looking for something to use as a face covering. Coming up empty in the many utility pockets, I unbutton the black shirt I threw over my t-shirt, shivering as cool air hits my chest.

Charlotte pulls an actual bandana out of one of her pockets, but Liz and Ivy come up empty. I slide a wicked serrated blade out of the belt holster and make quick work of my tee, tearing it into three strips to share with the other girls.

The black uniform shirt is scratchy against my bare skin when I slip it back on.

"I'll get us out of there." Garrett tosses a rag at Trey and gestures for him to follow.

"Watch him." I can't help tossing the warning at Trey's retreating back.

"I got this," he replies. "Watch out. They've got tasers now."

Ivy takes off down the hall, sticking to the wall and moving at a maddeningly cautious pace.

"Ew. You stink, bro." Liz's words are muffled and followed by a fake gagging noise under the strip of my shirt she tied around her face.

"Way to be mature." I roll my eyes at her.

We're almost down the long hall when our luck runs out. A pair of guards appear at the end of the hall. I duck my head down to see if we can sneak by unnoticed, but no luck.

"Logan? You're not supposed to be here."

I peer up from under the brim of my hat to lock eyes with a familiar pair. Northrup. Of course he ended up on the wrong side of the fence. He always was an ass and a bully when we went to school together.

Ah well. At least we're armed. No magic in here, but fists and weapons will do fine. I lunge at the guy who called us out. He's pulled a freaking long sword from a back sheath. Overkill, in my opinion, but then he was never known for his subtlety.

I brandish the dagger I never put away after disfiguring my shirt, running through my options. I know better than to bring a dagger to a sword fight. Not enough reach, but it might buy me enough time to get in there and disable him. I deke away from the swing of the blade, twisting around after the near miss to slam the butt of my dagger into his wrist. He's thrown off balance from his swing, so he can't avoid the jarring pain of my hit and his sword goes clattering to the floor with a ringing sound that has me wincing. If anything is going to catch unwanted attention, it'll be that.

"You always were a shitty fighter." I can't help smiling at the vibrant red shade his face turns at my words.

"You're going down, Armstrong," he says, rushing forward with a predictable lack of forethought.

He's an easy target when I spin a kick out at his temple, sending him crashing to the ground. It works in my favor that he hasn't bothered to improve his skills since we graduated.

Someone else took down unknown guard number two while I was busy. Loud screams from the reception area let me know that this delay could cost us our window of escape.

We take off, boots pounding down the hall. A handful of people spill through the doors, coughing. They're followed by a cloud of thick, bluish smoke.

We push past them, and I inhale a lungful before remembering to yank the makeshift bandana over my face. Not smart.

I cough so hard my lungs ache, but I push through, following my friends out the doorway. Smoke fills the room in such a heavy layer, I lose sight of them as they disappear one by one through the doorway.

An acrid smell fills my nostrils and my eyes tear up as we push on through, aiming for the door. It's open and the cold air coming through is dissipating the smoke.

Relief floods me as a wall of cold, fresh air hits my lungs and my powers snap back into place.

It's a relief to see everyone made it out, including Trey and Garrett. They made it out fast.

"Let's go." I urge them on, wondering why we're all just standing here instead of rushing off to finish our mission.

A chill runs through me at the fear in Liz's eyes when she turns to me. My little sister isn't afraid of anything. In fact, she has a tendency to be far too brave for her own good. I follow the length of her arm to the vast lawn fronting the compound.

My stomach drops at the sight. Black figures dot the lawn. Hundreds of them. There's a literal army here, ready to fight. No wonder we didn't encounter too many inside. They're all out here. Ready and waiting.

# Sophia

A dull ache is the only thing breaking through the hollow emptiness inside. It's like I've been carved out from the inside, left exposed and raw. A chill ripples through me as I blink in the dim light and try to figure out where I am and what's the matter with me.

It all comes back in a rush. Tobias, Garrett, the ceremony. My first attempt to push myself up fails, leaving scratches on my hands from the cold stone under my palms. Weak flickers from the torches provide the only light in the room.

I try reaching for my magic to light up the room with a little fire and fail. There's nothing there. Wait. Not nothing. A warm and comforting pulse beats within my chest and I'm flooded with a temporary sense of relief. Logan. He's still there. The bond is still in place. It's still strong and steady, having survived Tobias' brutal extraction of the rest of my powers.

His presence gives me hope, and I focus on the bond for a moment. He's close. Really close. That thought finally drives me into motion. I push my aching body into a sitting position and swing my legs over the side of the table. It takes a moment to adjust to the dim room, but when I'm able to take in the cavernous space, I realize that I'm all alone. The white candles that were encircling me have burned down to stubs, and everyone who was helping my uncle is gone. I guess now that I'm powerless, they don't consider me to be a threat anymore. But I'm not powerless. I may not have my magic anymore, but I survived the first seventeen years of my life without it. I can still fight. They don't know what they've done.

A sharp pain shoots through my ankles as they hit the floor and I have to swing an arm out to grab the table, steadying my wobbly legs. Apparently, the ceremony did a number on me.

Is Logan here? Did they start the plan early?

I slam my eyes shut to protect them from the daggers that accompany a burst of bright light. Booted feet pound across the floor, tripping my internal warning bells. After everything I've been through, I'm expecting an enemy at every turn. Fight back. I tell myself. Don't let them get you. I drop into my fighting stance and blink a few times, trying to see through the red glare that's taken over my vision.

I fling an arm out, landing a weak hit with a soft thud. A grunt sounds out as I make contact, but instead of the expected return blow, a pair of strong arms circle me, pulling me into a warm embrace. The familiar scents of cedar and lime invade my senses, accompanied by an overwhelming feeling of love and relief. I turn into a trembling mess in his arms.

"Logan." I blink to fight off the tears burning behind my eyes and the harsh glare fades, returning my vision to me.

His hand strokes my head in a soothing gesture.

"I love you."

The words send a thrill of warmth through me, even under the grim circumstances.

"I love you too." I nuzzle in closer to his shoulder, seeking his warmth.

"I love you too and I hate to break up the love fest, but we really should figure out our next step." Liz's voice chirps through, destroying the moment with a brutal reminder of our current situation. Logan squeezes me tighter, muttering under his breath.

She's right though. We need to get to my uncle before he hurts anyone else we care about. I may never get my powers back, but it'll be worth it if I take him down with me.

"What's going on?" A familiar, but unexpected voice cuts in. Someone I never wanted to hear in this place and under these circumstances.

I lift my head from Logan's shoulder, spotting my brother approaching. He's rubbing the back of his neck, glaring at Logan's back as if he wants to take him down with his eyes alone.

"Scott? What are you doing here?" I look up at Logan. "What's he doing here?" I untangle myself from Logan's arms and hurry toward my brother on legs that are still shaky.

"I got kidnapped. I have no idea what's going on. I think I'm losing my mind, or maybe they drugged me. I don't know. None of this makes any sense."

Horror rips through me. Tobias must have taken him to get to me. "I'm so sorry. This is all my fault."

Sadness fills me as he backs away in fear at my approach. I hold my hands out, palms up. "It's ok. It's me. I'm still me." I'm not sure how true the words are even as I say them. Am I still me without my magic? I'm not sure anymore, but I am still his sister. We're family and we always will be even if we're not related by blood. There are more important things than blood, as I've learned lately. My eyes fall on each of my friends in turn, narrowing when they land on Garrett. How dare he show his face here after he betrayed us. "What are you doing here?" I turn accusing eyes on him.

Ivy steps in front to shield him with her body. "It's fine. He's with us. He always was."

I take another step toward him. "How do we know that? How do we know you're not still playing us? You're not on team Zeus. How could you leave us like that?" I held back the tears before, but I'm not sure I can do it this time. I hate it but, I've always been an angry crier.

Logan's hand closes on my shoulder, holding me back. "It's true. He let us know you were here. He helped us get into the compound. He's really with us."

I don't think I would have believed anyone else's words, but Logan's hold weight. He's always disliked Garrett. If he believes him, then it must be true. I'm still pretty conflicted, wanting to punch him and hug him at the same time.

I turn back to Scott. He should be my priority right now. I need to convince him he doesn't need to be afraid of me. I'm all torn up inside. Confused, tired, and wondering who I can truly believe, but Scott has just been through some serious trauma. Tobias or his lackeys kidnapped my brother. He's probably seen people doing magic. I go back to my own feelings when I first found out about all the magic stuff. It's hard to believe it was only a couple of months ago. Feels like I've always belonged here, even if I never knew it. Even if I don't know what my place will be without my Archimage powers.

"Scott. You must be so confused. You must have so many questions." I take another measured step toward him. I'm dying to run at him and fling my arms around him, but the wary look in his eyes urges caution.

He doesn't back away this time. He's too busy glaring over my shoulder. "He said he was your bodyguard. What's going on?"

I swing my head back to make eye contact with a guilty-looking Logan. He holds his hands up. "I didn't know what to say to him?"

"I don't know. You could have told him you were my boyfriend. If you still are." Maybe he decided I wasn't worth it after I left him like that. I know that doesn't make sense. He wouldn't have rushed in to rescue me if he felt that way. Right?

"Wait. You're her boyfriend?" Scott's expression hardens. He's clenching and unclenching his fists. Great, that's all we need right now. A fight to break out over me.

Logan's wide eyes dart back to me, looking for help he's not going to get. "Yeeeesss." He's shifting from one foot to the other, and I'm not sure if he's more scared of me or my brother.

I take a step between the two guys, trying to keep the peace. "Yes. This is Logan. Logan, meet my brother Scott. Officially. Now we can totally talk about this later, but maybe we should get the heck out of here."

Scott's releases a sigh, and his shoulders sink. "Where are we even? And what's going on? Is he one of those… magic people?" Magic people? I twist my lips, pressing them together to avoid laughing out loud.

"Yes, we all are. Well, I was…anyway. It's a lot to explain."

"Right. I know you guys have a lot to work through, and I hate to bring it up, but does anyone happen to remember the literal army that's waiting for us out front? We might want to do something about that."

"I'm already on it." Trey stands at attention, his muscular arms crossed over his chest. "I called your parents while you were figuring stuff out. I'm glad you're ok, Soph." He gives me a nod.

"You gave him the rundown of their numbers?" Logan asks Trey.

"I did. Your dad wasn't sure how many he'll be able to get on board right now, but they're on their way. Hopefully, it's enough."

"It'll have to be. There's no other choice."

"My family will be in, and they'll bring the Witch community. My gran can summon an army with one stern look." Charlotte lets us know we've got back up from that side.

Garrett runs a hand through his sandy hair, glancing at the ground. I know he cut all ties with the Witch community after his family was killed. Is he worried about seeing them or is he feeling guilty because he's planning on betraying us if it suits him? I hate to think that's a possibility, but he abandoned us. He let Zeus take my powers. I want to believe in him after all we've been through, but I'm finding it hard right now. Maybe there will always be a part of me that will doubt his intentions now.

"An army? What the hell is going on here, Sophia? What have you gotten involved in? Where's mom?"

"I can explain more later but to give you the rundown, it turns out I'm a Mage. Apparently a powerful one. My biological parents gave me up to protect me, but they couldn't protect me forever. I have an uncle and he's kinda psychotic and power hungry. He stole my powers and is basically trying to take over the magical world, and we can't let that happen."

"A Mage???? What even is that?"

Logan's twitchy impatience is seeping through the bond. "Like this." He swivels his fist, spreading his fingers until a spark flashes and a ball of fire ignites on his upturned palm. The flames are bright in the dimly lit room. Of course he went for the showiest trick as usual. "See. Magic. Charlotte and Garrett are Witches. Not the same, but they do magic stuff, too."

He steps into my brother, ignoring the fear in his eyes, placing a hand on his shoulder. Scott cringes away, but Logan grips tighter, not letting him back away. "Listen, man. I know this is a lot, but we really don't have time to get into the whole thing right now. Like we said, there's a literal army out front. We can hide you away somewhere in this place until we're done, but we have to join our friends and family for this battle. You can come with us or stay here. It's all the same to me, but you better make your decision fast, because we are running out of time."

Everything in me is begging to leave Scott behind. I can't endanger my family any more than I already have, but the determined look in his eyes tells me a different story. He's not going to let us leave him behind. My goofy, athletic, amazing brother is going to stand with us. I get it. I really do, but it doesn't make it any easier. He's just a human, not a trained fighter, not a Mage or a Witch.

"I'm coming with you."

I give a nod to Liz, pleading with her to look after it. Her eyes dart from me to my brother and back again. *Please.* I mouth the word.

Scott cries out as she closes her arms around him, picking my brother up as if he weighs nothing and darting off. "I'm sorry, Scott." I yell at her disappearing back. She'll find somewhere to keep him safe. I feel bad locking him up after he just got out of a cell, but I know I won't be able to concentrate knowing he's out there.

Logan stifles a laugh, turning back to Trey. "So what's the plan? What did my dad have to say?"

"They'll be following the original plan, sending teams in at different points of entry. I let him know the situation with the tunnels, so they may send a larger force through there, given that the way is clear. He wants us to stay put until we see them enter through the front gates. At that point, we can join the forces coming in through the tunnel and back field. They'll think they've got it in the bag when they see the numbers coming through the gate and we'll surround them from behind."

"Sounds good."

"So now we just wait?" I look at all my friends, knowing we might not all make it out of here. "I love you guys so much."

"Love you too, sis." Liz makes a goofy face, trying to ease the tension before going serious again.

My heart warms at the endearment. In spite of the dire circumstances, it really feels like Liz has become a sister to me. I love everyone here. My eyes drop closed and I focus on the buzzing warmth of the protection bond that connects me to Logan. I can feel his fear, determination, and love through the twined threads that connect us. It helps ease the emptiness left behind by the theft of my magic.

Logan twists his fingers through mine. "Everyone. Let's head for the front entrance. We can wait there for the signal."

I nod at him and join my other friends when they start to walk through the doorway that will lead us out of this place and up the stairs toward our last stand.

I find myself held back by Logan's stationary form. He tugs on my arm, pulling me back until I'm facing him. We're separated by mere inches. I let his warmth surround me in a cloud of comfort, closing my eyes.

I look up when his fingers close over my cheeks, tilting my face until I'm looking up into those impossible eyes.

"Sophia. I just wanted to let you know…before we go up there. Before we get into this fight that…I love you."

My lips tilt up in a smile. "I know." And I really do. The skin on skin contact lets his thoughts and feelings swirl in my head, mingling with mine. *I didn't know you could feel this much for one person.*

"No. I don't think you do. I've never cared about anyone the way I care about you, and everything inside me is screaming to stop you from coming with me. To hide you away somewhere where no one can hurt you."

He presses a finger to my lips when they fall open to protest.

"I know I can't do that. I know you'd never let me get away with this. I know how capable you are, but it's not going to be enough. I'll do what I can, but I need you to make me a promise." He must see the protest in my eyes. "Hear me out before you say no. Just stay close to me. Please. While we're out there and you're vulnerable. Stay close to my side. I won't be able to focus if you're not near me."

I nod. "Of course. I'll stay close." I couldn't bear to be away from him either, so I get it.

"You are everything to me. I didn't expect this to happen, but from the first moment I laid eyes on you, I knew."

I laugh. "That does not track with the way you acted when we first met."

"Are you gonna throw that in my face now? I was stupid and scared. I knew then you had the power to bring me to my knees. To destroy me if that's what you chose. And that's what it would do to me if I lost you." His serious expression fades into the cocky smile I love so much. "And you wouldn't want to deprive the world of all this, right?" He tilts his chin, bobbing a dark brow.

Perfect. "Never. Pretty sure the universe would collapse under the weight of the loss of that gigantic head. It would throw off gravity on the planet and we'd go spinning off into space or something."

His grin widens. "Exactly. Don't let that happen."

He pulls me in closer, dipping his head down to meet my lips in a desperate kiss. An explosion of love floods me. That's what it feels like when he kisses me. Like someone lit the fuse of a stick of dynamite and it'll only be moments before the whole place explodes in the flames that engulf us. I can almost see them swirling around us, heating my skin and igniting my insides, leaving behind an ember that could combust at any moment.

Logan

The grim sight that greets us out the front window is more than enough to douse the heat I was feeling a mere moment ago while holding Sophia in my arms. The mass of soldiers lined up on the vast front lawn of the NAMC headquarters is meant to intimidate. It's not an unfamiliar sight, but any display like this I've seen in the past has been a training exercise, not a preparation for an actual battle.

It's almost like they know what we're planning. I can't stop myself from glancing at Garrett after that thought. Is he really on our side? Or has he been spilling our plans to the bad guys? I really focus on him. His face is set in the same hard lines as the rest of our group. We've been through a lot together these last couple of months and we've proven time and again that we're here for each other. Any room for doubts is over. We're all stronger working as a team.

Zeus knew we'd come for him. After I got away. After we slipped away from their pursuit. There's no way our parents and the other council members would stand for his takeover. He knew we would come for him and he's ready. Let's just hope that our side is just as prepared.

There's a weight to the air around us. Trey flips his phone over in his hand. He gives a nod. "They're in the tunnels. Won't be long."

Magic builds in the air like an impending thunderstorm, but I can't pinpoint the source. Hopefully, it's on our side. More likely it's both sides gearing up. There are still no signs of anyone in the distance by the front gates. We do at least have a good view from this building, which was built on the crest of a small hill.

A crash rends the air and the front gate flies apart in a massive explosion. Cars spill through the smoke and flames. Shards of debris raining down around them. I knew it was coming, and it's still surprising. The build up of magic was the product of the vast illusion woven together by Charlotte's family. I will never underestimate Witches again. Concealing our group from notice was no small feat. To take down the gate, the Mages used a combination of physical explosives and potions to conserve magic for the upcoming battle as was part of our initial plan.

The force on the front lawn moves into action, marching toward danger with guns and magic at the ready. I'm restless and almost as ready as my sister to bolt out the door to help defend our family and way of life. She's perched on her toes like a runner about to take flight. I reach out a hand to hold her back from jumping off the block too soon. Look at me practicing restraint. It seems like Sophia is the only one that can inspire me into foolish impulsiveness. I guess my father might have been right about that.

Our signal comes when a second group comes spilling out the doors of the prison building. This is it. I squeeze Sophia's hand, leaning in close to her ear. "I love you."

She tilts her head up. I hope she can read the words in my eyes as well as she can hear them. My father may have taught me to control my emotions and keep them hidden away, but there's a time and a place when they need to be set free, and this is it. This could be the last chance I have to say those words to her.

Her eyes are shining brightly, and her lips curve up into a hesitant smile. "I love you too." With a final squeeze of my hand, we're off to join the rest of the tunnel teams to approach the battle from the rear.

Eleven teams have emerged from the back entrance. My team would have been the twelfth if we hadn't gotten a head start with our early arrival here. We've been in contact with my dad and Houston, though, so they'll be expecting us, hopefully, with some extra weapons.

Sophia and I lead our team, jogging over to meet with Khalid and Tanner. They're the designated section leaders. I give them a quick nod in greeting. "Where do you want us?"

Khalid is the one to answer. "You'll be joining the right flank with me, as per our original plan. I'm not thrilled at the rushed state things, but we scraped together a powerful force." I can feel the judgment in his tone. I'm not sure if he's blaming me or Sophia, but we're definitely the culprits in his eyes. The ones that upset his careful planning. "Don't get in the way."

I bite back the angry retort on the tip of my tongue. Now is not the time or the place. He's the one in charge, and I know how to follow a command when need be. I guess we'll have to prove ourselves out there. Fine by me. He has no idea what we've been through together. We can handle this.

Our presence goes unnoticed by Tobias' army and it's not looking good for us the closer we get. My heart is racing in my chest at a terrifying pace, and Sophia's fear is piling on mine. I wish I could have convinced her to stay back, but I know her. She'd never let her friends fight her battles for her. Not to mention the personal vendetta she has against her uncle after everything he's done to her.

My parents are near the front of the army, each leading a team, but they're losing ground. Backing away. I can see Mom directing her team, anticipating the moves of the enemy before they happen. It's helpful to have a Psych for sure. Dad is hurling magic as fast as he's dodging the shots launched at him.

Thick smoke from all the small fires and explosions is making it difficult to see.

As we get close to the edge of the battle where we're supposed to be joining in a bright spot of color catches my eye. Rage passes to me through the bond and I know Sophia has recognized the person as well. It's her uncle in the thick of the fight, using magic that is rightfully hers against our family and colleagues.

My eyes widen as she veers off our path to head in his direction. "No, Sophia." I reach out for her, dodging a bolt of lightning and hurling a fireball at a Mage that's appeared right beside her. I take out the Phys before they have a chance to touch her.

I can't see my sister anymore. She's darted into the fray in a blur and it looks like she's... snatching guns out of the hands of soldiers who are probably mere mundanes. She's bending the deadly weapons into useless heaps of twisted metal. Smart. The more guns we get out of this battle, the better our chances of survival. The mundanes who've lost their guns look around in fear. Some of them just run while some of them try to defend themselves with their fists and legs. They've got no chance against her speed and strength, but the numbers are a problem.

Another Phys slams into her from behind as she's disarming the mundanes. My stomach lurches as my sister, who shouldn't even be here, flies forward. I'm frozen for a moment between running back to defend Liz and chasing after Sophia, who is weaving through the writhing mass of bodies intent on her goal.

I slam my sword down on the wrist of someone who approaches me from the side, then spot Trey knocking the Phys who attacked Liz off her feet. He's spun the guy up in a whirling gust of wind. After dropping the enemy, he maintains a protective whirlwind around them that prevents anyone from getting too close.

Satisfied, I turn back to find that Sophia has disappeared from view. Panic twists my gut as I rush after her. At least I know the direction she's headed in, but anything could have happened to her while I was distracted. I run after her, reaching through the bond to check on her. She must feel my inquiry because she spins around as I catch sight of her golden ponytail bouncing on her back. Her eyes widen a little too late for me to avoid the blow to my head. I stagger forward before righting myself to search for the culprit. There are too many people. I don't even know who hit me, but the throbbing in my head and blurry vision aren't lying.

"Logan, are you ok?" She's come back for me through the fighting.

"I'm fine. Probably be better if you didn't take off on me like that."

"I'm sorry. But I need to do this. I need to take down Zeus."

"I get it. I really do, but I think this is something we need to do together. We're stronger together. Not to mention I'm beyond distracted when you're not near me."

"Right. Sorry. But come on." She weaves her way back toward her uncle, pulling me along with her this time.

Now that she's by my side, I can focus on the threats around us sending off lightning, fireballs or fists whenever anyone gets too close. Trey's whirlwind seemed like a pretty good shield. I spin one up in a bubble that leaves the air around us still but keeps everyone around us from breeching our space. It'll get us to our destination, but it is draining on my energy reserves. I won't be able to maintain it indefinitely.

While my parents and other council members are in the thick of the things, I spot Lawrence and a few of his comrades staying off to the side out of the messiest parts of the battle. They're trying to preserve their own skins by letting others fight their war for them. Definitely not stellar examples of leadership. No wonder those cowards let Sophia's uncle do all the work for them. They think they can sit back and watch all the chaos they unleashed go down. Then they'll swoop in and take over. Good luck to them.

Something slams into my little protective wind tunnel and a hot poker of pain stabs through my thigh, stealing my hold on the magic. As our wind shield disappears, noise slams into me as hard as the electricity that caught my leg. It's chaos around us. Bodies shoving, magic flying, plants trying to trip us up. Sophia stumbles when someone gets shoved into her. She regains her feet and keeps moving forward, jostling through the crowd and leaping over the bodies that have fallen all around us.

Each step is painful now, sending a burst of pain through my thigh as if each step is stabbing me, but I push on, knowing we have to end this. We're the only ones who can. Sophia sends a wave of soothing calm through the bond. I'm not sure how she manages it amid this madness, but it helps. It helps me push through the odd thicket of bush that has sprouted up in the middle of the battleground. Fresh air hits my face. I feel like I can breathe for the first time as the crush of people around us gives way to space.

I don't even have time to relax when we hit the small clearing in the middle of the fight. There he is, right in the center of the almost peaceful space. Tobias, Zeus, Sophia's uncle. Whatever he's calling himself now, he's standing in the center of this circle, eyes bright with misplaced passion. The network of vines and plants keeping people out of this zone is on fire in some places, but the vines continue to knit themselves back into place. I imagine he's got some Bio Mages doing the work for him because I can't imagine he could maintain this intricate wall without draining himself.

He's using his protected area to watch the battle raging around him with a smile on his face. He's enjoying the chaos he's created. Psychopath that he is. A psychopath in a custom-tailored suit is still a psychopath.

"Nice suit." Maybe injecting that much sarcasm into the comment isn't my best plan, but I can't seem to help myself. Who wears a suit to a war?

"Ahhh. I've been waiting for you two. I knew you wouldn't let me down. Come here."

Sophia goes charging forward until she's far too close to her uncle for my comfort. She brushes an escaped strand of hair back off her dirt-smudged face.

"Why?" she calls out. "You got what you wanted. Why are you still doing this?"

Sophia

Maybe trying to reason with a madman is futile, but I have to try. The deep rage inside me has been simmering since I watched him take Xavier's life, but now that I'm here, seeing him pit everyone against each other. Watching people fall around me, I have to try.

"Niece. I thought maybe I could get you to understand. These people need to pay. All of them. Look at this. I didn't start this. I merely lit a single match and look?" He spreads his arm around him in a slow sweep that encompasses the battle all around us. "Fighting, killing, destroying each other. For what? Control of this council. Secrecy from the mundanes? Foolishness. We could rule this world. Why are we hiding away like scared rabbits when the wolves come out howling?"

"They're fighting for what's right. They're fighting for justice and progress. They're fighting for friendship and family."

"How idealistic. To think that people actually care about each other. Who was there to protect me when they stripped my powers away? Reduced me to a mere mundane. No one. Not my family, not your precious council. You can't even stay on the same side. Look how easy it was to divide this council. Just some small suggestions. Clearing the way. They're not here for you. They're here for chaos. There's no loyalty in this world."

"Not true." Garrett pushes through the hedge.

"See? This one claims to be on your side, but he was sure quick to come running to me when he thought it would benefit him."

I reach for my magic and come up empty. There's nothing there. An empty void where it used to rest. I want to shut him up before I start believing his dark view of people.

"I've always been here for her. I promise Sophia. I may have left, but I was always on your side." Garrett's hazel eyes plead with me to believe him, but I'm still unsure. If he'd only trusted me enough to tell me his plan before he took off. I thought I'd earned that trust from him, but apparently not.

A fireball slams through the hedge, creating a gaping hole that Liz and Trey step through. "Us too."

"Of course. But what exactly does that loyalty do for you? What does it do for your friends, Sophia? It gets them killed. That's what it does."

Zeus reaches for the sky in a move that makes him look like the god of thunder he's been pretending to be. He pulls lightning down in a column as thick as a tree trunk. The air crackles with electricity and the entire area is lit up like a baseball stadium during a night game.

Horror and helplessness war within me when he directs it at Garrett. "No!" I run at him, but there's nothing I can do. I don't have super speed or strength. I don't have fire or lightning. All I have are my friends.

I skid to a halt when I see the unstoppable lightning heading for my friend. Ivy bursts through the hedge, knocking Garrett out of the way. His body twitches and he stumbles when the current hits his calf, but he's still standing.

All these people. This battle. Why does he keep targeting me and my friends? "Why? You got my powers. Why do you keep going after my friends? I don't understand."

"Well, niece. You need to understand where I'm coming from. Once I've taken everything from you, then you'll understand. It was your family that took everything from me."

"My family is your family. It doesn't make sense." It finally hits me. He's not going to stop. He's going to take everything from me and leave me broken like he was.

"Then maybe you'll see things my way. Perhaps you'll even join me. But that's irrelevant at this point.

"Stop! Get away from here." Charlotte breaks through the hedge with a shout. Now it makes sense. He cleared this spot among the hedges to lure me in, knowing all my friends would follow. It shouldn't have been that easy to get through. He let them through. He let all my friends through so he could take them down one by one. In front of me. He's got some twisted idea in his head that I'm the one who has to pay for everything that ever happened to him.

Trey crosses his arms over his chest. "We're here for you, Soph."

My uncle's face twists in a grotesque mockery of a smile as he turns to them. "Welcome. I've been expecting you."

While Tobias has been spouting off his evil nonsense, Ivy has been busy. She's taken control of a section of the vines making up the barrier behind him. They twist in a slow crawl on the ground, creeping ever closer to him.

"Please guys. Turn back. He only wants to hurt me, and hurting you is the way to do it. Turn back and I'll handle it. It will be fine." I release Logan's hand, stepping forward.

"Never. We've got your back. That's what we do." Charlotte's comment attracts his attention, and he sends a bolt of lightning at her. The shot goes wild when one of Ivy's vines twines around his ankle, yanking him off balance. He laughs, sending another shot that slices the vine with a sizzle of electricity.

"You'll regret that." He turns to Ivy, and that seems to be the signal for all my friends to take action.

Without a word, we all advance on him. He bellows, sending fire and lightning at us from every side. When I step forward to join my friends, something seizes me from behind. It's the wall of greenery behind us. It's turning from a static blockade to a prison. The vines twirl around my arms and legs. I fight with all my regular old human strength, but my struggles only seem to tighten the vines around my limbs until I'm immobilized.

"Logan. Help me." I gasp out at his retreating form.

"Sorry. You're safer there. He's obviously not going to kill you." My stomach sinks at the determination on his face. He's really going to leave me here. He's going to leave me restrained while I watch Tobias kill my friends one by one. Rip out my heart piece by piece.

"Nooooo." I watch helplessly as my friends advance on my uncle.

Blue smoke rises from the ground around him and I'm not sure what he's trying to do until he sends a gust of wind that doesn't clear it. "You're not going to fool me, Witch." Charlotte must be creating an illusion to blind him. Smart. No surprise there.

I continue to strain my arms. If I can just reach one of my daggers, I can cut these vines away and make a break for it.

While Tobias is blind, the others get to work. Trey and Logan work together to build a wall of flames that spreads in a perfect circle around him. But Tobias sends a waterfall, causing the flames to flicker and go out. I can't tell who is sending more vines creeping along the ground until they tangle around Charlotte's legs, pulling her down. Her illusion breaks as she tumbles to the ground. Trey slices through them with a borrowed sword, helping her to her feet.

I've lost sight of Liz until she pops up behind Zeus, slamming a fist into his back before he sees her coming. He swings an arm, sending her flying, but she lands on her feet, advancing again to dart around in a blur that has him off balance.

It only seems to give him ideas, though. He's got that Archimage thing going on now so he can match powers with all of us. He blurs out from his spot, sending Garrett skidding back into the hedge. The raised sword he was approaching with clatters to the ground as vines wrap him up as tightly as me.

He knocks out my friends one by one using his speed. He hasn't killed anyone yet. I thought that was his entire purpose here. Unless. I turn to Logan, still on his feet. Zeus advances on him, intent on taking him out first. Causing the maximum amount of hurt possible.

Logan runs at him, dropping into a roll to avoid a volley of fire and leaping to his feet while returning fire. Zeus blurs out again, slamming the butt of a sword into his back. Logan staggers under the weight of the blow but pulls out his daggers. He sends them flying one by one, followed by a bolt of lightning and a gust of wind that sends Tobias stumbling back. He stumbles as a ball of fire catches him in the chest.

His face is twisted with rage as he builds a dancing cloud of electricity over his head. Then Logan dekes to the left to avoiding the bolts. Tobias darts in from the side, slamming his foot into Logan's back. The force of it sends him to the ground.

No. No, no, no. The bond is faltering and flickering when I reach through it. He can't. He can't die. He can't. I wouldn't survive that. I reach through the bond, trying to send him some of my limited energy. Grasping at anything that will help. Let him know I'm here. Let him know he can't leave me.

Logan's still there, weak, but still with me. His magic dances around the edges of our bond, just out of reach. His powers feel different from mine. More intense and sharp where mine have softer edges. Maybe because it belongs to me my powers feel more comfortable, but since we're connected in such an intimate way, his are still familiar. If I can just draw some of them away, maybe I can use them.

The idea takes hold, blossoming into a full-fledged plan in seconds. I can do that. I should be able to. We have, after all, shared magic on more than one occasion. From the very first time I used it when he helped me freeze the pillows in the air, to our most recent endeavor to share our magic, amplifying our own unique powers.

When I first try to grab hold of his powers, they slip away. He must feel me fiddling around because he sits up, turning to give me a small nod as we lock eyes.

As I lock on, Zeus slams a foot into his chest. The pain from the blow hits me like a gunshot, leaving me gasping for air and causing me to lose my grip on the strand of magic.

No. I push past the pain and grab it again. This time, I don't waste any time yanking the strand through the bond. It fills me up in an exhilarating rush that has me wobbling on my feet. It's a relief to have the current buzzing through my body again, even if it's not my own.

Zeus curls some vines around Liz's feet to keep her still when she stirs before returning to Logan. The sun glints off the brutal sword in his hand.

I grab onto Logan's fire magic and send it shooting through my fingers in a burst that scalds my jeans and turns the plant, holding me prisoner, to ash.

I take off at a run as Tobias lifts the sword above Logan in what will be a death blow. A frustrated whimper escapes my lips. I'm not going to make it. Without my extra speed, I'm not going to be fast enough. He's going to kill Logan before my eyes. This can't happen. I can't let it. I reach down deep inside, pushing with everything I have, and a soft tingle pricks at my brain. Is that? Is that my power? Buried deep within the magic I stole from Logan is a small snip of my Archimage powers. I don't have time to reflect on how that happened, but I pull on the small thread, infusing it into my racing legs, hoping that it'll work. It has to.

I slam into my uncle as his blade is descending. It's like he wanted to be stopped. He has the super speed too, right? Unless he was hoping for this fight.

White hot pain shoots up my arm where the sharp edge meets my skin. We wrestle for control of the weapon. I back him up a precious few steps from Logan, who's still lying there vulnerable in a way he would despise.

Even with Logan's magic and that tiny bit of my own powers, I'm losing ground. He's older, stronger, and way more experienced than I am. But the thought of my friends is enough to keep me on my feet even when I stumble.

I throw everything I have at him, but he's one step ahead of every move, as if he can read my mind. Maybe he can. Other than the odd thought, I've never really tapped into my Psych powers. It's like I've been afraid of them. That was foolish.

"That's right, niece. You're weak, and I'm going to win this fight because of that weakness."

His mouth twists into a grin as he shoves me. The hard packed snow jars my spine, radiating pain up my back. He looks over my shoulder, setting his sights on Logan again. I can't let him get to him. My vision is blurry thanks to fall, but I blink up at him. Distraction until I can get my body to listen to me again. "You think I'm weak because I've been cautious about using powers that have the potential for so much misuse?" Delving into people's minds is so invasive.

"That and your attachment to your friends. Look where that's gotten you." I flinch as the sharp tip of his blade points to me.

His triumph is temporary as he stumbles forward. Liz's heart-shaped face is a little worse for the wear but her trademark cocky smile is in place as she slams into my uncle. "I'd say it's gotten her a team of people who would trade their lives for hers. Where's your team?"

I drag myself up as he turns to fight with Liz, and the rest of my friends appear in various states of disarray. My heart overflows at the sight of them surrounding him defending me.

"That's right, Tobias. This is my team. My family. This is what family does. Nothing else matters. You may have stolen my powers, but you'll never be as strong as I am, because you're alone. None of those people really have your back. You've coerced, threatened or paid them to fight your war for you, but you have no loyalty."

"We'll see what good that does you when they're all dead."

He turns his back on Liz with zero concern for his own safety. He's spotted his target, and it's Logan. My heart. He may not understand love, but he knows he can destroy me with one blow.

I reach for the tendril of magic, willing it into every limb, praying for all I'm worth that this will work. That I can beat him to Logan. He can have my life. If I'm dead, he won't need to target them.

I push off into a run, but I'm not going to make it. He's apparently done with the sword. He's back to the electricity. He's built up another bolt, but he turns to look at me before sending it off, taunting me.

As he spins back around, someone else jumps in the path, blocking his blow. It's…Mr. Armstrong? Where did he come from?

Tobias roars as the current hits Logan's father rather than him. His body falls heavy on top of the son he was protecting.

"No!" The horrified shriek comes from Logan's mother. They must have broken through the hedge.

Everything is in slow motion. Tobias yanks Robert's body away so he can reach his actual target.

Not happening. My fury drives my magic into overdrive, and I slam into him in a blur. My entire body is electrified. Blue currents dance all over my skin with a warm tingle.

I wrap my arms around my uncle in our first and only hug and he gets the full force of my elemental magic.

His eyes fly open as his body jolts under me.

"I'm sorry." The words are a whispered truth. I didn't want to kill. I never wanted that. No wonder people fear Archimages. All this power at your fingertips. It could corrupt anyone.

I've got nothing left. Completely drained, even as the tingle of my magic awakens deep within. I close my eyes and fade away.

Logan

"Son." The dry croak doesn't bear any resemblance to my father's usual stern tone, but I've never been so grateful to hear his voice.

"Dad." I jump out of my seat. "I'll get Mom. She just went to grab something to eat."

"Wait."

I pause, turning back to him.

"Come closer." He curls his hand in a tired come here gesture.

"What's up? Did you need something?"

"Just to talk."

I approach the bed, crouching down so he doesn't have to work so hard to speak.

"I'm sorry, son."

"What? You don't have anything to be sorry for. You saved my life." He shouldn't even be wasting his breath right now. He almost died.

"No. Hear me out. I've been too hard on you. I know that. That's the way my father was with me. I thought that was the way

I had to be. I was wrong." His words are gaining steam as he recovers his voice.

"It's fine, Dad."

"I'm proud of you. I want you to know that."

My hand moves in slow motion. I'm hesitant to reach out that last inch, but he looks so frail in the bed. His shoulder is solid and warm under my palm when I finally make contact.

"Thanks, Dad." My chest swells with an unfamiliar warmth.

"Now go get your mother. I know you want to check on your girl."

I do. I'm itching to get back to her side. Mom needed to grab a bite, so I said I'd sit with Dad. This is the last thing I was expecting, but I'm glad we had this time. I'm sure he'll be back to his usual taskmaster self in no time, but we had a moment and there's no going back from that.

I skid down the hall to find Liz. "Liz, find Mom. Dad's awake." I yell the words as I run past her room, ignoring the pains in my leg, and arm, chest. Pretty much my entire body is in pain right now, but it's pain I'll recover from. Losing my dad before we had a chance to make amends. I don't know if I could have gotten through that.

"Got it." She zips downstairs in a blur.

I slow down as I get close to my room. Sophia's been sleeping off her power hangover and assorted injuries in there.

My hand goes up to grab the frame of the door and I lean in, not wanting to wake her up if she's still sleeping.

Her gorgeous chocolate eyes blink open as I'm peering in. "Come on in. Make yourself at home." She invites me into my own room with a smile, but it's the kind that breaks my heart. She looks devastated.

"On my way, Tempest."

Her nose scrunches up. "Tempest?"

"Yup. Because you're basically a one-woman storm."

"Am I though?" There's a question in her eyes. "Without my magic?"

I study her face. Does she not remember? "What are you talking about?"

"Tobias." Bright tears glisten behind her eyes as she says his name. It doesn't matter what he did, she's carrying a heavy burden of guilt for killing him, and she always will. "He took my powers. I'm not an Archimage anymore."

"You don't remember? They came back to you. I don't know where they came from, but you were using them at the end of the battle. I saw you."

Her eyes dart back and forth, and I reach out to see what she's seeing. She's running the final battle through her head, and it's hard to see the events from her perspective. There's so much pain, guilt, sorrow. Then her mouth drops open as it all comes back to her. "I got them back. You had some." She sits up too fast and I'm rushing forward to help her settle back. "You had a strand of my power from when we'd been practising. I must have taken it back and I don't know, amplified it? I have no idea, but..." she holds out a delicate hand, flipping it over to reveal a tiny flame dancing on her palm.

I close my hand over hers, snuffing out the flame. "Yes, you sure did, but maybe wait a minute or two to use them again. You pretty much destroyed yourself. I'm surprised you're already awake."

She gives me an irritated look. "I'm fine. Stop fussing." Her eyes widen again, and she turns them to me with a look of deep sorrow. "I'm so sorry."

"For what?"

"Your dad. I'm so sorry, Logan, I wasn't fast enough." Oh, she thinks…

I rush to reassure her. "No. He's fine. Well, he's not fine, but he will be. Tobias didn't hit him head on. He's going to recover."

A shrill cry escapes her. "He is? I'm so glad. I thought… How about everyone else? Where is everyone? Liz, Garrett, Trey, Charlotte, Scott."

"They're all fine too. Some injuries, some exhaustion, but everyone is going to be fine. Scott is super pissed that you had Liz locked up, but he's relieved you're alive. I think he'll come to terms with the magic stuff soon enough."

"And Lawrence?"

"We've locked up Lawrence and anyone else that was fighting on his side. Everyone will get a fair trial, but they sure won't be running the council anymore."

"I can't believe it's over."

"I wouldn't say it's over, but we've kind of got a blank slate now. We can start fresh. Rebuild the council. Better than ever. And the most important thing is you're safe."

I drop on the side of her bed, picking up the hand that holds my entire heart.

"It's hard to believe I'm safe. And I can do… whatever I want. I don't even know what to do first."

A smirk curls up the side of my mouth. "I can think of a few things."

She laughs again. There's a lot of sadness behind her laugh. It's not as exuberant as it was before, but it's still there. We'll help each other get through the trauma and we'll be stronger together, but as long as she's still capable of a smile, I know we'll be ok.

I'm lean down for a gentle kiss, but her hands are grasping my shoulders, pulling me closer until I'm kissing away all the hurt. I wrap my arms around her, pulling her tight against me in an embrace that's going to last the rest of our lives.

Epilogue – 1.5 Years Later

My hand flies up to scratch the irritating itch tickling at my hair. I was completely engrossed in the book I was reading. A soft chuckle erupts as my hand slams into something warm and familiar. I twist around so fast Logan has to duck away to avoid getting clocked again.

His face is a mask of mock outrage, but the twitching of his lips gives him away. "I thought you liked my face, Tempest."

"I like your face just fine, as long as it's not lurking around behind me when I'm trying to study. You should know better than to sneak up on a girl when she's reading. Well, this girl anyway."

He arches a dark brow at me in amusement, and he rubs a hand across his chest. Now that I'm looking at him, my eyes drift to the muscles his black t-shirt is clinging to. My eyes narrow. He did that on purpose. Distraction. "You didn't even feel me coming? I'm hurt."

"I told you. I was busy." His words draw attention to our bond that hums with a steady warmth. He's right. I should have felt him coming, but I've been working on an extensive project, and when I'm in the zone, a hurricane could rip through the library and I wouldn't notice. "I'm working on creating a unit about the use of wands." I've been taking mundane university courses online to get my biology degree. At the same time, I'm working with Ivy and Charlotte's grandmothers to create a new set of college-level courses about arcane magic, both Mage and Witch. It's amazing how much the Mages have missed out on all these years by dividing themselves from the Witch community. They both have so much to teach each other.

His mouth opens to question me and I wave off his incoming protest. "I know, I know. I've heard your opinions on the use of wands, but I bet I can change your mind. Did you know that different types of wood have unique properties that enhance or complement your magic? For instance, Maple can give you a power boost, while Ash has regenerative properties, so you don't tire as easily."

The smile has spread all the way up his face, crinkling his eyes at the corner. "I believe you, but do you think Mrs. Okamura could spare you for the rest of the afternoon? I'm sure these books will all be here when you come back tomorrow."

My mouth turns down at the corners. "But…" I look down at the pile of books in front of me.

A flop of dark hair falls over his forehead as he bends down to press his lips to mine. Heat spreads to my chest and my hands slide around his torso, pulling him down closer. When I'm breathless, he pulls away, planting a gentle kiss on my forehead. "Please."

"You don't fight fair."

"Of course not. You've got all the advantages. I have to fight dirty sometimes."

A snort escapes. "Sure." I run my eyes up his tall frame, hard with muscle. All the advantages.

"Come on. I promise you're going to like my surprise."

I sigh. "Fine." I glance around the cluttered room in the library that's become like a second home for me. There's no sight of Mrs. Okamura, which is kind of a relief considering what we were just doing in her library.

"I already talked to her. You're free." His hands close over mine, pulling me up out of the hard wooden chair. I reach my hands over my head in a big stretch, my shoulders are tight from all the hunching over books I've been doing.

"Pretty confident, aren't you?"

"My confidence is one of your favorite things about me."

I shake my head, turning back to clean up the spill of books all over the six-person table I've overtaken.

His impatience is nudging at the bond between us. "What's the big rush?"

"If I told you, it wouldn't be much of a surprise now, would it?"

When the books are neatly away on the cart, patiently waiting for me to get back to them tomorrow, I turn to follow him out.

His eyes have a glint of mischief in them, as if the sun is glancing off the ocean on a clear day. "Wanna race."

"I'm not racing you in the library. Do you even know me at all?"

He laughs, grabbing my hand to drag me along with him. I push past him to get out the front door first and let loose as soon as the fresh summer air hits my face, kicking off into a run.

"You don't even know where we're going." He calls out as he bolts after me.

I zip off, accelerating to Phys speed. The breeze cleanses my face, whipping my ponytail behind me. I can feel him reaching through the bond to borrow some of my power, so I push myself even harder. I skid to a graceful stop when I reach his car.

He's only moments behind me, but I'm perched on his hood, swinging my legs with my arms sprawled out behind me, propping me up when he arrives. I've got my face tilted up to soak in the sun's warmth.

"I win." I cheerfully proclaim.

"Cheater." He mumbles, tackling me and throwing me over his shoulder.

I'm laughing so hard my stomach hurts when he tosses me into the passenger side of his SUV. This one has managed to survive a year and a half already.

"Are we going home?" I ask, turning to see his profile illuminated by the sun.

"Yes," he says. A slight twitch of his right eye tips me off that he's hiding something from me. I send a feeler out through the bond trying to read his thoughts, but he's got a wall the size of a skyscraper blocking the way. "Don't even try it, Sophia."

I push my lip out into a pout.

"You missed your turn." I tell him when he drives right by the turnoff to his family's house. I've been living there since the big battle. The thought of what I did still sends an ache through me, and I think it always will. After the dust settled, they reestablished order with the council and then tore it down to rebuild it.

Logan reluctantly took over his father's position, but it's turned out to be a good fit for him. He worked with Ivy and the Witches to create a new and better ruling body for the magical community. And once things were solid again, they held their first vote, and he got voted on to the new democratic body. No more nepotism for the Mages.

Mom wanted me to go with her when she returned to our house, but I needed to stay here, so I moved in with the Armstrongs on a permanent basis. Logan needed me by his side as he took on his new role, and then I started working on the magical research. It made sense to be close to HQ.

We turn down a few more side streets until Logan stops in front of a large white house. It's got dormer windows, a red front door, and a neatly trimmed green lawn.

"What are we doing here?"

He says nothing, coming around to open my door for me. When I go to step down, he scoops me up under the knees, carrying me around the side of the house.

My arms fall naturally around his neck, and I lean in to whisper in his ear. "Are we trespassing? Should I have worn my combat gear?"

"Don't you think I would have brought extra weapons if that were the case?"

"True. Then what exactly are we doing here?" He's carrying me in a bride hold on this quiet suburban street in the middle of the day. Awkward.

He pulls a key out of his side pocket with his left hand and slides it into the glass-paned door at the back of the house. "Welcome home."

"What?" My heart has picked up to racing speed and my stomach is a tangle of nerves.

He sets me down inside a small room that houses a washer and dryer. The only other thing in the sunlit room is a set of polished pine stairs leading up to another door.

"Go on." He nods at the staircase. "Or do I need to carry you up those too, because I can, but you've already worn me out." He wipes a hand across his forehead.

I'm standing there in shock, not able to make my limbs move. I guess I take too long, because the ground disappears from beneath my feet again as he picks me up as if I weigh nothing more than one of Liz's cats. I think she's up to seven now.

Each step has me bouncing in his arms. My mind is racing. Home? We have our own place? I can't quite wrap my head around it.

He uses the key a second time to open the red painted door at the top of the stairs before setting me down. He spins around in a circle, arms spread out.

"Wait, this place is ours?" I try to take the apartment in. Gray wood floors cover the big open concept space. An island divides the kitchen area from the empty living room. There's a nook off to the side next to a window that will be a perfect sunny spot for a table for two.

We're going to have the best housewarming party, invite all our friends over. The ones that are close by anyway. Garrett has gone off to school on the other side of the country. At least he's still keeping in touch. I miss him when he's not around, but he's still working through his past and moving on with his new life.

"Yes, it's all ours."

"But what about your family?"

"They'll be fine. Mom and Dad could probably use a break from us, anyway. You've been hovering over them as if you're the concerned parent. Now that Liz is finished high school, she'll be going right into the MED training program and she's planning on staying at HQ, so she's not moving out anytime soon. Your mom is at her place, and she has David, so she'll be fine."

"But…"

"But, what?" He turns to me with concern. "Don't you like it? Shit, I should have asked you first. I should have let you help pick the place, right? I messed this up." He runs a hand through his hair. "It just came available, and I had to decide fast. I thought you'd like it."

"No, it's not that." Tears are burning behind my eyes, threatening to spill over. "I love it." I sniffle. "I just can't believe that we're…free." Even after a year and I half I still hold my breath, afraid the world is going to collapse around us again. Someone is going to decide I'm a threat and lock me up.

"Oh, baby." His calloused finger swipes at the tear under my eye. "I know. I know how hard it's been, but look where we've gotten. Things are good and they're only getting better. Not to mention you've got me. I don't know if you could get any luckier."

The return of his usual cockiness has a shaky laugh escaping me. "I don't know. I'm sure there's someone out there just as beautiful as you, minus that attitude."

"Awww, you think I'm beautiful? Thanks." Of course he goes straight there. It's good to know some things never change. "You'd be so bored with that jerk. Wait, wait, wait. I haven't even shown you the best part. Come on." He's so excited he's almost vibrating. I could almost mistake him for his sister.

He grabs my hand, pulling me along behind him again. The door flings open to another empty room. "Bedroom." I'm craning my neck back, trying to get a glance at our bedroom while we're off to the next door. Same with the bathroom.

"Now this. This one is all for you. I had to make a few additions before I brought you. I've actually had the key for a few weeks now."

I can't believe he's been hiding this from me for weeks. "You've been keeping this from me for…" The rest of the sentence vanishes when he opens the third door.

It's a little smaller than the bedroom, and it's the only space with any furniture. In fact, it's fully furnished. Bookshelves line every wall. White wooden bookshelves full of potential. Waiting to be filled with books in every color of the rainbow. There's a cut out space under each window with a white desk under one and a dark wood desk under the other, but my brain skips right over those to return to the shelves. My mind is already buzzing with how I'm going to organize them.

There's even a cheery yellow couch and matching chairs sitting in the middle of the room with a fluffy white rug set between them. I can already picture myself curled on the couch, head in Logan's lap, reading a book.

"Well, do you like it?"

"It's perfect. You're perfect." I fling my arms around him. "Thank you."

His voice goes husky. "You don't need to thank me. I love you. I'd do anything for you. You deserve the world, and if I could give that to you, I would, but I guess you'll have to settle for me and a roomful of dusty books."

"My books will not be dusty." I'm laughing and crying as I lean in for a kiss. "I love you too." I mumble the words between kisses, and for the first time in a long time, I feel like I'm really home.

THANK YOU TO READERS

Thank you so much for taking the time to read my novel. Reviews mean everything to indie authors, so I would appreciate it so much if you leave a review on Amazon, Goodreads, or wherever you purchased my book.

If you'd like to keep up with the latest news on the Archimage series, please sign up for my monthly newsletter. You can check out my website for sign up links and other information **www.nicoleaoliverauthor.com**

Or follow me on Twitter (@nicoleaoliver), Facebook (facebook.com/nicoleaoliverauthor), Instagram (@nicoleaoliverwriter) and TikTok (@nicoleaoliverwriter).

Never stop turning those pages

ACKNOWLEDGEMENTS

It's hard to believe my journey with Logan and Sophia is over. They've been living in my head for five years now and it's bittersweet to say goodbye, but I'm looking forward to all the new stories ahead.

I couldn't have published this book without my amazing husband who has supported me all the way. Thanks for putting up with me holing away for days on end. I love you always.

Thanks to Tina. Sorry about May, but I really appreciate that extra week off.

Kate and the Hamilton Book Crawl. Thanks for organizing events and helping me get to know lots of amazing local authors and publishers.

Nanowrimo. Logical Magic might never have come to be without a 2018 Nano win.

And of course Bookstagram and Booktok. I've met so many awesome authors and readers on these platforms.

Thanks so much to my cover designer Emily Wittig. I still have no idea how you turned my random jumble of ideas into the perfect cover.

And to my parents. You really inspired a lifelong love of reading that has led me to this place.

ABOUT THE AUTHOR

Nicole A Oliver is a Fantasy author from Hamilton, Ontario, Canada. A voracious reader, Nicole has always loved becoming lost in magical realms. She loves to travel, but she believes there is no better substitute than getting lost in a book world when that's not possible. Her passion for the genre and the power of words led Nicole to aspirations of becoming an author early in her life.

Nicole, her husband, and her two biggest fans, her twin son and daughter, love to hike and always have their eyes open for magical creatures when they do. During the day, Nicole indulges her love of coffee and fuels her writing by slinging mugs of java. Her family enjoys putting their heads together over jigsaw puzzles, spending time outside, and trying out the fares of local restaurants. Nicole is a horse lover and will admit to imagining herself as a fierce warrior heading into battle whenever she is lucky enough to get to the barn.

The Archimage Trilogy is Nicole's debut series.